Elissa felt choked by her own emotions . . . frightened by the sudden golden opportunity to say what she longed to say.

Clemence was not looking at her, but gazing out over the valley, dotted with farmhouses and trees ablaze with October colors. The great stillness of the mountainside silenced both of them. The soft breeze brought the scent of sweet grass from the meadow below. Elissa was aware that she would always remember this moment drenched in that scent.

Clemence said, "You remember, there were girls who had crushes on each other or some of the teachers — even in college that was so. I don't think this is the same thing."

Elissa burst out, "If this is a crush I have on you, Clem, it's going to last forever!"

She was disconcerted when Clemence laughed merrily. "You can't tell if it's forever till it's over, can you?" She reached over to take Elissa's face in her hands and kiss her on the lips. She seemed surprised when Elissa caught her in a tight embrace . . .

WORKS BY SARAH ALDRIDGE

THE LATECOMER	1974
TOTTIE	1975
CYTHEREA'S BREATH	1976
ALL TRUE LOVERS	1979
THE NESTING PLACE	1982
MADAME AURORA	1983
MISFORTUNE'S FRIEND	1985
MAGDALENA	1987
KEEP TO ME STRANGER	1989
A FLIGHT OF ANGELS	1992

A Flight of Angels

BY SARAH ALDRIDGE

The Naiad Press, Inc.
1992

Printed in the United States of America on acid-free paper
First Edition

Cover design by Pat Tong and Bonnie Liss
    (Phoenix Graphics)
Typeset by Sandi Stancil

Library of Congress Cataloging-in-Publication Data

Aldridge, Sarah.
    A flight of angels / by Sarah Aldridge.
        p.   cm.
    ISBN 1-56280-001-9 : $9.95
    I. Title.
PS3551.L345F55   1992
813'.54--dc20   91-38095
                                                          CIP

To
TW

I

Clemence sat on the marble bench under the young oak trees munching her sandwich. The small triangular park at the side of the National Gallery was dappled by the early September sun. The sky was very blue, the air sparkling, and the only people about were occasional strollers. She could see a group of tourists on the other side of the Mall, a group of adults and children on their way to the Smithsonian Castle, whose red brick tower she could glimpse among the trees. She liked this semi-solitude, punctuated only by the sound of traffic passing unseen on Pennsylvania Avenue on the other side of the Gallery. She liked the breezy, quiet stir of this outdoor spot as a contrast to the cool, stony splendor of the interior of the Gallery with its Greco-Roman atria decorated with green plants and gently splashing fountain.

"Shall I sit down or do you prefer solitude?"

She recognized the voice behind her shoulder. It was Elissa's, Elissa who in the last week had cropped up again in her life, emerging from the recent past of her college years.

"No, I'm not being anti-social. Sit down."

Elissa sat down. She was a tall girl and her larger bulk took up most of the rest of the bench. "You come here a lot?"

"It's a nice place to eat lunch. I'm surprised more people don't try it. I get tired of the cafeteria."

"I looked for you there and didn't find you, so I was on my way back up the Hill. And lo! and behold, you're sitting here." Elissa opened the white paper bag she was holding and took out a sandwich. "I thought I'd eat this walking back. It's much nicer to sit here."

They were silent for a while, munching. Then Elissa said, "Seen the *Post* this morning? Or don't you read the papers?"

"Yes, I read the *Post*. You mean McCarthy again?"

"Yes. He says the educational system in this country is full of communists. Now he wants all the school-teachers to take a loyalty oath, not just the college professors. He's not content with saying that all the librarians should be fired and the books burned because they're contaminating the minds of the children."

Clemence looked at her. Elissa had a broad face, usually impassive but sometimes aflame with indignation, lit up by a pair of shrewd, aggressive eyes. I've known her for years but I've never really got down to what makes her tick. "None of that's new, is it? Look what he's done to the movie people and the theater producers."

2

"That doesn't make it any more acceptable. What do people mean by accepting this stuff?"

"They don't pay as much attention as you do — unless it's something that affects them personally. Wouldn't you take a loyalty oath if it meant keeping your job?"

"No, I would not! Whose business is it what I think about politics and religion?"

"No, I don't suppose you would, even if you had an aged parent and six children who would starve if you didn't get your paycheck."

Elissa laughed. "You're at it again. It's what you used to do at Goucher. You can be pretty deflating, Clem."

"Well, 'Lissa, you always get so wrought up about abstract principles."

"Don't you think they're pretty important?"

"Of course. But there is no point in butting your head against a brick wall. You're not going to change McCarthy or the people who put him in office. He's paranoid. The trouble is he's paranoid at the public expense."

"He shouldn't be permitted to use the power of government to harass people he doesn't like."

Clemence looked at her curiously. "Do you know somebody personally who is being affected by this?"

Elissa shrugged. "Don't we all? This sort of thing is insidious. People lose jobs and reputations. Look at that Alger Hiss mess. Employers can be cowards and spineless, if they think you'll be a source of trouble."

She was gazing down at the ground at her feet. Clemence thought, Is she afraid for herself? "But you're safe enough in your job. He can't go hunting staff members on another congressman's committee."

"Oh, can't he? Don't you remember that last year the Senate censured him for harassing some of its own members? No, I'm not concerned about myself. The man I work for is his sworn enemy. It's not that. I hate spies."

3

"I don't suppose anybody really likes them," said Clemence drily. She took the lipstick out of her handbag and repaired the color on her lips.

Her tone brought a smile back to Elissa's face. "Ever the rationalist." As Clemence glanced at her sharply, she added, "I remember you back in Miss Carson's philosophy class. You always brought airy speculation down to earth."

Clemence crushed up the bag that had held her lunch. "Do you want to walk around the Gallery with me? Or are you short of time?"

Elissa gathered up her sandwich wrappings. "There's a committee meeting at two o'clock. I've plenty of time."

They walked slowly along the path through the shrubs and trees of the Gallery garden. Clemence said, "Seriously, are you worried about your job? I know there's no tenure in committee staff appointments. But they'd be silly to fire you just because —"

"Because I come from the Bronx and taught a class in Marxist theory at a settlement house? No, I'm not worried about that. There are other things I can do with my talents. What do your parents think of all this? I know your father spoke up in defense of Robert Oppenheimer."

"What do you expect they would think? They think McCarthy is a real menace to this country — much more of a danger than the people he persecutes."

"Do you still live with them?"

"Yes. That is, I am living in our apartment. They've just gone to Egypt. There is a whole bunch of scientists out in the desert waiting for some sort of heavenly occurrence."

"Your mother is just as keen as she ever was?"

"Oh, yes. She doesn't come down out of the stars for very long at a time." Clemence broke off and then said, "Well, here's where I go in, at this door. I'm glad you're here in Washington now, 'Lissa."

4

A faint blush colored Elissa's face. "I'm glad I found you. I had no idea you'd go in for art in a big way."

"Hardly. I'm in the administrative office. That's not what you'd call going in for art."

"You have to know something about it, don't you?"

"I'm learning."

"Oh, well. I'll come looking for you again."

"Yes, do."

The enormous marble-columned lobby of the Gallery was filled with a throng of people milling about. Clemence went into the side room where the information desk was located and the counters where guidebooks and postcard reproductions of the art treasures were sold. At least two sight-seeing buses must have emptied within the last five minutes. She turned away into the corridor that led to the staff elevator. Before she reached it she came face to face with the curator of Medieval Painting.

His name was Robert Alden and he was a fair, shortish man who gave the impression of being younger than he actually was. "Ah," he said, "our fresh air girl. Did you enjoy your nibble under the arbor?"

Clemence reminded herself that you shouldn't judge someone by his outward appearance, but she could not help it. He was dapper, wore rimless glasses, and his hair was closely trimmed. But it was chiefly the predominant expression on his face that bothered her. His small pursed mouth seemed to match the mocking look in his eyes glinting behind the lenses. Whatever he said seemed to carry an undercurrent of disdain.

"There is no arbor," said Clemence, knowing that he did not care, accuracy in statement not being important to him. She had known him only a few weeks, since, in fact, her first day in her new job, but she had learned that whenever he spoke he sought the elliptical, the unexpected.

He grinned. "The literal mind. How valuable it is when you're dealing with the fluidities of art identification." Then he abruptly put his arm through hers and began to walk towards his own office. "Come and talk for a moment."

Astonished, Clemence did not protest but went with him through the outer office where two women were seated behind desks, into the big panelled room overlooking the Mall.

"Sit down," he instructed her. He sat down behind his broad, bare desk and folded his hands on its shining surface. The gesture called her attention to the only sheet of paper on the desk, a copy of a printed leaflet circulated among the Gallery staff, containing the curriculum vitae of the new Director of Purchases. It stated that his name was Francis Hearn; that he was the nephew of a famous American architect; that he had graduated from Northwestern University; that he had served all through three years of the United States involvement in the Second World War; that he had been a junior officer on General Eisenhower's staff when the German army had collapsed and the discovery was made of the great caches of art treasures that Hitler's Fieldmarshal Göring had looted from the museums of conquered countries.

Alden was saying, "We're getting a new Director of Purchases, aren't we? What can you tell me about him?"

How like him, thought Clemence, to discuss such a subject with the newest girl in the office.

"I've heard about the appointment, Mr. Alden, but I don't know anything about him."

He laughed gaily, as if mocking her. "I knew you would say that! Why don't you know? Do we have to honor those old shibboleths about loyalty to one's elders and betters? I'm not one, of course. You need not call me Mr. Alden. I'm Robert. You're Clemence. What a classical name! You know as well as I do that the true course of events in our working lives are recorded in the rumors and gossip that circulate in the corridors, not in the official pronouncements of our superiors." The smile vanished from his face and a look of venomous dislike took its place as he spat out, "Superiors!"

Clemence was silent. Somebody had told her that he was a man who hated the idea of supervision. He was, they said, acknowledged to be the best man in Italian Renaissance painting, certainly in America, but the hunger that ate at his vitals was for the power to dispense with all authority but his own. He systematically attacked and ridiculed any man promoted over him.

He talked on. "Of course you know all about it. You must hear a lot of gossip. Have you met him?"

"No. I don't know anything about him, really, except what it says there." She pointed to the leaflet on his desk.

Alden jumped up and walked about the room. "What are they bringing him in for? His knowledge of the whole field of western art is mediocre, his experience is limited. Why? There must be other reasons. I'm sure you have heard discussions about him. Now, come, tell me, what do they say about him?"

She did not answer his questions and he stopped beside her to say, looking down at her sulkily, "I don't suppose you could really tell me what I want to know. The newspaper accounts say that he was summoned before the House Un-American Affairs Committee because his name appeared in a list of people who signed a petition a few years ago to let a Russian art expert into this country to identify paintings said to have been looted

by Göring from Russian art collections. By their logic that
makes him a communist or fellow traveler. Well, I did
that, too; they don't seem to have noticed."

Talking in this way seemed to have calmed his anger.
Impatiently he made it clear that he was eager now for
her to leave. He had been described to her as hasty and
unpredictable, suddenly enthusiastic and as suddenly
indifferent. His automatic good manners gave a superficial
gallantry to the way he walked her to the door, patting
her back as if in affection. The few times she had seen
him in the big office where she worked she had watched
him — a man nearly middle-aged but still very sure of
his appeal to young women, who he flattered with
impertinent gestures that meant nothing.

Every day, at shortly after five o'clock, she waited for
the streetcar at the corner of Fourth Street with a crowd
of other office workers. This evening, in the long light of
September, she watched for Charlie Olsen. He was taller
than most people, so he could easily be spotted walking
along Pennsylvania Avenue from the National Archives
Building three blocks away. She watched not because she
wanted to see him but because his daily arrival at this
time was inevitable and she wanted to be prepared to
greet him. The people she worked with assumed that he
was her steady — the word itself brought a condescending
smile to her parents' faces when they heard it. He fit the
description of a steady boyfriend, since he was always
underfoot, persistent in making himself her escort
wherever she went. All the young women she knew who
were not already married had someone with whom it was
supposed they slept at the end of each evening out. It
was the norm that such relationships led up to eventual
marriage. Nobody, it was said, wanted to leap in the dark

into the marriage bed with someone whose sexual compatibility they had not tested. She supposed she had been slow in completing this part of her education while she was in college. But she had not given it much thought. There had been much of greater interest — at least, to her — to occupy her attention. And looking back now at the couple of years that had passed since graduation, which she had spent idle at home with her parents, she had seemed to have spent the time in a vacuum, uncertain which path to take.

She saw Charlie, striding through the throngs on the street to greet her, a tall, thin young man with blond hair, wearing a lightweight wool suit with a natural elegance. Whatever I do, Clemence reminded herself, don't let him know my parents have left and I am alone in the apartment. She had tried every sort of subterfuge to avoid being intimate with him. He was aggressive, and since an important reason she had given him for not spending the night with him was that her parents expected her home early, it would not do to give him the opportunity of their absence.

He said now, reaching her, "Can we stop at the Harrington bar for a drink before you go home?"

Reluctantly she said yes. The bar of the old-fashioned hotel was dark and chiefly empty. He ordered and while they waited he said, "Did you see in the papers the FBI's latest? J. Edgar Hoover wants to know what you and I read when we go to libraries. That's just a step away from people who use the Archives." When she did not respond, he went on, "This is a sort of deadly Mad Hatter's tea-party. It's hard to believe that ordinary people are subject to this sort of harassment. I suppose partly it is a result of the Rosenberg trial. Everybody's a spy."

"It's mass paranoia."

"Well, it is. We have a devil of a time hiring

9

competent people, especially when we need people who know one of the rarer languages — like Russian. Being ignorant of any language but English is actually a plus if you're looking for a job in the Government. If you admit you know Russian, you're sure to be a spy looking for classified documents."

But Charlie's interest in the efforts of the spy hunters waned, as she knew it would. He moved closer to her on the seat and put his arm around her. She shrank inwardly from his fondling but tried not to show that she did. He insisted on going home with her as far as the garage where he parked his car. She was thankful that he had no parking space closer downtown, because then he would have insisted on taking her all the way home.

On the last lap of her homeward trip alone she thought, Why do I put up with this? She ought to be able to tell him that she did not feel the same attraction to him that he seemed to feel to her. She understood his intent, his technique. He would persist in pressing his bodily presence on her until through sheer perseverance he wore down her resistance. Eventually they would go to bed together, eventually that would lead to marriage, the kind of marriage most of the girls she knew made — a few years of childlessness, apartment living, theater-going, party-giving, and then a house in the suburbs and children. She knew this pattern very well from observing the girls she went to college with, the young women she worked with. Though sometimes this sequence stopped short of the culmination and the women were left waiting, fruitlessly, for a proposal of marriage that did not materialize and the time ran on while the man made excuses and sought someone else.

Well, anyway, she had avoided telling him that her parents were out of the country and she had the apartment to herself.

* * * * *

The new Director of Purchases was shown around the building and casually introduced to any of the staff who happened to be in sight. Clemence, who had known that his appointment had already been confirmed when Robert Alden had catechized her, watched him with curiosity. He was younger than Robert, wore good clothes carelessly, tended to slouch with his hands in his pockets while he was being talked to, said little in response but sent his dark eyes constantly traveling about. Robert was not (purposely, she felt sure) in the building. Francis paid very little attention to anyone he was introduced to, acknowledging the introduction with the merest nod. Perhaps he was afraid of compromising himself before he learned the lay of the land.

She found herself trailing behind the group that was accompanying him on his tour. She had not expected to do this, but the administrator in charge of the office where she worked had summoned her with a gesture as the group formed and she docilely obeyed. Perhaps, she thought, they needed numbers for a more impressive showing. The tour ended in the office of the Director of the Gallery and she and the others melted away into their own niches.

She was surprised, when the end of the day came and she was tidying her desk, to see the new man come into the big office and, with a nod to the others in the room, walk over to her and stand looking down at her.

"You are Clemence Hartfield, aren't you? You don't remember me, I'm sure, but the first time I saw you, you were three years old. You were with your parents on a visit to Paris. We were in the Louvre."

She felt the annoyance she always felt when someone claimed acquaintance with her, as her parents' daughter, when she had been too young to distinguish one stranger from another. It happened often enough, a natural consequence of being the child of parents who had achieved renown as scientists. Her annoyance faded a little when she met his eyes. They had a friendly beam quite unlike the black stare she had seen in them during the tour. She murmured, "Oh?"

He went on. "You know I'm Francis Hearn. Your father was very kind to me when I was a very young man, with no idea what I wanted to do with my life. He helped me sort myself out. How are your parents?"

"They're fine. They're in Egypt just now. There is a meeting of scientists there, in the desert —"

He broke in, smiling, "To observe some celestial event, no doubt."

He continued to chat, asking her questions about herself, how she came to be on the Gallery staff, did she look forward to a career in gallery administration. Finally he said, "I have to find somewhere to live. I was hoping your parents would be here. Just at the moment I am staying at the Washington Hotel. How about having dinner with me?"

With reluctance, after demurring and being pressed, she agreed. The evening turned out to be very staid. He seemed conscious throughout that he was the family friend responsible for her while she was with him. He met her in the lobby of her apartment house and when they got to his hotel, did not suggest the bar but offered her a drink at the table. In the interval since his invitation she had found another cause for anxiety. She was aware that the other women in her office had watched, first with surprise and then with curiosity, his singling her out. She wondered whether he, like Robert Alden, suspected her of knowing backroom gossip about his new appointment and that this had contributed to his eagerness to spend the evening with her.

But he did and said nothing that would indicate this. He spoke only about her parents and her own ambitions. "How does it happen that I find you in Fine Arts and not in the sciences? Isn't that a new departure in your family?"

"I'm not really in Fine Arts," she said. "I'm only in the administrative office."

"So you are not aspiring to be a painter or a sculptor or an authority on museum management?"

She thought he might be mocking her, in spite of his bland tone, but she realized that in fact he was talking to her as if she was a school girl. Perhaps this was his normal manner. "I don't think an aspiring artist would be interested in the sort of job I have. I've been out of college for two years. I haven't a head for science. There's no use pretending that I do. My parents accept that fact. I wanted something to do and someone suggested to my mother I might like working at the Gallery. I love paintings. Painting seems to express so much that words cannot."

"Ah. Perhaps you haven't found your field. There is a great deal to art, even if you don't paint or sculpt."

His tone had grown more sympathetic, though she interpreted his remarks as meaning that he supposed she would shortly marry and settle down to a family. A pretty girl, with a quick mind but no intellectual weight.

It was a long dinner, over which he seemed inclined to linger, and afterwards he took her home in a cab and said goodnight in the apartment lobby.

On rainy days she ate in the Gallery cafeteria, trying to choose a time when she could avoid the company of the people with whom she worked and yet anticipate the throngs of tourists who were admitted after the first hour,

13

which was reserved for the staff. Elissa was quick to learn this and appeared in whatever corner she chose to sit.

Today, putting her tray down on the table she had chosen, she saw Elissa halfway through the cafeteria line. She did not know what stratagem Elissa used to get past the guard at the door. Probably she flashed her security card. Clemence did not mind. She found relaxation in Elissa's company. She had not thought much about Elissa since leaving Goucher. Their backgrounds had seemed so different that when they no longer met every day in classes and campus events, she had tacitly relegated their friendship to a phase of her life that was over now. But now, having spent several hours with her over a week or more, she found herself falling back into the easy comradeship they had previously enjoyed. Of course, Elissa had nothing to do with the politics of the Gallery staff — which Clemence sought to stay out of — and this made her a better companion for leisure hours.

Elissa had reached her now. She took the dishes off her tray and sat down.

"Have you met the new man yet?"

"Yes. He says he first met me when I was three — when I was young enough that my mother trailed me along with her when she traveled. You know, I hate it when people claim acquaintance with me that way. What it really means is that they are friends of my parents and I'm just an appendage. This man says my father was a great influence on him when he was young. Of course, my father always had a lot of acolytes."

Elissa glanced up from her bowl of chili. "That's not something that would ever happen to me — not having parents anyone wants to know."

"He took me to dinner last night."

"Oh, ah!"

Annoyed, Clemence said, "No 'oh, ah' about it. He couldn't have been more starchy."

Elissa grinned. "Would you have preferred he hadn't been?"

"No. I have trouble enough with Charlie Olsen."

"Charlie Olsen?"

"He works in the Archives. He thinks he's my steady."

"Oh." Elissa was quiet for a moment. Then she said, "But don't you see, Clem, you've got a windfall. You know this man from outside your job. That's a very good gambit for in-house politics."

Clemence retorted, "I'm not interested in in-house politics. I try to keep out of them."

"That may be. But right now you have a great advantage in dealing with the people you work with. I expect you'll find you have a lot of bosom pals all of a sudden."

Clemence contemplated her for a moment. " 'Lissa, I realize you're a political person. You think in those terms all the time, don't you? But I'm not."

Elissa's smile was indulgent. "You're in Washington, Clem. Everything here is politics. What you mean is that you don't like to manipulate people or be manipulated. But you can't help it."

Clemence remembered Elissa in college: the indefatigable worker in extracurricular activities, in the Young Democrats Club, on the school paper, always at the head of any protest made to the faculty, as for instance about the wages of the black women who worked on the campus.

Elissa went on talking. "Hearn is a political character, from what I've heard. There was some maneuvering in getting him the appointment. I know everybody has to have a security check to get a government job, but his went a bit further because he was on Eisenhower's staff at the end of the war. He had dealings with some of the Russian officers when the Americans linked up with the Russian army. Of course, that made him a suspicious character in the eyes of the FBI. Just being in the same room as a Russian makes you a communist or fellow traveler. Ridiculous, isn't it? Look at the accusations against General Marshall. J. Edgar Hoover says he's probably a Red. What surprises me, really, Clem, is that Robert Alden ever got appointed. He's on your staff, isn't he?"

"He's curator of Medieval Painting."

"Well, the FBI did their best to prevent him from getting clearance. Don't you know all this, Clem?"

Clemence was silent. She had heard bits of gossip, to her mysterious, about scandals in Robert Alden's professional past. She was too new in her job to sort out the implications of much that she heard.

"Do you deal with these people every day?" Elissa was asking her.

"Who? Alden and Hearn? That's just routine. I do a lot of typing for Robert. He very often specifies that he wants me to type up his articles and things."

"Looks to me, then, that you're in an interesting spot to see what happens."

"I don't like the idea of being in the middle."

Elissa finished her bowl of chili. Suddenly she asked, "Are you going to be home this evening?"

Clemence thought of Charlie Olsen. "Yes, I am. Do you want to come around to my place?"

The invitation brought a bright smile to Elissa's face. "I'd love to. But I have to warn you. Very often I have to stay late at the office and usually I don't know ahead of time. But if I can get off at a reasonable hour, I'll be round. Perhaps if I'm early, we could have dinner together?"

"Of course. I usually leave at five but I could stay a

little longer and then walk up the Hill. I'll meet you at the streetcar stop in front of the Rayburn Building. If you don't show by six-thirty, I'll go on home."

"I think I can be there. See you then, Clem."

The late afternoon sun was warm as Clemence walked slowly up the footpath under the old, wide-spreading oaks and elms in the southern half of the Capitol grounds. She amused herself by reading the identifying labels fixed to the more exotic trees planted among them. There was a tranquility about this setting that pleased her. She had given herself plenty of time — she did not want to be available to the telephone, since, if it rang, it was likely to be a call from Charlie, frustrated at not finding her as usual at the streetcar stop. She stood for a while at the corner of the Capitol grounds opposite the door of the House Office Building, from which a steady trickle of people emerged. Elissa was not among them.

Elissa, walking down the corridor toward the outer door, saw her through the open doorway, a slight figure in a summer dress, her blonde hair blowing gently in the light breeze. Clemence hadn't changed much, she thought, since their Goucher days. The eager lift she felt whenever she saw her like this, unexpectedly, quickened her steps.

"Taking the afternoon off?" said the guard at the door, as she passed, using the time-honored facetious remark current among her fellow-workers whenever someone was seen to be leaving at the normal close of the business day. She was known to be one of those most likely to work several hours overtime.

She reached Clemence. "Made it. There isn't anything hot on the stove right now." She did not tell Clemence that she often stayed late because there was nothing to tempt her to leave, nothing to occupy a long empty evening.

It was a long streetcar ride into the westering sun to Washington Circle and New Hampshire Avenue.

17

Clemence's parents had a sprawling apartment in an old building without an elevator, inhabited chiefly by elderly tenants who had moved in there years before when the neighborhood had had a certain elegance.

Elissa, following along behind as Clemence mounted the stairs, remembered having been told about Clemence's parents in a cursory way. She had not known much about the parents of any of the girls she had known then. Partly this was because she said nothing about her own background and therefore did not elicit corresponding confidences. But Clemence could not hide the fact that she was the child of two famous scientists, recipients of many public awards. Clemence herself never referred to them except in casual comments, unless she was accosted by a teacher or school official and congratulated on some recent success of her parents reported in the newspapers.

Clemence, having reached the fourth and topmost landing, was searching in her handbag for the door key. She unlocked the door and entered the apartment and switched on the lights, because, though the long rays of evening still entered, gloom was gathering in the corners of the big living room.

Elissa sat down on the massive, shabby sofa. There was a sort of homely welcome in these surroundings. In her mind Elissa had formed an image of Clemence's parents as unworldly people whose minds were entirely taken up with the abstract principles of their discipline, above the petty dealings of lesser people. Vaguely she realized that this was a romanic concept, out of keeping with her usual attitude towards people she did not know. Generally, she suspected everyone of having ulterior motives, base designs, feet of clay, no matter how exalted might be their status in life. But this room seemed to bear out the image she had created, which was important, for it helped her understand Clemence. She had never known anyone like Clemence. When they had parted for the last time after the commencement exercises, she had been devastated by the realization that Clemence would no longer be part of her daily life. She had got into the habit of referring anything that came up in her mind to Clemence, for Clemence's judgment on it. Now there would be no Clemence. She had said nothing to Clemence about any future plans for meeting or continuing their friendship, and Clemence had said nothing in that line either. The possible reasons for Clemence's silence provided her with many tortured hours of conjecture. But then why should Clemence want to go on being her friend? She had very little to offer Clemence that Clemence could not have from other more suitable people. Clemence had always been kind, sympathetic, a patient audience for her tirades. But that did not mean that for Clemence there was any reason to prolong their association.

Clemence, who had gone into the kitchen, came back into the room with a tray and glasses and a couple of bottles, which she put down on the coffee table.

"I wish," she said, "they'd get over all this business of harassing people because of their personal opinions. I don't care what the Russians do with their own country. If they want to be communists, that is not my business."

Elissa laughed. "That's a pretty subversive statement. The idea is that we have to fight them so that they won't make us all communists." She laughed again at the distasteful expression on Clemence's face. "But what brought this up? Has somebody been talking about this?"

"Oh, one of the women in the office said that somebody she knew had been investigated by the FBI because she belongs to a book club that was re-issuing books by Russian authors. That's downright silly. Why, my parents could get into trouble because they use Russian sources when they write scientific articles."

"Probably they will."

19

"I just wish I didn't have to be hearing about it all the time. Oh, all right, you can tell me that I want an ivory tower. Yes, I do. Especially at work, so that I don't have to spend so much time keeping out of office politics." Clemence sipped her drink and then said, "That's enough griping. Let's talk about something else."

Elissa had been watching her. Clemence rarely showed annoyance or impatience with people who irritated her. "Such as?" Elissa asked cautiously.

"Old school stories," said Clemence promptly. "We haven't explored that subject since you turned up here." Where have you been since Goucher?"

"Out of the country."

"Where?"

"Latin America."

"What were you doing there?"

"I was with the USIA."

"And why did you come back?"

"A couple of reasons, I guess. One was that I got disgusted with the way things were handled — too many politicians. The other was that I got the feeling I was out in left field — that everything important was happening here."

Clemence smiled. "Yes, I can see that was something you just couldn't stand. You have to be in the center of things, don't you, 'Lissa? Well, you're here now, in the political arena."

There was a silence. Elissa's eye of memory saw Clemence in the big room at college where the seniors gathered for an afternoon break, silently watching some of the members of the student government group, herself among them, arguing about the current political issues. Clemence used to sit on one of the sofas, leaning back with her legs stretched out in front with her ankles crossed, holding her elbows, as if consciously holding back from the discussion.

Clemence suddenly asked, "How did you manage to come to Washington on a congressman's committee? Doesn't that take influence?"

"It was a fluke. I met somebody at an embassy party in Chile. In fact, it was a party for some visiting firemen — congressmen making a tour to see how U.S. funds were being spent. He said I had had some useful experience and would I like to come and work on the Hill. I didn't think much about it at first. After all, what you hear at a cocktail party is usually forgotten by the next day. But I was surprised. He called me up at the office and said his committee needed a staff member like me who had had some experience in the field. I can't explain why he chose me. Of course, I do come from his congressional district. He's quite serious-minded. I've learned since to have considerable respect for him. He's aware of such things as civil rights and how black people are usually short-changed when it comes to government money. He should be, since he has so many of them in his district, but it's unusual just the same."

"Are you happy you made the change?"

"We-ell, yes. Yes, of course. I want to be here."

"So what's the fly in the ointment?"

Elissa was thoughtful. "The fact that I'm a woman."

Clemence laughed in surprise. "That's not news, is it?"

Elissa was serious. "No. What I mean is that I've found out that women don't get listened to when they're dealing with men in groups. An individual man may listen to you, when you're talking to him alone. But in a group discussion, a woman is drowned out. If you try to make yourself heard, you're being too aggressive. I find myself most of the time gathering material for the men to discuss."

"The eternal handmaid."

"That's it. You can have an opinion and sometimes they'll listen to it with half an ear. But it's disgusting

21

when you know you're right and you can't get a chance to present your argument."

"Do you try?"

"When I really get het up. But they have a way of letting you know that you're just a woman, going off half-cocked. And then you find out that somebody has really listened to what you said and then comes up with it as a brand-new thought, something of his own."

Clemence watched as Elissa fell silent, immersed in her own indignation. She could see clearly what lay behind this lack of success in being effective with the men with whom she dealt. Elissa was a good-looking girl; there was something attractive about her long-nosed face, framed by the dark-brown hair that she wore trimmed to the lobes of her ears. But it would never occur to Elissa to use any feminine tactics to attract and pin down a man's attention. She addressed men as she addressed women, as rational beings whom she strove to interest in whatever subject she was discussing. Clemence remembered back to their college days. Some of the other girls — those with greater social talents and brought up to use their femininity as the normal way to achieve what they wanted in the world — had joked about Elissa's lack of common sense, by which they meant her lack of the ability to act like a girl. Clemence had often found herself in the position of defending Elissa, acutely aware of the fact that Elissa's sterling qualities outweighed those of some of her detractors. Some of the teachers recognized Elissa's intellectual capacity and strove to exercise patience with her frequent vehemence. But some felt threatened by her and exchanged smiles with the derisive girls.

"You mustn't get discouraged, 'Lissa."

Elissa shrugged. "I give them a chance. If they don't take it, I drop the subject. But that's not the right thing to do."

"Listen, 'Lissa. At Goucher you were supposed to be pretty hardboiled. Miss Benson said that you lacked the idealism proper to youth. But I think she was mistaken."

"Miss Benson of English Lit.? Did she say that to you?"

Clemence nodded. "She said it was a great pity, because if you don't have high ideals when you are young, you miss an appreciation of true greatness in the world around you."

"Why was she talking to you about me?"

"Because she thought I was your closest friend."

Clemence was surprised to see the slow blush rise in Elissa's face. Elissa finally said, "You know how I remember you best at Goucher, Clem? I remember you in class. We were fortunate, weren't we, to have some professors who liked to stir us up to thinking. Miss Benson was one of them. I remember once she interrupted an explication of Wordsworth poetry — was it the *Intimations of Immortality?* — and asked for opinions about the inevitability of genius being appreciated — whether a genius would inevitably be recognized, regardless of his own circumstances, whether or not he had a means of making himself heard in his community."

Elissa stopped, as if another thought had crossed her mind. "Have you noticed that we always say 'he' and 'his' when we're talking this way? Anyway, what her question was, whether there was something divine, beyond the human will, that touched someone to make him a genius and therefore this special gift had to find its way out into the consciousness of others. You were the one who said that finally. But you didn't say it till everybody else had kicked the question around till there was almost nothing left of it. I remember you standing up to have your say and Miss Benson looking at you as if she had been waiting for just that."

"Why do you remember that, 'Lissa?"

"Because it was what you used to do all the time. You just waited till the commotion died down — like the commotion in Proctor's class of Political Science, when Proctor began to question the virtues of socialism and the classless society. You waited and then you had your say — the still, small voice questioning the morality of a laissez faire philosophy. But sometimes you waited too long or the argument went on too long and you didn't get your chance."

Clemence was listening closely. "You must have been paying more attention than I thought you were."

Elissa looked surprised.

Clemence went on. "I always thought you were bored, as if you had heard all this before — because you came from a much harsher world and thought we were just a lot of schoolgirls from cloistered homes."

Elissa said, angrily defensive, "Well, you were. And most of you were just repeating what you'd heard your parents say. There must have been something different about your parents."

"Perhaps so. They never laid down any rules for what I should think. That has its disadvantages, sometimes, when you're growing up and need some certainties in your life."

They were silent for a while. The sky outside the windows was dark now, except for the glow of a street lamp below. Clemence glanced at the clock and asked, "Do you want to go out and eat now?"

Elissa felt a sudden disinclination to go out, to leave this apartment with its comfortable atmosphere, to break the web of harmony that seemed to enclose her with Clemence. How could she tell Clemence that she did not want to break this intimate closeness and go out among other people?

Clemence, as if she guessed her mood, said, "I don't

24

think I have anything to eat in the house, though I suppose there are things in cans."

Elissa got up when Clemence did and followed her out into the kitchen. Together they peered into cupboards at the cans and bottles.

"Soup is good enough," Elissa suggested, tentatively. "Do you like spaghetti? I see a package there."

In the end they ate the spaghetti, which Elissa prepared with anchovies and garlic. She had learned to cook it, she said, from an Italian neighbor. They ate heartily, suddenly hungry. When they finished, Elissa sat back and lit a cigarette. The kitchen, where they sat in what was obviously meant for a breakfast nook, was, like the rest of the apartment, spacious and shabby, as if the people who lived there had been there so long that they were used to it and had no desire to change it. She supposed that Clemence, in her parents' absence, ate most of her meals there alone.

She asked, "Do you get lonesome here all by yourself, Clem?"

"Well, yes and no. Yes, I suppose I'd like more of my parents' company — or somebody's company — somebody congenial."

"What about Charlie Whatshisname?"

"I don't invite Charlie here. In fact, I spend a good deal of ingenuity trying to avoid doing so."

Elissa laughed. "Anybody else?"

"No. I'm used to being by myself a lot, so that I can do what I want to when I want to. Or nothing, without anybody reproaching me. That's why I've been so long getting started on some sort of career. I'm not like you. I'm still marking time, being a government clerk, wondering what I want to do."

"Do you want to get married?"

"No, I definitely don't want to get married. You've

never had this problem, have you, 'Lissa? You've always been intent on reforming the world."

Elissa showed that she was vexed. "No, that's not what I want to do. What I want to do is something that will give me satisfaction — that makes me feel there is some reason for my being here, something I can do better than anybody else, something I'll succeed at, with tangible results that benefit the world generally." She suddenly stopped and blushed under Clemence's eyes. "Silly, isn't it?"

Clemence impulsively put out her hand to cover Elissa's. "Dear, you should not let anybody divert you from your own path. Nobody can have just the vision you do."

Elissa looked down at the table. Clemence withdrew her hand and stood up. "Let's go into the living room. It's more comfortable there."

"We'd better wash up the dishes first, hadn't we?"

Clemence looked down at the clutter of their meal. "Yes, I suppose we should."

Afterwards they sat in the living room and talked, lively and desultory by turns, till Elissa saw Clemence yawn and said she had better go home, and Clemence said, "We'd better call a cab."

They stood in the darkened doorway of the apartment house waiting for the cab. Elissa yearned to reach out and touch Clemence but felt the sudden tongue-tied shyness that had so often overcome her back in their days at Goucher. At the last moment Clemence leaned towards her and kissed her lightly on the cheek. Elissa, too surprised, did not respond. In the cab she thought, just the sort of kiss the girls used to give each other as they said goodnight in the dormitory and when they were going home for holidays. Clemence had never kissed her before.

* * * * *

When she got to bed, sleep seemed very far away. The evening had revived in pulsating quality all the feelings she had had for Clemence when they had been together day after day.

She remembered the first time she had seen Clemence, crossing the campus carrying an armload of books. She remembered that mild autumn afternoon, the scattering of fallen leaves tumbled by the wind around the legs of the slight girl dressed in a pleated skirt and Norwegian sweater, her blonde hair blown about her face. She knew who she was because somebody had said that that was Clemence, the daughter of Harold and Clara Hartfield, the team of married scientists who had just won the Nobel Prize for Earth Sciences.

She had forgotten what her first reaction had been to this piece of information. It was the sort of thing that got across her nerves in those days, raw as they were from this abrupt plunge into surroundings so far outside her life's experience. Ever since she had been informed by the school board people in New York that she had won a full scholarship for her junior and senior year at this prestigious women's college, she had been in conflict with herself — whether she should take it or turn it down contemptuously, seeing it as a sort of bribe offered her to join the prosperous middle class she despised from afar. But the temptation carried her along, preventing her from making a gesture which she recognized to be absurd. She could not explain to anyone that underneath everything there was this great joyousness at the thought that she could leave behind the narrow, self-destroying world she had been born into, the world that had no value for achievement of any sort, that denied that value to anyone who aspired otherwise. In her earliest years she had gone

27

from foster home to foster home, until she had found her way through the public schools to use her mind to escape. By the time she had reached her second year of college she had long since become independent and self-sustaining. The scholarship was, after all, only the reward for her efforts.

But at a price. She found that, confronted with the girls and women of this very different world, she felt called upon to assert her own value, quick to see disdain when perhaps none was intended. She knew that this inner conflict sometimes gave a vehemence to her behavior that others found downright ludicrous, that embarrassed some girls like Clemence who had been trained to act in a much more temperate way. Girls like Clemence, but not Clemence, who seemed to understand something of what drove her into these intemperate outbursts.

She had not spoken to Clemence for a little while after that first glimpse of her walking across the campus. When they did meet she nodded stiffly and caught her eye only in a lightning glance. But one day in English Lit. they were talking about Charlotte Bronte and Elizabeth Gaskell, and Miss Benson had asked questions about the difference in the way these two writers confronted the social inequalities of their day. Her long brooding had broken out into an impassioned diatribe against the narrowness of middle-class mores that hampered any writer no matter how sympathetic she might be to the woes she described. Several minutes passed before it was borne in on her that the room had become perfectly quiet except for her own voice; that, taking their cue from Miss Benson, the others were listening silently and attentively, some of them staring at her in astonishment. Again, except for Clemence. Clemence seemed to be listening as if this was a viewpoint that she needed to hear and consider. Ashamed of her outburst she had stayed sullenly silent for the rest of the class period and walked out as soon as Miss Benson dismissed them, walking off by herself in an agony of humiliation at the idea that Clemence had found her uncouth.

But Clemence had caught up with her. After her first furious burst of speed she had unconsciously slowed down, the stress of her inner feeling giving way to a familiar despair.

Clemence asked at her elbow, "Don't you want to go to the snack bar and have something to drink? Miss Benson's class always makes me thirsty. I suppose we all talk a lot."

Elissa stared at her, slowly absorbing what she said. "Oh, all right."

When they sat in the snack bar she had unaccountably told Clemence that she did not know why she had made such a fool of herself.

Clemence had looked at her in surprise. "Whatever makes you think you made a fool of yourself? That's the sort of thing Miss Benson wants. She has a hard time stirring the other girls up to involve themselves in what they are reading. What you said was right. We're all too complacent. Miss Benson is always telling us that we should read these books and understand them in the context of our own time, not just read them as something required for a good grade." Clemence had paused and then said, "You feel very strongly about social injustice, don't you? It must be because you have a different background from the rest of us."

Elissa remembered retorting bitterly, "You mean, I don't belong here."

"I don't think that's right. When you're dealing with ideas, everybody should belong, in any discussion. You've got a good mind and you want a college education. You belong here as much as anybody. 'Lissa, you shouldn't let feelings like that get in the way of what you want to do."

At the time Elissa did not know how much Clemence echoed the ideas her parents had instilled in her. The very thought that one had parents who exercised that responsibility was alien to her. But when she knew Clemence better she realized what was the source of Clemence's notions: the tolerance of diversity of opinions, respect for intellectual achievement, regardless of social and economic class, the importance of moral integrity over material advantage. She felt at sea until, coming to know Clemence better, she learned to understand Clemence's difference from so many of those around her.

From then on her college life was dominated by Clemence, by a reliance on Clemence's opinion, by Clemence's gentle and unobtrusive efforts to help her respond to this strange environment. She thought Clemence had no idea how completely she came to depend on her approval. She saw Clemence every day, yet she always seemed a little remote, characteristically serene in any situation.

When graduation came it turned out that she and Clemence were the only two girls whose parents would not be present.

"Don't you mind?" Elissa demanded.

"Well, it would have been nice to have them here. But, after all, they'll be back in a couple of weeks and we can celebrate then."

Clemence had never asked anything about Elissa's own parents and this fact in itself told her that Clemence was in this instance exercising her extraordinary gift for letting dangerous and painful subjects lie undisturbed. She remembered the last time she had seen Clemence, boarding the train for Washington, while she herself stood on the platform waiting for the northbound New York express.

When Clemence walked into the Gallery's administrative office she was instantly aware of some sort of excitement in the air. The usual lethargic awakening to the day's activities so characteristic of a formal, tradition-bound office was missing. She glanced briefly at each of the women who shared it with her. They were silent, almost as if they had been talking among themselves, saying something that in some way referred to her. She was used to this sort of furtive discussion of what her role might be in the events taking place day by day in the Gallery. She was much younger than most of them. Her path to an appointment had been different, and she was truthful when she said she had no particular training for a job in an art museum. She wondered whether this time it had something to do with Francis Hearn. Or was she becoming obsessed with the enmity that had become so obvious between him and Robert Alden?

She took the cover off her typewriter and arranged things on her desk, ready for the morning's work. When she sat down Flora Kelso came over and stood beside her. She knew Flora as the only woman curator in the Gallery; a woman in such a position was still a rarity in the museum world. Flora was a middle-aged woman, grey-haired but still with a youthful figure, which she dressed to emphasize.

"You won't believe what has happened, Clemence. I think I should tell you about it before you hear it from others. The Giardini has vanished."

"The Giardini?" Clemence repeated stupidly.

"Yes. Vanished." Flora was smiling as she spoke, as if at a good joke.

"Do you mean it has been stolen?"

Flora went on smiling and raised her eyebrows. "No one seems to know. It vanished overnight, but the guards are not talking about it."

Baffled by her attitude, Clemence said, "Well, what is being done about it? The Gallery has never been robbed before, has it?"

"Not that I know of."

Flora paused and in the pause Clemence's mind went to the painting. Flora knew it was a particular favorite of hers. She felt a sudden sense of loss at the thought that it was no longer where it had always hung. It was a big canvas by a fourteenth-century painter known only as Giardini; nothing had ever been learned about him nor any other paintings identified as his. It depicted a landscape, lush, treed, with flowering shrubs and in the foreground a path on which a band of pilgrims traveled, evidently on their way to a shrine. But though this foreground was pleasing, the glory of the painting was in the scene above their heads — a brilliant sky with soft clouds and in the midst of them a host of angels, ethereal beings in floating draperies, their bare feet treading the translucent air, aloof from the throng below and at the same time protective of it. She could not say just what it was that had trapped her imagination in this painting.

The subject was one similar to others of that age, portraying biblical scenes or the ecstacy of the devout. It was the angels who held her attention. They seemed so real and yet so otherworldly, not blazing forth but wrapped in a soft radiance that seemed to come off the painted surface. She had noticed it in one of her first trips through the galleries and it had drawn her back time and again. She had expressed her enthusiasm for it to her parents and had seen in their faces the fond indulgence they always showed when she burst out with one of her rare demonstrations of deep feeling. She knew that they, tolerant agnostics, saw her as a romantic, not attributing her enthusiasm to religious fervor but to the attraction of the ideal.

She became aware that Flora was looking at her with curiosity. "Does it mean so much to you, Clemence? Why?"

Clemence faltered. "Yes. But why the Giardini?"

Flora shrugged. "Why, indeed. Except that it is in Robert Alden's jurisdiction. You know, he is the one who convinced the trustees that it was a painting they should acquire. He had to overcome the rumors about its authenticity."

"Then why should the thieves choose it to steal when there are so many other paintings more valuable?"

"Well, it is after all unique — the only Giardini. And I don't know that it is a question of thieves. The painting is simply not hanging in its usual place. Nobody seems to know where it has got to."

"Do you mean it has been removed — perhaps for cleaning?"

"There has been no requisition order for that. Besides, it was restored just a few years ago, when it was acquired. It was among the paintings that were recovered from the Germans at the end of the war. Does it mean so much to you, Clemence?" Flora asked the question a second time.

Clemence did not return her gaze. "I think it is the most glorious painting. I don't know what you mean about its authenticity being questioned. I know that the painter has never been properly identified. But whoever he was, he has captured something that very few painters have."

Flora nodded. "I have heard other people speak about how affecting they find it. Well, it is not on the wall where it should be." She paused again and then asked,

"Has Robert Alden by any chance said anything about it lately?"

Surprised and vexed Clemence replied, "No. He doesn't discuss his plans and intentions with me. I wish that people understood that."

Flora reached out to pat her hand. "It is annoying, I'm sure. But to many you seem to be on a special footing with Robert. Probably it is because you are new — and young and pretty."

She smiled again and turned away to walk out of the room.

Not immediately but after a while, when the women around her seemed absorbed in their work, Clemence left her desk and went into the gallery where the painting usually hung. In her mind she had christened it A Flight of Angels, since it had no official title, being listed only as Landscape with Pilgrims and Angels. It had hung by itself in a space between two long rooms filled with Italian paintings. Though she was prepared for its absence, she felt a shock at the emptiness of this anteroom, which had always before greeted her with a luminousness. Now it was simply a hiatus between two doorways, with a bare wall that might never have held a painting. She stood for several minutes, calling up in her mind the image of the painting, remembering the feeling of exhilaration it had always induced in her.

Finally she sighed with disappointment and began to walk back to the office. The marble passageways were thronged with tourists in small groups or large parties, gazing respectfully if sometimes uncomprehendingly at the objects around them. She turned into a small bare passageway and came face to face with Robert Alden.

There was a scowl on his face and she thought at first that he was going to shoulder his way past her without speaking. But suddenly he stopped and switched around to look at her angrily.

"You've been to view the scene of the crime, haven't you?"

Mutely Clemence nodded.

He glared at her fiercely. "There is no crime. There is no robbery. I'm in charge in that gallery and I've seen fit to remove the painting from public view. My reasons are my own business. You can go and tell your friends in the administration that I told you so."

He spun around again and walked rapidly away, his heels clicking sharply on the marble floor.

Clemence stood still, too astonished to leave the small corridor. After a while she walked slowly back to the office. What on earth, she wondered, made him attack her as if she had something to do with the frustration that he obviously felt in dealing with the people who ran the Gallery. She remembered what Flora had said: that she was supposed to be on closer terms with him than the other people she worked with. It was puzzling enough that her co-workers should think that about her, but that Robert himself should act as if he considered her a go-between —!

It was a relief, that evening, to tell Elissa what had happened. Elissa listened intently, not interrupting, and then said, "You remember. I told you you'd find yourself involved in office politics. With Francis Hearn here it would be inevitable."

"But why? I know Francis because he is a friend of my father's. I do a lot of work for Robert, at his request. Why should that make people think that I'm bosom pals with either one of them?"

"Not being in your office I can't say. But I can make some guesses. You're the newest girl in. You're there because your parents have connections. Remember,

Washington is a place where connections are important and everybody is aware of them. So naturally people begin to speculate. You're young and pretty and you're bright and these are two men."

"That's what Flora thinks."

"Flora?"

"She is the curator of Ceramics and Pottery. She makes a joke of the fact that since she is the only woman curator here, naturally she has the collection that lives in the basement."

"She has a point." Elissa thought for a moment. "You say that all you know about Francis is what he told you, that he is a friend of your father's."

"He said that my father changed the course of his life. Apparently he went through some kind of crisis. He started out to be an architect, in his uncle's office. Then the war came along and after that he decided that the fine arts were more his line. So because of the way he feels about my father, he makes a point of being friendly to me."

"People are apt to look for more than a platonic basis for friendship in your situation."

"Just the same, why do they think I have a special relationship with Robert?"

"Do you like him?"

"I don't really know. Sometimes I feel sympathetic towards him. He likes to talk when I'm with him and a good deal of what he says is very interesting. It's really amazing how much he knows about painting — artists, history, methods, all that. And when he is talking like that, he becomes completely absorbed, so that he has you hanging on the ropes listening to what he's saying. That is one thing everybody seems to agree on — there is not a better qualified man in his field anywhere. He has something more. He has the knack of conveying his feeling — and it is obviously very deep — about paintings to you. You know, there are lectures here in the Gallery every week and he is the most popular speaker. People come back again and again to listen to him. The funny thing is that he's arrogant most of the time but when he's answering your questions, he's amazingly patient in explaining. He'd make a marvelous teacher."

"Then why is it you don't like him?"

"I didn't say I don't like him. But a lot of people don't and I can see why. When he's not talking about art, he can be very nasty. He makes a point of saying that he does not respect laws and moral commandments. He says everybody cheats — that is, when they think they can get away with it. He sneers at people who have scruples, says they don't really, they're just putting up a front. He seems so petty then. That's the only way to put it."

"Does he tell you that you're a hypocrite like everybody else? Does he jibe at you?"

"No. He treats me very well. He always acts as if I was a sort of sounding board, not really a person. I don't really mind that. Sometimes he is in such a savage sort of humor that he needles me. I think he can't resist doing that to everyone at one time or another."

"It sounds to me as if it's the size of his ego. It takes up all the space around him."

They were sitting, as they had fallen into the habit of doing, in the living room of the apartment. Charlie Olsen did not like this new arrangement. When he found himself more and more often excluded from her company, he had pressed Clemence more urgently to spend the evenings with him. He was suspicious of what she did instead. When he learned that she preferred to spend them with Elissa, he demanded to know who she was, and when Clemence said, a friend from her college days, he wanted to know what was so fascinating about her.

Surely he said, she had outgrown this adolescent dependence on girl friends. It was time she acted her age, a grown woman with a place in her life for men.

Clemence had wondered at his vehemence. Why should he be so angry at the idea that she had a female friend with whom she preferred to spend part of her leisure time? Her first impulse was to ask Elissa what she made of this, and then it occurred to her that she had grown into the habit of consulting Elissa, in fact or imagination, whenever she was puzzled by the reactions of the people around her. Elissa had become a sort of source of understanding, as if Elissa herself would have no reaction to what she asked. Instinct held her back now. This was one situation in which Elissa might not respond as objectively as she expected.

"Well, what is the situation, then? Has Robert kidnapped the painting?" Elissa was asking.

"Not exactly. He ordered it removed from the place where it has been hanging and put into one of the storage vaults. He won't answer any questions he's asked about why he has done this, especially without consultation with any other Gallery official. The Gallery administration is threatening to suspend him from his job. He ignores what they say. Flora says that he has always been in conflicts like this and that he seems to thrive on this sort of controversy."

"Will they fire him?"

"They're afraid to. If they try, you see, they know he will make a public scandal. He won't hesitate to attack them in the newspapers and art journals. He doesn't mind that sort of notoriety for himself and he knows that they cringe at the very idea. He has a world-wide reputation, you know."

"I suppose Francis Hearn is watching all this."

"I am sure he is. He may even be egging people on to

act against Robert. I wonder why they are such enemies. But Francis won't come out in the open."

Elissa looked at her in surprise. "You've not got a very good opinion of him, then."

Clemence hesitated. "I really shouldn't say something like that because I don't really know what he is like. It is just a feeling I have. Francis has not been in the office since the painting was removed. I keep thinking that I should warn Robert to watch out for him. But I don't know why."

"Don't you think Robert suspects him already?"

Again Clemence hesitated. "I don't know. Robert is riding high. He's wrought up by the excitement, he thinks he's invulnerable, that he can smash anyone in his way. According to Flora, he has ridden through some pretty bad storms in his career. He thrives on this sort of thing, but it's hard on my nerves."

"Why, Clem? Why are you so upset by this?"

Clemence did not answer and Elissa, seated beside her on the sofa, put her arm along its back. She longed to touch Clemence. Clemence did not move, still deep in thought.

At last Clemence said, "It's hard for me to explain this to you, 'Lissa. Partly it's because of the painting itself. I call it A Flight of Angels. It is hard for me to explain to you the feeling I have when I look at it. Can you understand, 'Lissa, that a painting like that could change your whole mood, linger in your thoughts after you've looked at it? It has a religious theme: pilgrims being watched over by a host of angels in the sky. But it is not really a religious feeling I have. It is a sort of exaltation, as if for the moment you've been liberated from the confines of the world around you. Oh, it's hopeless for me to try to describe it. You've never seen it, have you?"

Elissa shook her head. Clemence turned and looked at her and Elissa was paralyzed by the feeling of wonder as she returned the look. Never before had she heard Clemence speak so simply, so fervently of her inmost feelings. This was not the composed Clemence she was used to, kindly but remote from the emotional stresses that affected other people.

There was a long silence. Elissa was afraid to speak or even shift her position for fear of breaking this rare, this extraordinary moment with Clemence. Clemence seemed lost in her own thoughts. After a while she sighed and seemed to return to the present.

Elissa waited for a while. Then she said, "By the way, there is something else I've been meaning to tell you. Do you remember Regina O'Phelan?"

"Oh, yes. I get a note from her every so often."

"She called me the other day, said she was going to be in Washington for a while and could we have lunch together. It seems she called me because she thought you'd gone out of the country with your parents and she knew I worked on Capitol Hill."

"Well, the last time I wrote to her I did say that I might go abroad with Father and Mother. That was before I got my appointment at the Gallery."

"What do you say we have dinner together, all three of us? She is much more your friend than mine."

"Oh, yes. That would be nice. Why don't you arrange it? You have a telephone number for her?"

Elissa nodded. "I said I would talk to you about it." Elissa paused. "Why did she transfer to Goucher in her senior year? That was unusual."

"She wanted to spend a year in a non-Catholic school before she went on to graduate work in psychology."

"That's a funny reason. And why did Goucher agree to this?"

"Regina is a brain. The faculty recognized that and

besides, you know Regina has a charming way about her. It's not such a funny reason. She had always gone to Catholic schools — parochial school and then to a convent of Ursuline nuns. Regina is brilliant. She would be a credit to any school. But she's not at all arrogant. I'm sure you remember how she used to be in class."

Elissa thought wryly, Yes, I do remember and how I resented her because she always seemed to know what to say and how to say it and always listened respectfully to what everybody said. You never knew what she really thought. Elissa remembered her physically also; in fact, a sharp image of her came up in front of her eyes when Regina phoned and she recognized the honey-like voice. Regina was a classic type of Irish beauty: dark, silky hair, large grey eyes, thin dark eyebrows, a porcelain skin with a bright dash of red in each cheek. She was also finely bred, her manners never less than impeccable. Around her you would feel awkward except for her subtle and constantly exercised gift of erasing any sense of conflict between herself and you. How many times, Elissa thought, I wanted to be rude to her but she never let me be. Some of the girls nevertheless disliked her — envious, probably, and made ill-at-ease by her obvious intellectual superiority. But not Clemence. Clemence did not seem to feel any reason for dislike or envy.

"But why did she wait till her senior year?"

"Because of her family. They did not approve. They thought she should continue her way through Catholic schools."

"She probably felt claustrophobic."

Clemence, aware that Elissa's outlook was strictly non-religious, said patiently, "Naturally her family wanted her to stay within the fold. I suppose they were nervous because she is so exceptionally gifted. She has an IQ close to genius. She could never quarrel with her people, so she had to wait till she could talk them round."

41

"You mean her parents?"

"Her mother, really. I think her father has been dead for some time. I suppose there are other relatives — there usually are in clannish families — who thought they should have a say in what she chose to do." Clemence remembered Regina, pensive when they were alone together, excusing the absence of her usual courteous cheerfulness by saying, "Call it Celtic melancholy, dear."

Elissa was saying, "You say you've heard from her from time to time. Has she finally broken loose?"

"I don't really know. Her letters are about her academic life. She doesn't go into details about her personal affairs. Right now she is working on her dissertation for her Ph.D. It is based on experimental research about memory — why we remember and how we do. She's worried because there are questions being raised about the validity of the results — whether the work she is doing, along with other researchers — will stand up under scrutiny. Getting her degree depends on these results."

"Well, I'm glad we'll be a party of three."

Clemence laughed. "You sound as if you're afraid of her."

Clemence picked up the sheaf of papers from her desk. She had just arrived and she had taken them out of her desk drawer where she had placed them the evening before. This was work she had done for Robert and it had been too late to take it to him then. He insisted that any papers he gave her or that she typed for him should stay in her hands until she could give them directly to him. She went down the corridor to his office and walked through the outer room, nodding to the two assistants who sat there. She had expected simply to lay the papers on his desk and go out again, perhaps without a word from him, if he was immersed in work. Lately he had completely abandoned the satirical gallantry with which he was in the custom of greeting her. But this morning when she entered he was sitting at his desk waiting. When he saw her he threw down his pen.

"Ah, the messenger from the enemy camp. What news do you bring? What are they saying behind my back?"

She looked at him in astonishment, partly because of the black look on his face and the fierceness of his tone of voice. She must have walked in on some argument that was raging in his mind. She was at once scared and dismayed. Robert never showed his hand like this. If he was breaking down under the strain of being beleaguered, she did not feel capable of coping with his collapse.

"Why, I don't know," she stammered.

"Oh, yes, you do. You must hear what everybody is saying."

"Well, I suppose everyone is wondering what you intend to do with the painting."

"I would suppose that. But are they digging up all that old business about its authenticity? Do they say I've hidden it so that they can't have it tested again to see if it's genuine?"

"Robert, I don't know what is being said. I try to keep out of that sort of thing. I am just unhappy that the painting isn't hanging where it belongs. I miss the angels."

He jumped up from his desk and paced around the room. What she said now seemed to penetrate through the mass of thoughts that filled his mind and he stopped and stared at her. "What did you say?"

"I miss the angels — the flight of angels. That is what I call if privately. It is so wonderful."

"How amazing!"

"It is amazing. It is amazing how the painter had

captured such a feeling — the flight of angels and the pilgrims below in the shadows —"

"The heavenly host hovering over a darkening world. What a wonderful concept. No, I meant how amazing that you should respond so to that painting." Robert seemed to forget the venom that had filled him when she had first come into the room. His mind now was taken up with the recollection of the painting, the marvel of the painter's skill. "How difficult it is to look into the mind and emotions of an artist, to know for a certainty what he is seeking to project in a form that can transmit his vision to another human being. We have reams and reams of interpretations, rationalizations, syntheses of great paintings and yet, if you're honest, when you look at a painting for yourself, you wonder how far off the mark you can be. Perhaps Giardini is fortunate. Very few people have sounded off about his painting. It is fresh, almost neglected —" He stopped and looked at her again. "You talk about that painting as if it means something special to you. Does it?"

"Yes. Ever since I first saw it I've come to feel that it is more and more part of my world. There is something about the group of floating figures that catches at me — as if they shed a heavenly light —"

"I'm sure Giardini would be delighted to know that. That must have been what he wanted to convey — not just the vision of angels but the sense of heavenly grace that filled that vision." Robert fell silent and stalked away from her across the room. When he turned round he said, "But how beyond the comprehension of our colleagues such a concept is."

Clemence saw that his old feeling of ill-will was coming back. She waited for what he would say next.

He struck the top of his desk with the flat of his hand. "All they are concerned about is that I have found reason to believe that I have made a mistake in acquiring

44

the painting and that I have sequestered it to hide this fact from them. That's absolutely the feeblest rubbish I ever heard."

Clemence realized that he must be referring to something that had been said in a meeting of the arts council that advised the trustees.

He went on. "The idea is that I've done the Gallery out of a large sum of money — the price paid for that painting — and cost it besides a lot of prestige through having a fake hanging on the wall for five years. It's up to me to make reparations."

"What did you tell them?"

"That the painting is not a fake and that I didn't connive with a certain dishonest dealer to acquire it."

"Why do they think it is a fake?"

"They don't know whether it is a fake. They're not well-enough informed to make such a judgment. They are just frightened by the idea that it might be. In reality they are afraid of me. This is all Francis Hearn's idea, of course. He is clever at manipulating them."

Venom dripped in his voice. Clemence spoke timidly. "Has Francis accused you of knowing that it is a fake?"

Robert made a grimace, half angry, half contemptuous. "He would never come out in the open and accuse anyone of anything. He puts an idea in someone's mind and when that person speaks of it, he agrees with them."

He turned away from her with a dismissive gesture. But she lingered long enough to ask, "Why did you take the painting down?"

He turned back to her and said sharply, "So you really want to know? Because I wanted to stir up this nest of the complacent. I wanted to bring this all out into the open before Hearn has a chance to build a trap for me in the dark." He paused and glared at her. "You can go and tell him so."

Clemence was offended. "I am not a particular friend

45

of his. I talked to you about the painting because it means something special to me. It cannot possibly be a fake, can it?"

He looked at her for a moment, his mind obviously divided between the subject of the row about the painting and her own reaction to it. "Well, don't get upset, Clemence. No, it is not a fake. No threats are going to change what I am going to do." He picked up the papers she had placed on his desk. "Thanks for these. I'll call you when I want something else."

She walked slowly out of the room and back to her desk. Whatever had been the fact before today, it was now true that she did have an inside track with Robert, whether she wanted it or not.

"You ought to get out of that sorority you spend most of your time with."

Charlie Olsen had insisted that she spend Sunday afternoon with him at a ball game. The team from his alma mater was playing Georgetown. They weren't favored to win, he said, because the odds were always on the home team. When she said she knew nothing about football and could not follow the game, he swept her objection aside and said that she should learn to enjoy watching robust masculine sports.

When the game was over they went to a tavern in Georgetown and sat in a corner booth surrounded by boisterous parties. Since the weather was still mild, the air was oppressive from the crowded bodies.

"What do you mean, sorority?"

"All these girls you spend your time with — sorority, a band of sisters. It's Latin."

She was offended. "I know it's Latin. But what do you mean?"

Charlie laughed, pleased to have riled her. "Why, I mean, why are you so exclusive with these female friends of yours?"

"I don't think it is any business of yours who my friends are or how much time I spend with them."

Charlie's bantering tone vanished. "Now, look, Clemence, you're getting downright bad-tempered. What's got into you?"

"I'm not in the mood for corny jokes."

Charlie looked nonplussed. He had an open, ingenuous face, not handsome, but attractive because of the aura of good health he projected. He had a snub nose and ginger hair and somehow promoted the feeling in others that he was honest, wholesome and not likely to cheat or be revengeful. "But, really, Clem, I thought we were beginning to get really close and now all of a sudden I have all this female competition."

"It's not all of a sudden. It's just that these girls I knew at Goucher keep coming to Washington to work for the Government and want to pick up where we left off. Don't you have a lot of old college pals?"

"Well, yes. But most of mine are married and wives don't seem to like their husbands' old friends. It's natural. You go on in life to meet new people, find new interests."

Clemence did not answer at once. Charlie, as if seeking some neutral topic, said, "What's this gossip I hear about a scandal brewing at the Gallery — something about a painting?"

Clemence glanced at him. "You've heard gossip?"

"Aha! Then there's something to it. I know somebody who works for the Fine Arts Committee on the Hill and he says there's a feud going on between one of your curators and the trustees. What's it all about?"

Clemence sighed and took a sip of her drink. "I don't want to talk about it — certainly not on my leisure time."

For a few minutes Charlie was silent. Then he said,

leaning forward a little, "I think I can make a good guess that it's something to do with Robert Alden."

"Why would you think so? What do you know about him?"

"Well, he's a favorite subject of gossip at cocktail parties. I don't know him but he is a curator, isn't he? I remember that there was something in the paper about him back when he was appointed to the Gallery. That was before your time. The FBI took a dim view of him."

"That's all in the past."

"Nothing's ever in the past as far as the FBI is concerned. Do you work for him?"

"Yes, I do some of his typing, as I do for other people. I'm not an assistant of his, if that's what you mean."

"Do people think you're his girlfriend?"

"Well, I'm not."

"I should hope so! He's not married and I've heard rumors about him."

"I don't know anything about his private life. Now, can we stop talking about the Gallery and Robert Alden?"

He agreed reluctantly. They finished their beer and went to dinner in a nearby restaurant. Charlie was truculent when she refused to spend the night with him.

Clemence said to Elissa, "Charlie Olsen says I should shake loose from my sorority."

"Your sorority?"

"He says I shouldn't spend so much time with women. I'm always putting him off."

"Men don't usually like it when you put female company ahead of their own. Don't worry about it. They always hint that you may not be normal."

"Normal?"

Elissa was suddenly embarrassed. She did not know

how sophisticated Clemence was when it came to sex. "You remember, at college, there were some girls who got talked about because they had crushes on other girls or some of the professors."

"Oh, that! Well, what I do with my leisure time is none of his business."

"Of course. But Washington is a place where there is always a lot of gossip about such things. About men and about women."

"About men?"

"Yes. Especially about men. Some people say that J. Edgar Hoover is a fairy, you know — that's one word they use. He pretends to hate homosexuals — perhaps he really does. But he has a male friend he treats as if he was his wife. The FBI is great at trying to entrap suspected characters."

Clemence was silent for so long that Elissa decided to change the subject. "Have you been seeing Regina? I haven't seen her since our dinner together."

"I've talked to her on the phone. She seems to want somebody to talk to."

"You know, I think about her every so often. She seems sort of at loose ends — as if she is groping for something. I suppose that's not surprising since she's just come to town and probably doesn't know anybody."

"Oh, but that's not true! Her mother lives here, has lived here for years, out in the northeast part of town, near the Shrine of the Immaculate Conception — what the Catholics like to call the Christian part of town. That's what they say in the classified ads for apartments out that way. Regina's father worked for the Government."

"Well, then, she shouldn't be lonely. But she strikes me as being sad — as if she has something on her mind."

"She'd say that was just Celtic melancholy. But she does have something on her mind. It's a problem concerning her dissertation. The research she has been doing is breaking new ground and I think there is some criticism of its validity. I don't understand it very well, but that is what she talks about chiefly. What she needs is more frivolity in her life. Regina is too serious."

"I don't really know her but I wouldn't dispute you."

They were silent for a while and then Clemence suddenly said, "I think I should throw a party. That's the way to solve everything."

"A party? What kind of a party?"

"Oh, I suppose you'd call it a cocktail party. That's the thing to do in Washington, isn't it?"

"Ah! The Washington cocktail party. Who are you going to invite?"

"The people I work with and whoever else at the Gallery wants to come. And you and Regina. Especially Regina. I think that one of the things she is afraid of is that, without new friends of her own, she'll be drawn back into the family circle. Evidently she finds it pretty deadly. She's so nervous about her dissertation and she has nobody to discuss it with except the other researchers."

"She's nervous all right. I almost got indigestion sitting next to her the evening we had dinner."

"She is so reticent. She seems to be appealing to me for help or sympathy but she can't bring herself to speak out about what's bothering her."

"Too inhibited. Her work in psychology doesn't seem to have helped her much."

"It is easy to understand things in the abstract without being able to apply what you know to yourself."

"Where will you have the party?"

Clemence looked around the big living room with its old-fashioned, shabby furniture. The apartment had been built years ago — it was one of the first in Washington — when the people who moved into it still thought in terms of houses. Clemence said, "I think I'll have it here. It would be expensive to have it in a hotel or restaurant and not nearly as effective for what I want to do."

"Well, that will be different, certainly." Elissa wondered how Clemence would manage. She was sure that Clemence had never before arranged a large party. She had always been simply the docile daughter of parents with an easy-going attitude toward social entertaining. "Are you sending out invitations? Or doing it by word of mouth? That's easy enough here. All people need to hear is the rumor of a cocktail party and they're on your doorstep. I'll spread the news around my bailiwick."

Elissa was right, thought Clemence on the appointed Sunday.

Elissa had arrived early to give a hand in arranging the plates of little sandwiches, the supply of glasses and bottles. Clemence had hired her mother's cleaning woman, Vinnie, to serve as waitress. Vinnie was accompanied by her husband, a dignified man who worked in the daytime as chauffeur for officials in the Government agencies. Elissa recognized him. She had met him often at other cocktail parties. It was wonderful, she thought, how the messengers and chauffeurs you saw every day in the halls of Congress and other government establishments greeted you in the evening at somebody's house. The fund of personal information about official Washington they gathered must be enormous.

Regina was one of the first to arrive, wearing a filmy cocktail dress that emphasized her usual air of delicate fragility. The fact is, thought Elissa, she is the very type of the Princesse de Lointaine, remote and seductive even as she chattered cheerfully with the other guests. Her dark silky hair, her transparent skin with its flush of red over the cheekbones, her slender neck whose delicacy was accentuated by the thin gold chain that held the religious medal hidden beneath her dress — it was so obvious that the effect sought by so many women through the use of cosmetics had come to her through the gift of nature. Her thin dark eyebrows moved constantly as she talked, laughed. She was the same height as Clemence, who beside her looked the robust outdoor type. When she was closely engaged in conversation her slim body seemed to tremble with the nervous force that flowed through it.

Regina did not arrive alone. With her was her sister Kathleen. Elissa had not known she had a sister but this seemed to be no surprise to Clemence. There could not have been a greater contrast between the two sisters. Kathleen was taller and must surely, thought Elissa, weigh half again as much as Regina. She was not fat, simply robust, with reddish hair and an air of being uneasy in strange surroundings. Her voice was louder, her manner of speaking positive, a sort of natural aggressiveness that quenched Regina's presence. Their only feature in common, thought Elissa, was the fresh perfection of their complexions.

When Clemence had told Elissa that she had invited both Robert Alden and Francis Hearn, Elissa exclaimed, "Clem! You didn't!"

"Yes, I did." There was a stubbornness in her expression that told Elissa that she had deliberately chosen to take a chance. "I couldn't invite one without the other and I couldn't leave them both out."

"Well, I hardly think they'd start a fight — unless they have too much to drink. I've seen things like that happen."

Robert was in fact the first to arrive after Regina and Kathleen. Clemence herself was a little surprised, having supposed that he would wait until the party was well underway before making his entrance. His attention immediately fastened on Regina. He sees her, thought Clemence, as an Italian Renaissance beauty.

She heard him ask, "Are you new to Washington, Miss O'Phelan?"

The color in Regina's cheeks intensified. "Oh, no! I was born here. But I have been away quite a while."

"That's interesting. Away —?"

"Oh, at school, college. I'm working now on my graduate degree."

"In what discipline?" Robert, Clemence knew, was not a man to mouth some stupid remark about what should a pretty girl like you be doing working for a graduate degree.

"Psychology."

He raised his eyebrows. "That's interesting! Why?"

Out of sheer nervousness Regina laughed. "Because I want to make it my profession."

He nodded as if he found the answer satisfactory. What was it about Robert, Clemence wondered, that made it so difficult to pin down your opinion of him? In his manner towards Regina there was only a sort of kindly interest, while his eyes dwelt on her beauty as if he was examining a rare object of art. Clemence knew how he behaved at the office — making amorous gestures towards the women who worked there, gestures that seemed automatic, perfunctory, as if required. Now he was talking to Regina, listening attentively but as if absentmindedly to what she was saying in answer to his questions.

After Robert the guests began to arrive in twos and threes and Clemence was kept busy welcoming them. The servants, used to these affairs, moved unobtrusively through the crowd, offering trays. Clemence was not aware that Charlie Olsen had arrived until she found him in a corner watching the throng. Elissa must have greeted him at the door.

"Hi, there, Clemence," he said. "This is quite a bash. Where'd all these people come from?"

"Why don't you circulate and find out? Here, you can start now. Kathleen, this is Charlie Olsen. He's in the Archives. Charlie, Kathleen O'Phelan. She's Regina's sister. You've heard me speak of her. That's Regina over there. She's one of my sorority sisters."

She looked him in the eye as she said this. When she turned away, Kathleen said, looking him over, "What did she mean by that? I didn't know that Regina and Clemence were sorority sisters."

Charlie's face reddened. "Oh, it's just a joke. Can I get you a drink? That one's gone." He pointed to the glass in her hand.

But the waiter appeared at his elbow and handed them both fresh drinks. When Clemence looked in their direction fifteen minutes later she was surprised to see them still together in animated conversation.

Francis Hearn arrived when the party was at its height. He came across the room, finding his way carefully through the crowd of bodies to where Clemence stood. Having greeted her, he said, "I thought I would find your parents here."

"Oh, no. They're still out of the country. I don't expect them back a while yet." She was acutely aware that Robert was somewhere behind her. She waited anxiously for Francis' gaze, wandering systematically over the throng, to light upon him, but if Francis saw him, he gave no sign.

Instead she found herself introducing him to Regina, who had come to her side to escape from the close ring of men competing for her attention. Regina frowned at his close stare, which presently, remembering common politeness, he turned away from her. He began talking rapidly about anything that came into his head, as if clinging to a plank in the sea. Regina was her usual self-possessed self. It was not for nothing, thought Clemence, that she had spent her adolescence in a convent school run by Ursuline nuns, elite women whose social upbringing survived their immersion in conventual life.

When she did see Robert, Clemence knew at once that he had spotted Francis. Robert was standing beside a man who was talking to him with energy, whom he was obviously trying to ignore. He glowered and his face was red. Surely he had not had that much to drink, Clemence worried.

She glanced over at Francis. Francis likewise had seen Robert and for a moment he seemed undecided. Regina had again been surrounded by a group of men, of which Francis was one. Then he slowly began to make his way toward Robert.

When he reached him he said, "Hello, Robert," but his voice was not cordial.

Their confrontation was so obvious that the chatter of the people closest to them died down. Clemence, standing near Robert, held her breath. Robert did not speak. He seemed to swell with suppressed anger and for a moment, to Clemence, time stopped. Then he put out a hand at arm's length, as if to push Francis aside but without touching him, and walked past him, shouldering his way past people to the front door of the apartment, opened it and went out, letting it close behind him with a thud. The party chatter resumed, like a wave of sound closing over a vacuum. Someone who had had too much to drink broke out into a loud laugh.

The party began to subside as people left. When most of them had gone, Charlie Olsen lingered, still absorbed in conversation with Kathleen, whom he had followed around the room as she moved to talk to other people.

Now, as Kathleen said to Regina, "Hadn't we better go now, 'Gina?," he spoke up, "Why don't you let me take you two home? I have my car here."

"We live pretty far out," said Kathleen. "Out in the northeast."

Francis, standing behind Regina, struck in, "Why don't we all go to dinner — all six of us?" He glanced at Clemence and Elissa as he spoke.

Clemence shook her head. "I can't go now," she said. "I must stay here till Vinnie and her husband have cleared up."

In the end the foursome left for a good restaurant that Francis recommended.

Clemence said, "Are you hungry, 'Lissa? You could have gone with them."

"No, I ate so many of those little sandwiches that I don't want dinner."

Clemence nodded, listening to the sounds from the kitchen. Vinnie and her husband did not take long. Years of practice had made them efficient and quick. Finally the door closed on them.

Elissa said, "That was quite a party, Clem."

Clemence turned away from the window where she had been standing gazing out at the teeming rain. The fine afternoon had dissolved into stormy weather. "I'm so glad that you were here with me, 'Lissa. I'll admit I was frightened about how it was all going to go."

"That was a sticky moment when Francis bearded Robert, wasn't it?"

Clemence sighed. "I suppose I shouldn't have done it."

"Well, it went off all right. Did you notice that Charlie Olsen is fascinated by Kathleen?"

"Not really." Clemence spoke absently as if the subject

was on the periphery of her mind. She was still standing at the window. Presently she said, "You might as well spend the night here. You'd have the devil of a time getting a cab in that weather."

Elissa held her breath for a few moments. She searched Clemence's face for information but found none. Still abstracted, Clemence walked away from the window and sat down on the sofa. Elissa sat down beside her. Clemence raised her arm from the back of the sofa and laid it across Elissa's shoulders. "Stay with me, 'Lissa. I need you here tonight."

Sitting so close to her, Elissa felt sudden warmth penetrating her body. Wildly she wondered, what would happen if I said, "I love you, Clem?" But the mere idea of daring this checked her and the old familiar distrust of herself took hold.

Surprised by her silence, Clemence said, "You will, won't you?"

"Of course. It doesn't make any difference to anybody at the boarding house if I don't show up. The cook isn't there on Sundays."

"You can have my room. I'll sleep in my parents'. I'm edgy tonight and I can't tell you why." Then she added, "I think it's just a general feeling that things aren't very satisfactory."

"Why not, Clem?"

Clemence shifted around to look at her. "You'd never feel like this, 'Lissa. You've always got something that takes up your heart and mind. But I'm at a loose end. Why do you suppose I've taken this job at the Gallery? I don't need to earn my living at something like this. My parents won't mind if I go on living with them for the rest of their lives. I think they'd like it better if I developed some burning interest in life — the sort of thing they have. But I can't and there's no use pretending. I took the job to fill up some of the twenty-four hours in a day. I suppose I had the idea that I might stumble onto something if I was among people who had a real interest in what they were doing. But most of the people I work with don't really care what they earn their living at. Robert is the only one that isn't that way. To him, art is the most living thing in the world. As far as he is concerned, no matter how unsatisfactory people are, there is always art. It must be wonderful to feel that way."

"He does mean something to you, doesn't he, Clem?"

Clemence's attention came quickly down to her. "Not in a romantic way. He just seems to me to be such a real person. He could be male, or female, or black or white or green. He is what he is and he doesn't change for anyone."

"And a lot of people don't like him for that very reason."

Clemence nodded. "I don't say he is very easy to deal with, because he isn't. He's —"

"Sublimely indifferent to what anybody thinks," Elissa said, as she hesitated. "Well, he knows you like him better than most people do. He'd be stupid if he didn't."

Clemence interrupted her own thoughts to look at her. The trace of jealousy in Elissa's voice was unmistakable. Clemence thought, that odd, intimate demand that she always makes on me, remembering innumerable occasions back at Goucher when Elissa had become sulky and ill-tempered, had walked away from her when some other girl's friendliness intervened. She said, "I've told you, 'Lissa, I don't have a sentimental interest in Robert. He'd laugh his head off if he thought I was falling in love with him. The trouble is that the women in the office think just that — that I'm infatuated with Robert and that he is playing me along to make a fool of me. It seems he has done that with other women."

"Clem —" Elissa began and stopped. She was in a

turmoil of emotions and as usual she could not express them in the cool, rational way that Clemence seemed to expect. She felt Clemence looking at her. She could not turn to look at her.

She felt Clemence's hand on her shoulder, burning her skin through the cloth of her dress.

Clemence said, " 'Lissa, I've asked you to stay with me. If you would rather not, just say so."

"No, no!" Elissa cried. "I want to stay!" She felt that she was choking with the tension that had built up in her, and was surprised that her voice came out so calm. Oh, Clem, she screamed silently, will I ever be able to tell you what you mean to me? How I want to rant and rave and tear out my hair, letting you know what a marvelous, unbelievable thing your "friendship" is to me? How I want to seize hold of you and squeeze you till you feel something of what I feel?

But none of that would be acceptable to Clem and she must spend the rest of the evening — and later, alone in Clem's bedroom — suppressing the raging torrent of words and arguments that welled up in her.

Clemence got up and turned on the radio to the good music station and they spent the rest of the evening listening to Guy Lombardo and his band.

II

Elissa laid the Government Printing Office document on Clemence's desk. Clemence glanced at it. It was in the usual two-column format of reports of Congressional committee hearings. She picked it up and looked at Elissa, standing beside her. The lunch hour had begun and they were alone in the Gallery's administrative office.

Elissa said, "I've had a glimpse of the transcript of the FBI files in 1949 when Robert was being investigated before his appointment to the staff here. He was interrogated several times but I couldn't read much of the transcript, so I can't tell what they asked him or what he said. But there was a reference to this document of the 1947 hearings before a subcommittee investigating the use of Army funds for nonmilitary purposes. Robert was one of the witnesses."

Clemence looked at the document again and then, opening her desk drawer, slipped it inside the pouch she used as a briefcase. Without being told, Elissa understood her intention to take it home to read away from the curious eyes of her office mates.

Clemence got up and they walked together down to the cafeteria, seeking a table where they would not be surrounded by tourists. When they had placed their trays and sat down, Elissa said, "Robert was well-known in 1947 as an art expert. That was why he was called as a witness. He had been hired by the Army to help identify and restore the art treasures that had been discovered by Patton's army at Berchtesgaden."

"Yes, I know that. He held several curatorships in big museums before he came here, all over the country. And he has been in Europe a lot. He was always going from one place to another, because he would never accept supervision. He said it would compromise the integrity of his freedom to speak out. But everybody wanted him in spite of his high-handedness, even though they knew he might walk out in a rage over some petty dispute. Everybody knows he can't be equalled in his field. There is nowhere he has ever been that he hasn't left behind a finer collection than he found. He's arrogant but he's audacious, too, and he has the courage of his convictions. There are a lot of articles and a couple books about him. He's not afraid of wealthy people, the sort who spend their money collecting art and donating it to museums. The Gallery was very anxious to get him. You know, the Gallery has only been in operation since 1941 and it needs someone like him to open up the future."

"You certainly have his history down pat." Elissa

spoke before she could bite back the comment. She
hurried on, to cover up the sharpness of her tone of voice.
"You'll find a lot about him in these hearings. You can
spend your time with him when I'm working overtime."

Clemence glanced up at her, but all she said was,
"You do work a lot of overtime these days, don't you?"

"Yes. Ever since President Eisenhower had his heart
attack." After a pause she said, "How about Charlie
Olsen?"

"I don't see him very often now."

"Isn't that a change?"

"Well, yes. He's interested in another girl."

"Oh? Who?"

"I don't know. It's just my guess."

Elissa looked at her but said nothing.

That evening, Clemence, arriving at the big, empty
apartment, poured herself a drink and sat down on the
sofa in the living room. To be alone like this, without
Elissa, had become a rarity, unwelcome when it happened.
She reached down to the pouch at her feet and pulled out
the hearings report. 1947. At that time, eight years ago,
she had been in preparatory school, only just thinking
about college. She read the heading and ran her eye down
the first column.

The questioner asked, "Your name is Robert Alden
and you give your profession as art expert. You've been a
curator in a number of museums and art galleries. Is that
correct?"

"Yes."

"Where were you in June, 1945?"

"Paris."

"France? What were you doing there?"

"I was attached to the U.S. military government to
give technical advice on the identification and restoration
of art objects and paintings that had been discovered after
the liberation of France."

"Were you a member of the armed forces?"

"No. I was a civilian."

"What do you mean by art objects that had been discovered?"

"I mean art that had been looted by the Nazis from all the countries they invaded. Hermann Göring was the man who did this — Hitler's Reichsmarschal. He gathered a huge collection of art objects and paintings. In April, 1945, General Patton's Third Army found a salt mine at Merkers, a village near Eisenach, where some of these things had been hidden."

"And where was that?"

"In Germany. It was the birthplace of Johann Sebastian Bach and Martin Luther lived there at one time."

Reading, Clemence smiled. How like Robert! Handing out these nuggets of information in his blandest voice, mocking his interrogator, who probably suspected that he was being mocked but was unable to put his finger on exactly how. She went back to the report.

The questioner said (no doubt testily, Clemence thought) "Well, we aren't concerned with those people right now. What was in that mine?"

"The gold reserves of the German government and stacks of German and foreign paper money. There were also hundreds of pieces of art. Generals Eisenhower and Bradley and Patton saw all this."

"Did you?"

"No. I wasn't there. I saw the paintings when they had been taken out of there. They were in very poor shape. But I was at Berchtesgaden when the American army took over the place and found Göring's art collection buried in caves and tunnels under the castle where Göring surrendered. He had taken it there from Berlin. It took four days to empty the place. These things were in deplorable condition, injured by damp and covered up with tapestries to protect them from water dripping from the roof. The tapestries themselves were priceless treasures."

The questioner (obviously, thought Clemence, intrigued in spite of himself by Robert's narration) said, "You mean to say these things were all taken away from other countries?"

"Yes. The Russian commander Marshal Konig found the treasures looted from Dresden in a limestone quarry in Lingenfeld near the Czech border. The Sistine Madonna was among them, surrounded by pools of stagnant water. It will take years to repair this damage."

The questioner interrupted. "We don't need all this irrelevant detail. What were the Russians doing there?"

In her mind's eye Clemence could see the surprised look on Robert's face. "Why, they captured that area. The Russian army was driving west to meet the Allied forces."

"So they got to this place first? You say you weren't at this place when those things were found? This is hearsay?"

"Naturally I wasn't with the Russians."

"Who was in charge of the work you were doing?"

"Mr. James Rorimer, the director of the Metropolitan Museum of Art in New York. He was Monuments and Fine Arts Director for the U.S. Army and he recommended that I be hired to help in preserving these treasures."

"Why did he recommend you?"

"I suppose because he had heard of my work in the past."

"How did you get to Paris in June, 1945? Did you travel with the military?"

"I was already there."

"You were already there. Were you collaborating with the Germans?"

Clemence, reading, could hear the expression in Robert's voice. "May I remind you that art is my profession, my life work. Like other people in my field, I had been aware throughout the war years that the great treasures of Europe were in extreme danger, not only from the destruction of cities by bombing, but from looting. A good many treasures were lost — and remain lost to this day — through thievery not only by invading armies but by individuals who saw a chance to steal in the confusion of warfare and its aftermath. A number of masterpieces were undoubtedly brought home by American soldiers."

"Are you accusing American GIs of being thieves?"

"The facts speak for themselves. Sometimes people stole and then sold what they stole, sometimes for a pound of butter or a loaf of bread, when starvation stared them in the face."

He's well away now, thought Clemence, reading on through Robert's tirade, which was eventually cut short by his exasperated interrogator. Robert was no more patient then than he was now, obviously, with those he thought stupid and no more careful not to offend them, though they might have the power to harm him and the wish to, from resentment or revenge for subtle humiliation.

Clemence put the hearings report down and sat pondering. The report had certainly thrown a clear light on the Robert of ten years ago. Elissa had said that this report had been referred to in the FBI investigation. There were several things that might rouse the FBI's interest. How had Robert reached Europe before the liberation of France? He could have been in England, of course. Or had he escaped there from somewhere in occupied France? And how had he learned about the Russians' rescue of the Dresden treasures? These were things Robert had not divulged and did not intend to.

* * * * *

The following Sunday was a clear, brilliant sunny October day. Elissa had a car, a Volkswagen she had bought second-hand when she came to Washington.

"Let's go out into the country," she said, after a late breakfast in Clemence's apartment. The Sunday papers were spread around the living room floor. "I'm tired of reading about Congress trying to sabotage the civil rights act."

They drove in a leisurely way through the mellowness of the Virginian countryside, till they were within sight of the Blue Ridge Mountains. There was not a great deal of traffic on the secondary roads they chose and the warm browns of the fields and the blue of the distant hills was soothing. Elissa finally pulled off at a wayside that had a view across a valley to a lower ridge of the mountains. In the shade of a brilliant red oak they sat for a while enjoying the stillness.

Presently Elissa asked, going back to the subject they had been discussing earlier, "Do you think that Robert and Francis met back then in 1945?"

"They could have, very easily. Francis was on Eisenhower's staff when the Germans surrendered. Seeing all those wonderful treasures that Robert described may have been what made him decide to make the fine arts his field."

"So he might encounter Robert, the outside expert. And Robert might have snubbed him as an ignoramus."

"Well, I suppose so. After Francis was demobilized he became interested in museum management. He became director of a small gallery in the midwest. That was only ten years ago. Since then he has gone straight up the ladder till he became a curator at the Metropolitan Museum of Art and then he has come here. There could be some family influence in that. He has a cousin who is a state senator and some other relative who is in the Congress. He has acquired a very good reputation in gallery administration and people respect him, even if he doesn't have long experience. I suppose part of the answer must be that he knows how to get along with people — he doesn't make enemies, like Robert."

"In other words, he knows how to deal with people who have money and power — and with politicians."

"Yes, that must be so. But —"

Elissa prompted her, "Yes, but what?"

"He is very competent. Everybody thinks so. But he lacks something that Robert has. Robert feels passionately about art, about the value of art. He feels that if he doesn't fight for what he thinks is right, he is betraying the Muses. He feels he has a sacred trust to guard — actually to guard against people like Francis, who have a more mundane view of the place of art in society. I don't think that Francis would ever understand that, no matter how efficient he is in dealing with art objects."

Elissa watched her as she spoke. This was the Clemence she had sometimes seen at Goucher, arguing in support of some abstract principle. "Judging from what you say, I should say that Robert has the power of swaying people, nevertheless."

"Of course. That is the strength of his integrity where art and art standards are concerned. He can overwhelm you when he gets on that subject."

"Does he know how you feel about him?"

Again Clemence's ear picked up the trace of jealousy in Elissa's voice. It penetrated through the wall of her own enthusiasm. "What do you mean?"

"You certainly are his great defender."

Clemence replied testily, "This has nothing to do with any personal feeling for him, 'Lissa. I don't like to see anyone attacked behind his back. But I don't like the things that Robert is apt to do and say. He has no sense of honor in personal dealings. He thinks that sort of thing is nonsense. Everybody should watch out for him or

67

herself and anybody who doesn't put himself first is a fool. And he doesn't suffer fools gladly. Art is pure to Robert. No human being is."

"What do you think about Francis, then?"

Clemence was slow to reply. "I don't know. He seems to be a more — more respectable person than Robert. He's more adaptable. But —"

"But?"

"I can't convince myself that I like him."

"Why is that?"

"I don't know. There's just something that makes me want to side with Robert."

"But Robert wouldn't thank you. And your father likes Francis."

"That's true. And my father is a very good judge of character."

There was a long silence while Clemence's mind seemed to run on the problem. Elissa sat quietly, yearning to bring her attention back to herself, yet afraid to trespass on Clemence's musing. She gazed at the mountain range in the distance, absorbed in the gradations of blueness in the clear air. She was startled when she felt Clemence's hand on her arm and turned to see a smile on Clemence's face.

Clemence said, "It's lovely out here alone together, isn't it, 'Lissa?"

Elissa burst out, "Oh, Clem, I'm so happy when I'm with you!"

"Well, so am I with you, 'Lissa." She passed her arm around Elissa's shoulders and brought her face close so that she could lay her cheek against Elissa's. " 'Lissa, do you remember, back then, when we all used to talk about the sort of lives we wanted to live — what sort of women we wanted to be —"

Elissa, thrilling throughout her body to the touch of Clemence's skin against her own, thought wildly, yes, and how I wanted to tell you that I wanted to be with you forever — that I didn't want any of that stupid business of marrying a man and setting up a family, as the other girls foresaw for themselves. You didn't talk that way. You say, how "we" used to talk. It wasn't "we" — you and me. You never said anything but just sat there listening with a sympathetic look on your face and I listened as long as I could stand it and then picked up and left. Aloud Elissa finally said, controlling her impulse to seize hold of Clemence, "You and I had some idea of what sort of women we wanted to be, we ourselves. The rest were all for joining the young married set as soon as possible."

Clemence laughed lightly. "There were some exceptions, 'Lissa, though I must admit, most of them wanted just that. But I didn't talk because I didn't know what I wanted to do." She sat up and turned to face Elissa. " 'Lissa, there have been cases of two women who have lived together for years and years. Do you suppose they were as happy as if they did the usual thing and married men and had children? Or was it just a compromise — making do with what's available, so to speak?"

Elissa felt choked by her own emotions. She managed to say, "I think some of them certainly were happier than if they had married men. In fact —" She choked on what she was going to say, frightened by the sudden golden opportunity to say what she longed to say.

Clemence was not looking at her, but gazing out over the valley, dotted with farmhouses and trees ablaze with October colors. The great stillness of the mountainside silenced both of them. The soft breeze brought the scent of sweet grass from the meadow below. Elissa was aware that she would always remember this moment drenched in that scent.

Clemence said, "You remember, there were girls who

69

had crushes on each other or some of the teachers — even in college that was so. I don't think this is the same thing."

Elissa burst out, "If this is a crush I have on you, Clem, it's going to last forever!"

She was disconcerted when Clemence laughed merrily. "You can't tell if it's forever till it's over, can you? Oh, now, 'Lissa, don't get upset! What we feel for each other is pretty solid, isn't it? After all these weeks, spending every free moment with you, I feel as if it's always been this way." She reached over to take Elissa's face in her hands and kiss her on the lips. She seemed surprised when Elissa caught her in a tight embrace and thrust her tongue into her mouth.

After a few moments, when they relaxed, Clemence said, "I wouldn't want to do that with anybody else. Charlie Olsen tried it once. I found it disgusting." She ran her hand down the back of Elissa's neck. "Circumstances alter cases, don't they?"

Elissa did not answer but began to search under Clemence's blouse, undoing her bra and taking her breasts in her hand, at the same time entering her mouth once more with her tongue.

Clemence pushed gently against her and turned her face away so that her mouth was out of reach. "I like it with you, 'Lissa — so warm and soft and — and searching. But not so fast. You are getting me all stirred up. Why, you're on fire!"

Still Elissa did not answer, too concentrated in venting the desire that had built up in her for so long. She pulled Clemence against her more tightly, with her free hand undoing the band of her skirt and thrusting inside her panties, searching for the space between her thighs. Clemence, fascinated by this new experience, opened her legs to receive Elissa's thrusting fingers, abandoning herself to the climax that swiftly engulfed her, yet wanting to escape from the demanding fingers and at the same time eager for the half-painful pleasure to continue. Elissa, feeling her combined cringing and eagerness, pressed closer.

At last, gasping, Clemence lay limp in her arms, her head on Elissa's shoulder. Elissa said breathlessly, "I've been wanting to do that ever since I first saw you."

Clemence looked up into her eyes. "So that's what made you so cantankerous sometimes." She sat up and pushed Elissa against the seat back. "Two can play that game." But even though Elissa, clumsy with eagerness, helped her undo her own clothes, Clemence could feel her climax already throbbing under her inexperienced fingers.

When they returned to a realization of the outside world, they saw that the shadows of evening were beginning to gather on the floor of the valley below them. As had been the case all afternoon long, there seemed to be no other people around them, only the far-off movement of vehicles on the distant roads.

Clemence said, "I think we'd better go home now," and Elissa, rejoicing, knew she meant the apartment.

Whenever they spent the evening together, which was as often as possible, the sensuous closeness of the evening went on into the night. Clemence was aware of Elissa's eagerness for them to go to bed, of her suppressed impatience at the time spent in getting ready for bed, of the difficulty she had in restraining the driving force of her desire. She herself did not feel this overwhelming urgency. She enjoyed the quieter moments of their settling in together under the covers, the nestling of their bodies so that the coolness of her skin gradually absorbed the heat of Elissa's body. This preliminary harmony was to her luxurious; this intimacy with another body dissolved the feeling of solitariness that she had not hitherto been aware of. This caused her to hold back and she knew that Elissa sometimes felt that she held back purposely to tantalize, to exercise the emotional dominance that she knew was hers.

At first she did resist Elissa's impetuousness because the persistent probings of Elissa's fingers and mouth, inexorably leading to orgasm, produced in her a sort of reluctance, until the orgasm itself swept away that reluctance. She knew that Elissa was aware of this ambivalence in her and that sometimes this caused Elissa to hesitate briefly and suspend her dedicated efforts to bring her to a climax.

When they reversed their roles she realized that it took very little effort for her to produce in Elissa an overwhelming climax that resulted in Elissa crushing her in a breath-stopping embrace. Elissa was always just on the brink of fulfillment at the very start of their lovemaking.

The first few nights when they went to bed together, Clemence was absorbed in learning the nuances of this new experience. Until her climax swallowed up every thought and plunged her into the enormous stress of physical pleasure, Clemence's mental processes were alert. In a way, she thought, it was as if she was clinically observing physical phenomena she had heard described but never witnessed or experienced. What was happening to her was a sort of necessary phase of maturing, a passage into adulthood. She admitted to herself that it was enjoyable beyond anything she had ever imagined, that she reveled in the touch of Elissa's hands, the feel of her body in a way that could not be described.

But after several of these night-long sessions of lovemaking and deep, comfortable sleep in the warmth of their conjoined bodies, she began to realize that there was another element entering into their relationship. Perhaps, she thought, the novelty of the experience was wearing off for her and she was beginning to feel something that lay beneath the prolonged physical contact. She found, on the occasional night when Elissa was not with her, that she not only missed Elissa herself, the comfort of her company, but also the pleasure of released desire. Sometimes desire awakened in her when she was alone but she was not prompted to seek some other person with whom to satisfy it, as she realized now some people did. She still felt repugnance at the idea of sharing with anyone but Elissa the sort of intimacies they enjoyed together. She also realized that she was not quite the same Clemence she had been before Elissa had moved in on her physical privacy. She now knew another body as intimately as she knew her own. This added a dimension to the world that she had not beforehand understood.

One day when she was musing about this difference in herself, she was brought up short by the thought that she had slipped into this new situation without really having made a decision to do so. She had not consciously elected to take Elissa as her lover. It had been Elissa who had taken her by storm. She had dropped into accepting this intimacy without considering the whys and wherefores of it. Was this love and the way love came about? Did she love Elissa in a way she had never loved anybody else? She knew that this was indeed the fact. But it troubled her that she did not feel the overwhelming strength of emotion that gripped Elissa, who seemed sometimes ready to burst with the passion within her. Did this mean that she herself was of a colder nature and that she could never really respond to Elissa as Elissa deserved? But she could never now do without Elissa.

But the dilemma was there. It would not exit if Elissa was a man. No one would question the naturalness of her acquiescing in a man's desire for her. But Elissa was another woman and here they were in a situation that could not be acknowledged. Off and on she mulled over the problem, seeking a clue to the way ahead. Elissa seemed to have no doubts about the rightness of their love and its expression. Perhaps she simply lived in the present moment. So it is up to me, thought Clemence, to find the solution for us. Her parents had never imposed on her the idea of propriety of behavior beyond the one rule that she should never consciously or willingly damage someone else's self-esteem. You behaved, wherever you were, in a manner appropriate to the occasion, unless principle demanded otherwise. And principle did not operate here.

More and more often Regina came to the Gallery cafeteria to join Clemence at lunch. She seemed prepared for the fact that Elissa might also be there. When Elissa came and found them together or when she and Clemence were together and Regina joined them, Elissa saw — or thought she saw — an expression of impatience quickly cross Regina's face, a fleeting glimpse of what Regina's real feeling might be. But otherwise, when the three of them were together, Regina covered over any discomfort she might feel by talking about her dissertation, or the research on which it was based, and frequently, about the philosophical and ethical questions that might be raised by it. At first Elissa found this aspect of scientific research strange. Scientific inquiry, she thought, was not subject to considerations of religious and ethical problems, being in a pure sphere of its own, free of any limitations not arising from within science itself. Gradually she began to realize that this was a naive view. Science consisted of phenomena observed by human beings and therefore was subject to all the failings of human beings.

At first, irritated by what she saw as an intrusion into her time with Clemence, Elissa tried to talk Regina down, discussing at length newspaper accounts of the FBI's activities or the struggles in Congress and elsewhere over the civil rights act. But she was quickly aware that Clemence did not like her to do this. Also she sensed that there was some innate sympathy between Clemence and Regina and that Clemence was ready to listen to Regina's problems, which seemed to extend beyond the questions involving her scientific work. She took to leaving the lunch hour early when Regina appeared, inwardly angry that Clemence was willing to give part of their time to Regina but humbled by the thought that she had no right to monopolize Clemence. She often left them together rather than to betray her own feelings of jealousy and indignation.

When Clemence and Regina were alone together, Clemence became more and more aware that there was a certain yearning in Regina, a yearning to reach out to her. She remembered that when she and Regina first met in college, she had at once been aware that there was a bond between them that did not exist for her with any of the other girls. She found that she was not alone in noticing this. One or two of the professors seemed to observe an affinity between them and, to Clemence's surprise, put it down to the fact that the two of them had a religious bent that the others lacked. When Miss Benson of English Lit. said casually that there seemed to be a bond of faith, an understanding of mysticism between them, Clemence had fallen silent. For several days she had mulled over the comment. She knew Regina to be a devout Roman Catholic. Regina was polite but firm in emphasizing this fact whenever the occasion arose. But about herself Clemence wondered. When she was a little girl her mother had sent her to the same schools she had attended herself — Episcopalian schools that reflected her mother's family background. But her mother had been as surprised as her father — who had abandoned his own Quaker background — when, as a teenaged girl, she had decided that she wanted to be confirmed in the Episcopal Church. They were surprised but, in keeping with their view of toleration of the beliefs of others, they had not objected, beyond a mild inquiry into why she felt that way. She had not been able to explain. Her mother was suspicious at first that she had fallen victim to someone else's proselytizing, but when she had assured herself that this was not the case, put it down to a wayward impulse of adolescence and had said nothing more about it. They assumed she had made her own choice and that the matter rested there.

But Clemence knew she had nothing like the strength of religious conviction that Regina had. And yet, after Miss Benson's comment, she realized that her own outlook, her own emotional outreach, matched Regina's closely enough for them to be able to understand each other on many questions. This was undoubtedly the reason why Regina now sought her as confidante and comforter.

Sometimes Regina talked about her family, commonplace talk that did not include complaint but did give Clemence the feeling that Regina was turning a critical eye on those among whom she had lived her whole life. Clemence had always known that Regina was quick to defend her mother and sister from any implied criticism and knew also that only with her could she speak plainly without seeming disloyal to them. The first time that Regina made an acerbic remark about Kathleen, Clemence was surprised. Beneath the invariable sweetness of Regina's manner there was now a nervous impatience that Clemence had never seen before.

"Kathleen," Regina said, pursing her thin, perfectly defined lips together before she spoke, "has no idea of the difference between the world she thinks she lives in and the world that surrounds her. I find it impossible to enlighten her. She believes absolutely everything the nuns ever taught her, everything Father Vincent says, without a glimmer that there might be another view."

Clemence, abstractedly eating her salad, wondered whether she should say something or merely remain the silent listener. Regina did not wait for her. "Kathleen thinks that everything is either black or white — you're a good person and believe in whatever you've been taught, or you are wicked. If you're good — and her definition is very narrow; it means chiefly that you believe in everything that she believes in — that you're normal and you'll eventually go to heaven — that is, you'll be saved from the consequences of any sin you may have committed, if you make the proper acts of contrition — and sin is what the Church says is sin, which is chiefly sexual transgressions." Regina made a sound of disgust. "It's impossible to bring fresh air into her mind. She's only two years younger than I."

Disturbed by seeing her so unhappy, Clemence said, "But, Regina, why are you so upset now? You've always known this, haven't you? At least, I think so, from what you've said to me before."

"Of course. I've known her all my life from the age of two. Yes, of course. Oh, Clemence, I used to long to talk to you about this when we were together at Goucher. You were quite different from the other girls. I felt as if you would understand what an awkward situation I was in — which I had placed myself in, I admit. I couldn't talk to any of the girls I went to school with. Nor to the nuns in the college where I went for my first three years. They would have told me that I was losing my faith. That is the only way they could see it. And I am not concerned about that at all. My faith is not so fragile. I know that there are basic beliefs that must not be questioned. I know that there are boundaries to thought and action beyond which one must not go. I know that God's word and church doctrine are not subject for interpretation by unschooled individuals. I know all that. But it is assumed that, since I am engaged in scientific inquiry, I will forget these things and therefore endanger my immortal soul. Father Vincent is very persistent in his warnings about this. He deplores the fact that I've made it necessary for him to open such a discussion with me. He forgets that I'm not a child — which, as a woman, I should remain in intellectual matters."

Regina stopped talking and stared unseeingly down at her plate. Clemence said, "But you're not a child and you must use your mind to understand your faith." Or is that, for her, heresy, Clemence wondered.

If so, Regina disregarded it. "Oh, Clemence, don't you see why I can't possibly talk to anyone but you about myself?"

Clemence said gently, "I think you give me credit for a great deal more discernment than I have. I do have my own faith. I grew up in a doubting environment, but I have found the essence of what I need. That is as far as I can go in explaining. I do understand what all this must mean to you."

Regina sighed. She pushed aside her lunch tray and rested her elbows on the table. "There is something that has brought all this to a head. I've been wanting to tell you about it. I've debated whether I should — whether I should burden you with this."

"Oh, yes! If it will help you, Regina."

"It is about Kathleen. Kathleen thinks she is in love."

Surprised, Clemence said nothing.

"She is in love, actually for the first time. I never thought Kathleen would ever fall in love. I mean, really fall in love, so that her usual complacency would be upset. I'm not criticizing her. But I've always thought that if you really are in love, you are swept away, beyond your usual boundaries of feeling." Regina paused and gave Clemence a weak smile. "A hopelessly romantic idea, isn't it? And I've always thought that Kathleen was too practical and level-headed to be swept away by anything. She grew up thinking she would meet a man who fit all the requirements, religious and otherwise, and have children. So far this has not come about. She is attractive — you've seen her — and men are attracted to her — for a while and then it seems to peter out. Kathleen gets very dogmatic when she is in any sort of discussion. She scares men off with that, I guess. She won't listen to me when I say anything."

"Can't your mother give her a few hints about being more easy-going?"

Regina shook her head. "Nobody can give Kathleen hints. It takes plainspeaking to make any impression on her. My mother has told her she should be tactful but Kathleen thinks that is being deceitful. The Irish are quite puritanical, you know. Any man who wants to marry Kathleen must understand completely what she believes and must agree with it, not just pretend to."

"Then she has found someone like that now?"

"No! That is the trouble. The man she thinks she is in love with is a Protestant. She can't possibly marry him unless she makes a convert of him first."

"Is he a likely candidate?"

"I don't know. He really seems to be in love with her. She seems to have captivated him. He responds to her, thinks everything she does and says is wonderful. I think he is in such a fog that he really doesn't hear much of what she says or if it's strange to him, discounts it. It's Kathleen he wants. The fact that she isn't an intellectual doesn't bother him. He isn't either. I don't mean he's stupid. He is not, and he has a good education and a good job. I'm sure he'll always be a good provider. In fact, you know him, Clemence. He met Kathleen at your party — Charlie Olsen."

Clemence, astonished, was silent, absorbing this information. So that was why she had not seen much of Charlie in the last few weeks. Her surmise was correct. He had another girl.

Regina went on. "He sees her almost every day. In fact, he's underfoot so much at my mother's apartment that she complains about it to me. He is not very tactful and he annoys her sometimes. My mother is sensitive about ill-manners and calls him a bog-trotter — a good Irish term for someone like that. But he's very good-hearted and she realized that Kathleen is in a state over him. What do you know about him, Clemence?"

Clemence said carefully, "I really can't tell you a great deal about Charlie. I went with him for several months. He considered himself my steady boyfriend. He's a decent sort of fellow but he wants the sort of things from girls that most men want. You know, Regina, men like Charlie, when they go with a girl on a regular basis, expect her to sleep with them — a sort of try-out for marriage, so to speak. I never went that far with Charlie, but it wasn't because he didn't try. In fact, that was part of the reason we stopped going together."

Regina's fine-shaped nostrils drew in. "I see."

"I'm wondering how Kathleen is going to handle that."

"I can't imagine Kathleen accepting that. But, then, I don't know what Kathleen will do under these circumstances. Perhaps that is the way reality will come to her."

The lunch hour had fled and Clemence said she had to return to her desk. Before they parted Regina asked in a tentative voice, "Clemence, you don't mind that I've told you all this?"

"Oh, no! Only, there is so little I can do to help."

Impulsively Regina leaned over and kissed her on the cheek. "You don't know how much it means to me to have you for a friend."

Leaving the Gallery, Clemence walked across the Avenue in the fading glow of a fine sunset. No Elissa tonight, she remembered, as she joined the small throng waiting at the car stop. Elissa had said that there was a special staff meeting that evening and probably a special assignment afterwards. She had come to depend on their evenings together and she had a bit of news to tell her. She had had a letter from her mother, saying that they would be abroad for a while longer; perhaps they would be back for Christmas. If not, her mother said, why didn't she take a leave of absence and come over to London to be with them?

"Well, fancy finding you here!"

She looked up, startled. Charlie Olsen. She had forgotten how once she had expected him every evening, watching for him to appear coming through the crowd.

She said, "Why, hello, Charlie."

He said, "I haven't really seen you since your party. Are you free tonight?"

She told herself she should have said no, but her instinct for telling the truth betrayed her and she answered promptly, "Yes."

"Well, come and have a drink with me."

They went to the hotel lounge where they had so often gone before. Clemence was annoyed that she had let herself in for the sort of evening she had lately been able to avoid. But Charlie was in a very good mood and he overlooked her edgy silence.

He was even jovial when he asked, "How's old Robert

doing? Is he still sitting on that painting? You have to hand it to him. He doesn't scare easily. What is going on between him and Francis Hearn, anyway?"

"Is there anything going on between them?"

"From what I hear."

"From whom?" Clemence asked suspiciously.

"Oh, the grapevine."

"And what grapevine is that?"

Charlie gave her a hard look. "You are suspicious, aren't you? Kathleen seems to hear quite a bit from her sister."

Astonished, Clemence exclaimed, "Regina!"

"The very same. She seems to be as thick as thieves with Francis." Charlie looked pleased that he had made an impression on Clemence. "It seems to all have begun at your party."

Trying to hide her bewilderment, Clemence said, "Robert and Francis don't like each other."

"That's the understatement of the year. At your party it really looked for a moment as if they were going to have a fight. Did you invite them both to see what would happen?"

"Of course not. It was poor judgment. I'm grateful to Robert for walking out before anything happened."

Charlie sipped at his drink and chewed a few nuts. "Do you see a lot of Robert these days?"

Clemence said warily, "I see him every day in the course of business."

"Does he tell you what he intends to do?"

"About the painting? Of course not. I'm not in his confidence, though everybody seems to think I am."

"My, we're touchy this evening! Well, I know you're good at freezing somebody out when you want to. You've changed a bit, Clem. Are you sure you're not Robert's girlfriend?" His glance at her was speculative and his tone was provocative. In the old days Charlie had sometimes been provocative for the purpose of getting her attention. Now he seemed to be baiting her.

She decided to be bland. "If I am, it's not your business."

She saw by the surprise in his face that she had scored a point. "Oh, oh! The new Clem." He went on, talking rapidly, "The real question, I suppose, is why he did it. Seems to me he could be accused of appropriating public property for his own use."

"Don't be silly. He hasn't stolen it. It is stored in the Gallery vaults."

"How do you know it's still there? If he hasn't let anybody see it, he could have spirited it away."

"Charlie, this kind of nonsense isn't funny. Where would he take it and what would he do with it?"

"Ah, he has a reputation for shady dealings with pictures in the past. Well, anyway, it makes for lively conversation. People like to gossip about him. I suppose they tend to identify with him because he has the guts to do something like this."

They were both silent for a while. Clemence was startled when Charlie suddenly said, "Say, you've been friends with Regina for a long time, haven't you?"

"Since my senior year at Goucher. She's one of my sorority sisters that you objected to, remember?" She could not resist the jibe.

Charlie laughed. "Well, it's not Regina I'm interested in. It's her sister Kathleen."

"I hardly know Kathleen. I met her for the first time when she came to my party."

"She's not like her sister. Kathleen is a real woman. She has plenty of vim."

Clemence looked at him askance.

"I mean, when she believes in something she lets you

know about it. She's a real devout Catholic. I've never gone with a girl like her before."

"She comes from a very devout family."

"Oh, I know that!" Charlie mulled over the statement. Then he said, "Have you ever wondered why some people get so fanatical on the subject of religion?"

"Why, I suppose usually it's the way they're brought up."

"Well, we don't all do just what our parents did. My folks are Lutheran. Their church is pretty important to them, especially my mother. They don't like it that I've sort of fallen away. But I don't disagree with them. On the other hand, I can't get worked up about religion. It has its place, of course."

Clemence looked at him from under her eyebrows. "It could have something to do with belief, couldn't it? Going to mass isn't the same thing for Catholics, though. It's something that is required, not something of choice."

"Belief?" he seemed uncomfortable with the idea, but not as if it was new to him. Yet she was sure that, up to the last occasion when she had spent any time with him, he had never given much thought to the idea that religious belief could be overriding.

Suddenly he demanded, "Do you go to church?"

"Quite often. You know that, Charlie."

"Yes, I remember that now. I met you down at St. Margaret's once or twice. But that's it — sometimes. That's normal. I used to go to Sunday School when I was a kid. But there aren't all those constant reminders around the place — religious statues, symbols, that sort of thing."

"You weren't a Catholic."

Charlie did not answer for a moment. "The people I know take their religion for granted — take it or leave it, so to speak — whether they're Jews or Protestants or even Catholics. They don't shove it under your nose all the time."

"Are you talking about Kathleen? I imagine she takes her religion pretty seriously."

"She keeps talking about the fact that I have to think more about God and my soul and so on. It bothers me. Every time I see her she brings it up."

"Then if it bothers you, why do you go to see her?"

Her question was received by a long silence. Charlie was not looking at her. It was obvious to her that he had removed her from the position she had held with him in the past, that the woman he had pursued so perseveringly had faded from his consciousness. She was now just a trusted confidante for his present dissatisfactions. She was still Clemence but she was no longer the focus of his interest. How typical he was, she thought, in his maleness. He assumed without question that she would enter sympathetically into his problems of the moment. The idea that this might cause her heartache and even jealousy did not cross his mind, or, if it did, was discounted as of lesser importance. It's a good thing, thought Clemence, that I never really wanted him.

Finally Charlie said, "That's not the answer. She's very good company, otherwise. She's lively and I think she's really interested in me. I think maybe I can get her to forget this religious stuff after a while, when we get more intimate."

"I hardly think so."

He pounced on her. "Why not? She probably never met anyone just like me before — just the same as I've never met anyone just like her."

Clemence looked at him with a feeling of helplessness. It was her duty, as a true friend, she thought, to try to awaken him to the reality of his situation with Kathleen. But she could see no chink in the armor of self-confidence that he had wrapped around himself. Regina was right. Charlie was indeed in love with Kathleen as Kathleen seemed to be in love with him.

One Sunday Elissa went to New York with other members of her committee, on committee business. Fortunately, Clemence thought, because for the first time Regina wanted to spend Sunday afternoon with her. They spent a couple of hours at a Hitchcock movie and returned afterwards to the apartment. Clemence was aware that some all-absorbing subject held Regina in its grasp — something she wanted to talk about but nevertheless could not broach.

When they settled down in the living room Regina was silent for a while, a frown on her face. She was looking down at the floor, immersed in her own thoughts. Suddenly she looked up at Clemence and asked, "You work with Robert Alden, don't you? I remember that he was at your party."

"Yes. He and Francis Hearn nearly had a fight. You may not have realized how close they were to it. I should not have invited them both but I could not invite one without the other."

Clemence saw the color heighten in Regina's cheeks. Her head jerked up at the mention of Francis. "Oh, I don't think Francis would be as gauche as that!"

Francis! The first name, coming from Regina, surprised Clemence. She was taken aback at the confidence with which Regina said it, as if she was on familiar territory. Regina was usually quite formal in speaking of people she did not know well. "Mr. Hearn" would have sounded more normal.

"You don't think so?"

Regina's blush deepened. "Well, of course, I don't know

86

him as well as you must. I only met him a couple of months ago, at your party, of course. But he doesn't strike me as the sort of man who would quarrel with someone in the midst of a gathering at someone else's house."

Clemence, aware now of the strong feeling that Regina was carefully controlling, said mildly, "Francis and Robert rub each other the wrong way. They seem to have a feud going on that dates back a good many years."

Regina was silent again for a while and then said, "You've known him quite a long time, haven't you?"

"Francis? No — well, let's say he has known me for quite a while. When he was a young man my father befriended him. He has always kept in touch with my father and when he came to the Gallery he made a point of seeking me out. I sometimes do some work for him, though not as much as I do for Robert. Sometimes things get difficult since they're such enemies."

Regina asked, in a very careful voice, "Is he married?"

"He's divorced. That happened to a lot of people." Watching her, Clemence tried to gauge the effect of this information. Regina was again looking down. Her mobile face often reflected her inner feelings, especially in unguarded moments like this one. She was sitting on the sofa with one elbow resting on its back and her hands clasped. Clemence saw that she interlaced and freed her fingers and interlaced them again in nervous preoccupation.

After a long pause, Regina asked, "Do you like him? He is a very intelligent man. He seems to be well informed about a lot of things. He has a very good reputation as an art scholar, doesn't he?"

"Yes, that's true. He doesn't have quite the professional reputation that Robert does. But then Robert is extraordinary. And then Francis has been in this art field for a much shorter time than Robert. Otherwise, I

87

haven't seen enough of Francis to have more than a superficial impression of him. I must confess that I'm always a little annoyed with someone who claims acquaintance with me as my parents' child."

Regina raised her eyes to look at her. "Yes, I can see that that would be a nuisance." She gave a little laugh and the twinkle that Clemence had always seen as characteristic of her came briefly into her eyes.

"It's a silly reaction, I know."

Regina said soothingly, "Dear, I do sympathize with you. But perhaps Francis doesn't realize you feel that way."

There it was again, thought Clemence: Francis. "As I said, I don't see much of him. When I see him at the Gallery, it is strictly business. He's not like some of the men. He doesn't exchange a lot of silly talk with the women. He's much more reserved. And as I've told you, the bad feeling between him and Robert makes things difficult for me. The trouble is that Robert has taken to talking to me a lot more than he used to. He complains to me about how he is treated, as if he's sure that I'm on his side in this controversy."

"Are you?"

Clemence thought for a moment. "I suppose I am more his friend than most. I don't understand Robert's actions or the motives for them. But I do feel a certain sympathy for him. I seem to be propelled into defending him. But this is an irrational sort of thing."

Regina smiled a tolerant smile and said gently, "Dear, you can't always be rational, you know. Do you think you are in love with him?"

Clemence stared at her in astonishment. "In love with him? How on earth could you suppose that?"

Regina was still smiling at her. "Love is an irrational thing. Romantic love, that is. It isn't something you can justify. You just suffer it."

Clemence, anger welling up in her, shot back, "I'm much more likely to be in love with you!"

The smile vanished from Regina's face, which turned white. "Oh, no! Oh, no! That would be impossible!"

"Why would it be impossible? Because we are both women? That is not true. Some women do love other women. You know that, Regina."

Regina dropped her head into her hands. "Oh, Clemence dear! I didn't mean to make you angry! Don't say things like that. You're really the only understanding friend I have."

Still angry and wishing to hurt, Clemence retorted, "So therefore I can't love you."

Regina suddenly grew calm and said, "No, that's not so. Of course you could love me and I could love you — feel for each other everything most women feel for men. Yes, Clemence, that is so. It wouldn't take very much for me to desire you in that way. But I need you more as a friend — I badly need you to save me from the consequences of irrational love."

Clemence looked at her silently and Regina looked away, profound unhappiness showing in her face. Finally Clemence said, "Regina, I am your friend — we've always been friends since we first met — close friends —"

Regina broke in desperately, "Yes! Yes! I've always felt I could talk to you about the things most important to me — the way I have never been able to talk to anyone before — my mother, the nuns, certainly not Kathleen. Nobody I've ever known can think, can understand, beyond what they've been taught to believe, as if they are afraid of what they might find out about themselves. You've always held out a hand to me, Clemence, to help me through the tangle of thoughts and feelings I've struggled with for so long. You never jump to conclusions about what I've told you, and you've listened."

She stopped and gazed at Clemence with an

anguished expression on her face. She had got up from her seat on the sofa and was standing close to Clemence. Suddenly she put her arms around Clemence's neck and buried her face in her shoulder.

Clemence stood perfectly still, astonished at this embrace and yet aware that it was the expression of some depth of feeling between them that was not an erotic appeal. Yet she realized at the same time that it could easily have been possible for her to love Regina as she now in fact loved Elissa. She said slowly, "Regina, you must tell me what is really the matter. There is something else, isn't there, that you haven't told me."

Regina raised her head and stood back a little, slipping her hands down Clemence's arms. "Yes. Yes. I must tell you, because otherwise I shall lose all my self-control. You will understand."

Clemence looked at her closely. "Understand what?"

Regina looked at her directly. "It is Francis. I cannot get him out of my mind — out of my —" She dropped her head. "What am I to do?"

Clemence took a few moments to absorb what she meant. "Do you mean that you are in love with Francis?"

Regina looked up at her. "Is that what it is?"

Clemence put her arms around her and held her in a loose embrace. "Regina, I have no idea. You mean that since you met him at my party you've fallen in love with him?"

"You remember that he and I and Charlie and Kathleen all went to dinner that evening. Since then he has called me frequently and we have spent the evening together. He is a fascinating companion. I think about him when I'm not with him. I wonder what he is doing and what he is thinking when we are not together. But I have no idea what he thinks about me. Does he go out a lot with other women?"

Clemence shook her head. "I can't tell you that

because I know nothing about his private life. But, Regina —" She stopped, at a loss about how to phrase the thought in her mind.

Regina straightened up and moved away from her. "Yes, I know what you're thinking. Of all the men for me to get involved with! He is not sympathetic to religious feeling, except as it concerns the subjects of paintings, medieval paintings. I'm sure you know that he is a very well-informed man and therefore he knows a great deal about religion as a matter of history. But he says frankly that he has no feeling for religious belief and that he thinks faith is a self-delusion."

"You mean, this subject has come up between you because you know that you cannot marry someone who is at least not opposed to your religious belief."

Regina looked stricken. "Clemence, how can I even be imagining marrying him, when I know nothing about his real feeling for me? But, yes, you are right. It is something that I cannot avoid considering. We don't discuss my family, of course. But when I say that I find it difficult to talk about religious belief, he says that comes from my upbringing — that someone who is brought up in strict observance of religious rituals and who then questions those rituals is like someone imprisoned in a room who, when the door is opened, is afraid to go through it for fear of what lies beyond." Regina laughed briefly. "They say, you know, that you can keep a hen imprisoned in a circle drawn in chalk on the ground around her. She thinks there is a real barrier."

The bitter note in her voice jarred on Clemence. "It seems to me that he is being pretty ruthless. Has he met your mother?"

"Oh, no. He hasn't been to my mother's."

They lapsed into silence for a while. Clemence went into the kitchen and returned with glasses and a bottle of scotch and some ice. Regina, she knew, would sometimes drink a very light whiskey with plenty of water. She prepared it and handed it to her. Regina took it from her in an absentminded way.

Then, after a moment, Regina said in a voice that, coming from her, sounded harsh, "I do wish, Clemence, that I was in love with you — that I hung on every word you said, forgot to eat because I was mooning about thinking of you, waited every day for a phone call —" Regina's voice became openly mocking. "It would be so much easier for me. Of course, for two women to go to bed together is a mortal sin. But even that would be easier for me. You're so much closer to me." Her manner changed as she reached out her hands toward Clemence. "Clemence, you do understand me, don't you?"

"Of course. I'm afraid, only too well."

"She's really in love with him, 'Lissa, hopelessly in love with him."

Elissa frowned. "I've seen that happen with girls who have never been exposed to the possibility before."

"But Francis! It would be a disaster, 'Lissa."

"It often is, haven't you noticed? I suppose because the people involved are blinded to reality." Like me, but not you, Elissa added to herself.

Clemence, moving about the living room, automatically straightened the pile of magazines on the small table at the end of the sofa. It was her instinct for orderliness operating at her subconscious level, thought Elissa; she has no idea that she is doing that.

Clemence said, " 'Lissa, I can't let it happen."

"Let what happen? Oh, I see. In any case you can't stop it. You ought to know that you can't make somebody wake up when they're in a dream world like that. She'll have to work it out on her own."

"Then it will probably be too late. Don't you see how devastating it will be for her when she does wake up? Oh, anybody but Francis!"

Elissa looked at her judiciously. "Is he so much worse than most? Besides, he may show her a side of himself that he doesn't show you or me or anybody else." She saw that her words were not convincing to Clemence.

"You don't understand. Francis is a cold fish. He'll break her heart because he doesn't have any warmth to give her and Regina needs warmth. That's what she is seeking now — some sort of human warmth."

Which is why she comes to you, thought Elissa. "Do you mean that she wants to marry him? I don't think she's the kind of girl to have an affair. Her religion would get in the way. But do you think Francis would want to marry her? Or anyone? Isn't he content to be free now that he's divorced?"

"Francis will get married again eventually. He prefers the life of a married man. And Regina interests him because she is both beautiful and brilliant. He would think that she is just the sort of ornament that would be appropriate as his wife."

"I see. Well, I don't know him at all and besides, I'm not much inclined to size men up as husband or lover material. Has he been interested in you?"

Clemence was thoughtful. "I think perhaps he was, in a tentative sort of way — chiefly because I'm the daughter of my parents. He would like to have my father as his father-in-law. Of course, this business with Robert has put an end to his thinking about it."

"Robert?"

"Oh, I've told you that everybody seems to think I'm Robert's special friend." Clemence broke off and said testily, "I'm tired of being somebody's special friend."

Elissa smiled and put her arm around Clemence. "Mine?" she teased.

Clemence relaxed in her arms. "That's something different. 'Lissa, we're a special case, aren't we?"

Elissa looked at her seriously. "We're not unique, if that's what you mean." Her grasp tightened on Clemence, as if to reassure herself against the vague doubt that Clemence's question had raised.

Clemence pulled away so as to look her in the face. "You've just said that lovers live in a dream world. Perhaps our situation isn't reality, either."

But Elissa would not let her go. "It is to me. Isn't it to you? What has happened, Clem?"

Clemence relaxed deliberately. "Of course it is. Don't get upset. I don't know just what we are doing or what we are headed for, but you're something I never thought about before you happened to me." She took Elissa's face in her hands and kissed her deeply on the mouth. Presently, she said, "I don't know how to fit you into my life. But you do fit somehow. I've always been waiting at the door for someone to come. Well, now you're here."

Elissa's gaze still held uncertainty. She was elated by Clemence's words, but behind the elation there was the doubt: what had happened to make Clemence come so boldly forward?

Clemence, instantly aware of the doubt lurking in Elissa's response, grasped her shoulders and shook her slightly. " 'Lissa, can't I even tell you how important you are to me without you thinking that there is something I'm holding back?"

Elissa, hugging her to her, said, "Oh, Clem, Clem," and began kissing her all over her face, savoring the little nibbles that Clemence gave her in return.

For a while they made love, fondling and kissing each other. Then, as the evening shadows grew deeper, they roused themselves and went to fix supper. Afterwards they turned on the radio and picked up a concert by Burl Ives. A spontaneous, all-exuding happiness possessed them

94

and they danced together around the room to the Tennessee Waltz, Que Sera Sera, and finally, finishing off with Mr. Sandman, they went to bed in Clemence's bed.

"You'll come, won't you?" Regina pleaded over the phone. "My mother likes to have people in on Sunday afternoon. She'd be delighted to meet you. It seems incredible that during all the time I've known you you've never met her."

"I don't think there was ever an opportunity," Clemence responded, thinking, you were not eager to have me or any of your college mates know your family.

"I suppose not. In any case, you'll come this Sunday, won't you? I'll tell you how to get there. You can take the streetcar downtown and then transfer to a bus that goes out past Catholic University, near the Shrine. If you'll tell me the time more or less you expect to get there, I can meet you at the bus stop. It's not far from our apartment house."

"Oh, I can find my way!"

"Ah, but I should like to have the chance to talk to you while we walk there."

Sunday afternoon was grey and chill, typical December weather, thought Clemence, shrugging her shoulders at the wind sweeping by the bus stop. There were few people on the bus and the trip seemed long and tedious, past the back of the Union Station, around the Old Soldier's Home grounds. She was glad when she saw Regina standing on the pavement waiting for her. Part of her depression came, she knew, from the fact that Elissa was not with her.

Regina kissed her. It was remarkable, Clemence thought, how there was so often a radiance to Regina, even when she was, as now, nervous and talkative. Of course it was this that captivated people — that beautiful, radiant face with its expression of soft compassion. Clemence remembered how, when Regina first appeared at Goucher, this image had disconcerted the other girls. They had wanted to find it fake, assumed, silly, misplaced in a girl when there were no men around to be impressed by it. Yet they found it difficult to believe any of these things about Regina. Clemence realized that she herself had very soon come to know Regina in other moods — angry, unhappy, scornful of the shortcomings of others, moods that the other girls never witnessed. Some of them, like Elissa, were wary of her, uncertain how to approach her, daunted in spite of themselves by the evidence of her extraordinary intelligence. Others, resentful, had been critical and back-biting, eager to find reasons to laugh at her. But Regina had never openly noticed that she was the special focus of anyone's attention.

Now she put her hand through the crook of Clemence's arm and turned her to walk in the direction of her mother's apartment house. She said, "I don't know who may be here today. Some of my relatives, of course — there are always some of those — Irish clannishness, you know, and also of course, Charlie Olsen. It is always open house on Sunday afternoon at my mother's."

Clemence wanted to ask whether Francis Hearn might be there, but she did not. Instead she said, "Is Charlie still underfoot?"

Regina laughed. "More than ever. I'm really amazed at how Kathleen has mesmerized him. I would never have believed that my little sister could have learned such sophistication in dealing with a suitor. You remember I told you how she usually treats men. Of course, the boys have always clustered around her since she was in high school. But she is always so forthright about her obedience to what she has been taught. The nuns always said she was such a comfort. They never had to worry about Kathleen being led astray."

"But they did worry about you."

They walked a few steps before Regina answered. "I think they did, chiefly because they found it hard to understand me. They tried hard to do so and I tried to reassure them. Perhaps that was one reason why they worried so about my losing my faith. Some of them were sophisticated women, probably with some personal experience in a worldly sense before they took their vows, and they knew about the hazards of temptation, especially intellectual temptation. I know that two or three of them, who had been my teachers and were eager for me to succeed in the academic world, were quite unhappy when I told them I wanted to attend a non-Catholic school. They listened sympathetically when I explained my reasons and they wished me Godspeed when I left but I know that they were full of misgiving."

"I remember when I first met you, you told me something about this. You seemed troubled by the idea that you might disappoint them. What do they think now? Are you in touch with them?"

"Yes. I do hear from them sometimes. You know that I have spent a couple of years working at the University of California in an environment very different from theirs. I've tried to explain the research I am doing. But lately I've not mentioned it, because — well, I'd been told that Catholic theologians have expressed doubts about some of the implications of the research, saying that it must be evaluated from the viewpoint of doctrine."

"Oh, no, Regina! Your work isn't threatened, is it?"

Regina hesitated and Clemence saw anxiety in her eyes. "I don't know."

"How does your mother feel about this?"

"My mother does not concern herself with this sort of

thing. As far as she is concerned, the teachings of the church are not for her to question. She would expect me to acquiesce in any decision made by the church hierarchy."

She stopped talking and said, "We're here."

They were standing in front of an apartment house, six stories high and of red brick with white facings around the windows. Regina led Clemence up the shallow entrance steps, through the lobby to an elevator. They got off at the top floor and walked down a corridor to what was obviously the apartment that took up the front of the building.

The door was opened by Kathleen and Clemence was struck again by the contrast between the sisters. Junoesque, she supposed, would be the word used to describe Kathleen, who was a little taller than average and calmly self-assured. When she became a matron she would be solidly buxom but still handsome. Now she was still youthfully slender but she did not have Regina's air of fragility.

Kathleen said, "Hello, Clemence. So nice to see you again. Come on in. You haven't met my mother, have you?"

She put her arm through Clemence's and led her into the living room, leaving Regina to follow. It was a big room, with windows overlooking a park, so that the effect of spaciousness was accentuated. Clemence was conscious of religious symbols displayed: a statue of the Virgin Mary in a corner, with a rose in a vase before it; a painting of Christ ascending into heaven surrounded by angels.

Mrs. O'Phelan was seated in an armchair by a tea table in front of the windows. Kathleen said, "Mother, this is Regina's friend Clemence."

Mrs. O'Phelan smiled and waved a hand towards the empty chair beside her. She looks like both her daughters, thought Clemence, or they both look like her. In build she was like Regina; in coloring she was like Kathleen, a faded fairness in her skin and hair. She said, "I'm so happy that you were able to come, Clemence. Regina speaks of you often. I feel we should be friends already."

Clemence said, "I'm glad to be here, Mrs. O'Phelan. Regina talks about you to me, too." She glanced around quickly to see where Regina was and saw that she was on the other side of the room talking to an elderly priest. Obviously these people were relatives and close friends of the O'Phelans, people who probably came to spend every Sunday afternoon with Regina's mother. She supposed she was the only stranger there. She was aware of brief, discreet glances that came her way and as quickly turned away.

Mrs. O'Phelan was looking at her with a kindly expression on her face, but her blue eyes behind rimless glasses were alert, curious, shrewd. In the course of polite chat she asked questions about Clemence's parents — such renowned people, where were they now; she was interested in reading about them in the newspapers; did they expect Clemence to follow in their footsteps?

When Clemence said no, she was more interested in art, Mrs. O'Phelan said, "Oh, yes, Regina has told me that you are at the National Gallery." Clemence braced herself for questions about the Gallery's scandal, but Mrs. O'Phelan veered away to another subject.

Then, in the same discreet, unemphatic way, various of the people in the room came casually over to be introduced to her, summoned, she supposed, by some slight gesture of Mrs. O'Phelan's. Each of them stayed to exchange a few commonplaces, then withdrew. It was a relief to Clemence when the doorbell rang and Kathleen, going to answer it, came back into the room followed by Charlie Olsen. He did not try to hide his surprise at seeing her, exclaiming even before he greeted Mrs.

O'Phelan, "Why, hello, Clemence!" He went on talking to several of the people standing nearby as if he had met them several times before. Clemence watched him as he went around the room, greeting people, before sitting down next to Kathleen. Somehow his voice was too loud for the room and his heartiness too overpowering. Glancing at Mrs. O'Phelan, she caught an expression of impatience on her face, as if she found Charlie too noisy.

It seemed a long afternoon. Clemence was relieved when Regina came over and sat down beside her.

"Mother," she said, "Clemence knows Francis Hearn. I've told you about meeting him. He is Director of Purchases at the Gallery."

Regina, while speaking to her mother, was looking at Clemence. Clemence tried to interpret that level gaze, uneasy that she might not respond as Regina wanted her to.

Mrs. O'Phelan said, "I understand that he is a very distinguished man, very well-known in his profession."

"Yes, that's true," said Clemence.

Mrs. O'Phelan pressed on. "Regina says that he is a friend of your family."

"My parents have known him since he was a very young man."

"You work with him?"

"I am in the administrative office, so I often prepare material for him." Clemence thought: she intends to get some sort of character assessment of him from me. She glanced a little desperately at Regina, who was still gazing at her. I'm to say he's okay.

But before Mrs. O'Phelan went any further, another voice joined their conversation. Clemence looked up to see a tall priest standing beside her. Regina turned away to introduce him. "Clemence," she said, "Father Vincent wants to meet you." She got up as she spoke and moved away from them. The priest sat down in her chair.

100

He was a robust man with an air of authority. His eyes focused on Clemence, he said, "You are connected with the National Gallery, aren't you? I am acquainted with Robert Alden, the curator of Medieval Painting. Do you know him?"

"Oh, yes," said Clemence.

He continued to scrutinize her and she thought he might be going to say something about her parents. Instead he said, "I am especially interested in the Italian paintings in the Gallery. I find Alden to be an extraordinary curator. He has a great sensitivity when it comes to understanding the spiritual value of these paintings. They are among the world's greatest treasures not only as art but also as an illumination of our faith. Yet he himself is not a believer."

He paused as if to give her a chance to say something.

"He is well-known."

The priest nodded. "Certainly. But what has he done with the Giardini? Can you tell me when it will be replaced?"

"I don't know."

"It seems strange that it should be removed without notice. It is a painting of great power. Whoever Giardini was — I understand that nothing is known about him — he had a vision of tremendous enlightenment when he painted it. I have not seen Alden lately. I was devastated when I went into the Gallery a few weeks ago and found it missing. Whenever I have business in that part of town and have a few minutes to spare, I go to look at it. When I gaze at it, it gives me great spiritual refreshment. You have no idea when it will be restored to its place?"

He seems to be holding me responsible, thought Clemence, uneasy under his scrutiny. "I have no idea," she said. "I've heard nothing."

The priest took his eyes off her and said with an air

101

of resignation. "I have thought of writing to the Director of the Gallery to express my dismay. Perhaps if he receives enough protests something will be done. There must be many people who feel as I do."

In spite of herself Clemence felt an impulse of sympathy for him. Whatever religious interpretation he put on the painting, obviously he felt as she did the subtle but overwhelming power of the concept it embodied. She said, "I'm very sorry also that it has been taken down. It is a favorite of mine."

"Ah!" His eyes came back to her in a bright flash. "You feel its strength, too? That wonderful vision of the divine grace reaching down to us from above, embodied in those angelic forms!" He went on talking for a while, keeping his eyes fixed on her as if gauging her reaction to what he said. Mrs. O'Phelan listened to him with absorbed attention.

She left the apartment with Charlie Olsen, who came and said goodbye to Mrs. O'Phelan when he saw her about to take leave. They walked along the quiet street in the almost-dark, as the gusts of wintry wind sent a few dry leaves scraping along the pavement ahead of them.

Charlie demanded, "How did you like Sunday afternoon at the O'Phelans?"

There was a satirical tone in his voice and, not wanting to fall into the role of his confidante, she answered neutrally, "I found it interesting. We're sort of outsiders to them, aren't we?"

Charlie laughed boisterously. "You can say that again. I've heard about how clannish the Irish can be and now I know."

"You must admit they're hospitable enough to heathen like us."

"Heathen? Oh, I see what you mean. The weight of the Church certainly hangs over them, doesn't it? I'd say the atmosphere there is pretty claustrophobic. I'm getting used to it, though."

"Do you go there a lot, Charlie?"

"Well, yes. I don't have much luck getting Kathleen to go out with me. She says she's too busy and she isn't used to spending a lot of time in bars. She won't come to my place."

"You mean she lets you take her to bars?"

"Oh, stuffy kinds of places — not the sort you've been to with me. She's wrapped up in this teaching job — a lot of little kids. She's a lay teacher in a parochial school. She says she likes teaching little kids — the littlest ones who still love their teachers. I wouldn't know much about that but I tell her she doesn't get enough time off."

"What does she say to that?"

"She says she doesn't feel exploited. She likes her job too much for that. Here we are. I'm parked here." He stopped beside his car and put the key in the lock.

"I was going to take the bus," said Clemence.

"You don't want to stand and freeze in that wind waiting for the bus. They're not frequent on Sunday. Come on, get in."

He opened the door for her and then went round to get into the driver's seat. Clemence, thinking how long it was since she had ridden in his car, wondered uneasily what he had in mind.

Charlie was cursing under his breath. The engine started but died immediately. He struggled with it for several minutes before they were finally in motion.

"I've got to trade this heap in on something newer,"

he declared. He was not talkative on the way to her apartment. When they got there and he got out to open the door for her, he seemed to linger as if waiting for her to invite him in. As she hesitated, he said sarcastically, "I'm not going to make a nuisance of myself. That's all over between us. You've probably noticed. I just want a drink — and I'd like to talk to you."

Clemence thought, he has never had much grace of manner but at least he's forthright. So she answered as warmly as she could, "Of course, Charlie. Come up and have a drink." So now, she thought, he has achieved what he never had before, an invitation into her home.

She left him in the living room while she went to fetch glasses and ice. He made no attempt to follow her to the kitchen. When she came back he was sitting in one of the armchairs, smoking. He looked up.

"When are your folks coming home?"

"I don't really know. Every time they say they are winding things up, they write again and say they're postponing."

Charlie took the glass from her and said, "Cheers!" as she sat down. As if to emphasize his need for a drink, he downed half the glassful in one gulp. "Ha! That's better."

"Is Kathleen a teetotaler?" Clemence asked.

"Oh, no. She likes a drink. It's just that I get fed up to here —" he drew a finger across his throat — "with these Sunday affairs."

"Why do you go? Can't you see her some other time?"

"She says she has to be there on Sunday afternoon. It's an established thing, as I guess you've been told. She says she owes it to her mother to be there and help make all the aunts and uncles and cousins feel welcome. They've been doing this since the beginning of time and they can't — I suppose they don't want to stop now. I don't see it myself. These people don't have anything to say to each other. Nothing new ever happens to them.

They just sit there most of the time. Being in the same room together seems to be what counts. And there are always nuns or priests or seminarians there."

"The priest who was talking to me — Father Vincent. Is he there a lot?"

"He's a special favorite of Mrs. O'Phelan's. I don't think he's a relation but he seems to have a lot of authority. I can't stand him; he's too dictatorial. But Kathleen won't let me say what I think about him. By the way, he doesn't approve of Regina. He thinks she's altogether too independent for her own good. He thinks Kathleen is a much better example of a good Irish lass. I wish she was more like Regina."

"Well, Regina has tried to get out more into the non-Catholic world."

Charlie nodded and held out his glass for a refill. Clemence poured him another drink. He made a gesture towards her with his glass and took a large swallow. "I don't see how anybody can put up with that sort of pressure. Why do they accept it?"

"You mean Regina and Kathleen? Why, they've been brought up to be obedient."

"Yes, but they are grown women. When you get to be an adult, you ought to know your own mind. You tend to ask questions. At least, I did. You don't have to be a slave to your family's prejudices."

"They don't see their religious teaching as prejudices. But, Charlie, if you feel this way, don't you think you'd better consider whether you and Kathleen can be really compatible? She'll never change her mind about her religion. I'm pretty certain of that."

Charlie set his empty glass down on the little table beside his chair. "I'm not giving up on this. Kathleen really means a lot to me. I'm not going to let a bunch of crows get between us. Kathleen is beginning to think about things now, things she hasn't questioned before. I'm waking her up. She's got to learn that there are other points of view in the world — in spite of what Father Vincent says."

Clemence showed her doubt. "He's got all the arguments on his side. He strikes me as a very determined man."

"Autocratic, you mean."

"I'm sure he has no doubt that he's right. He's a very well-educated man. He seems to know a lot about art, especially the early Italian painters."

"Well, that's natural enough. Right in his line of business, you might say."

"Oh, Charlie, don't be so crass! He's not a run-of-the-mill parish priest. You've got quite an adversary there."

Charlie, feeling the alcohol he had drunk, said belligerently, "You seem to know a lot about the Catholic clergy. Anyhow, he's a friend of your pal, Robert Alden. That's probably where he gets his information. By the way, I heard a bit of news about Robert. Do you know he's a pansy?"

Shock kept Clemence silent. It was a word that Elissa had used. Charlie went on, not noticing her reaction to what he had said. "That explains a lot about him, doesn't it? He'd better be careful. That sort of reputation doesn't do him any good with the FBI. How the devil any guy can be a pansy is beyond me. Makes you wonder about the people he goes with."

Still Clemence did not answer. She was relieved when he wandered off to other topics. He stayed for another hour, consuming more drinks. Then the liquor began to make him morose. Clemence, growing ever more uneasy, sighed in relief when at last he left, with only a brief, half-hearted attempt to kiss her.

* * * * *

Elissa wandered slowly along F Street, looking without much interest in the shop windows. She felt bereft. She hated these long Sunday afternoons when she could not be with Clemence. But Clemence had said that she had to go and visit Regina's mother. Why? Elissa had demanded, and Clemence, out of patience, had said tartly, "Because Regina has asked me to. Sometimes I do have to do things you don't like. Regina needs moral support just now. I couldn't turn her down."

Elissa sulked, but at the same time she felt guilty because she could not suppress the shaft of jealousy that pierced her. She told herself that Clemence had every right to be annoyed. She did not own Clemence. They did not own each other. She had often fulminated about women who clung to a partner, jealous of every sign of interest that partner showed in someone else. You could smother a friendship, she said. You shouldn't allow yourself to act that way. But that was before she had found Clemence. Clemence had to be hers. And Clemence, with her extraordinary patience, had endured a number of scenes she had made over this fact.

She had not been able to occupy herself indoors this Sunday, her unhappiness making her restless. So she had gone out, to walk around downtown and try to take her mind off the waste of the day. There was nothing open except the movie houses. She walked down F Street and read the announcements on the marquees: an Anna Magnani film she had already seen at the Columbia; a Hitchcock film at the Palace, also not new. It was a grey, chill day, adding to her depression.

She reached the end of F Street, or at least that section where the stores were situated. Beyond Ninth Street there were only the burlesque houses and dilapidated buildings occupied by secondhand stores of various kinds. It was a familiar region to her. She used to, when she was still at Goucher and had nothing to do on weekends, take the train from Baltimore to Washington and come to prowl around here, with a sort of perverse nostalgia for the city streets she had grown up in. There was a particular store she had discovered which had drawn her back again and again: Mrs. Braunschweiger's secondhand bookstore. Mrs. Braunschweiger never closed her door before nine o'clock at night, any day of the week. Her spirits brightened as she thought of this and went in search of it.

The bookstore was housed in an old building dating from the time of the Civil War, when it had been a private residence. Going up the flight of iron steps guarded by a battered railing, she stepped into what had been the front and back parlors of the original owner. They were now a jungle of iron bookshelves reaching from the floor to the ceiling, set so closely that it was difficult to pass by someone standing reading under the naked light bulb suspended from the ceiling. She pushed her way to a back window thick with grime that let in very little light from the airshaft into which it opened. Here there was a large table with high sides attached to it to hold stacks of prints and engravings, many of them gutted from old volumes no longer resalable. She began to search through these in a leisurely way, more interested in looking at the scenes depicted — reproductions of paintings by the Hudson River school showing heavily forested banks of the river in the early nineteenth century, of drawings by eighteenth century artists of Rome and London — than in finding some treasure she wished to acquire.

"Well, how do you do, Miss Elissa?"

She turned to look down at the man at her elbow. He was a hunchback who had to peer up at her through thick distorting lenses.

"Well, hi, Mr. Sanders. How are you?"

"Good enough, good enough. Haven't seen you here for quite a long time. Been busy?"

"Yes. A lot of overtime. Have you some new stock?"

"Oh, yes, new things all the time. You'll have to look for them. You know how Mrs. B. is. She believes if you want something, you ought to hunt for it."

"Is she here now?"

"Oh, yes. In the back room, as usual. Is there something special you are looking for?"

"No. Don't bother with me. I'm just filling in time."

He nodded and turned away, to move crablike down one of the narrow aisles. Every time she saw him, she thought the same thing: how pale and fragile he looked, like a plant that never saw daylight. But she knew his appearance was deceptive. She had seen him climb the ladder to find books on the upper shelves with more agility than she could have shown. And she knew that he was there in the store every day, like Mrs. Braunschweiger herself. It was his choice to do that, she knew; Mrs. Braunschweiger had hired him when nobody else would but she certainly did not demand that kind of service from him. Elissa supposed he had somewhere to sleep and that he sometimes ate, but otherwise he seemed to live there in the bookstore as if it was his natural habitat.

She edged her way back along one of the narrow aisles to the open door at the back, leading to a room that had been the kitchen of the original dwelling. It was now Mrs. Braunschweiger's private office. Like the rest of the place it was crowded with piles of books, in the midst of which was a big, battered desk. Mrs. Braunschweiger, an enormous woman in dingy garments, sat behind it. To herself Elissa compared this sanctum to the throne room with the queen upon the throne. Mrs. Braunschweiger had been selling secondhand books for many years. Her clientele was chiefly scholars and people with compelling hobbies, who sought her out for help in finding rare books on many subjects, some of them esoteric. Her own range of knowledge — superficially, at least — was enormous, and many of her customers came to her store often just to chat with her about their own specialties or the events of the day and current politics.

Now Elissa put her head around the doorjamb and peered into the dirty room, lit only by the faint daylight from the grimy windows and the gooseneck lamp that threw a brilliant beam down on the desk. Mrs. Braunschweiger looked up at once — she had an unusually sensitive ear — and said in her deep voice, "Come in, Elissa."

It was only then that Elissa saw that there was someone else there, sitting in the battered armchair opposite, a blond man wearing a heather-colored tweed suit, sitting at ease with one leg draped over the arm of the chair. He did not move when she came into the room but sat staring at her in an unwelcoming way.

Mrs. Braunschweiger said, "Am I still looking for something for you, Elissa?"

"No, not now. I just dropped in." Elissa put her hands in the pockets of her suede jacket and stood easily in the center of the room. If she wants me to leave, she's going to have to tell me, she thought.

But Mrs. Braunschweiger, leaning on her crossed arms, said, "You ain't been in here for a while. Too busy, I suppose. There's a lot goin' on on the Hill these days, from what they say in the papers."

Elissa nodded and looked more closely at the man seated in the chair, telling herself that he looked familiar, but how and where had she seen him?

Seeing her scrutinize him, he got up, picking up his tweed hat which he had placed on the floor beside him. "Well, I'll be on my way, Mrs. B. Enjoyed talking to you as always." He nodded briefly to Elissa as he passed by her, giving her a keen look as if trying to place her.

Suddenly remembering, Elissa exclaimed, "Mr. Alden!"

He stood still. "Yes, I'm Robert Alden, but I must confess —"

Elissa said, "Elissa Sampson. I'm a friend of Clemence Hartfield. I met you at her apartment."

"Ah, yes. You were at her party. Quite an affair, that. Well, I must leave you to Mrs. Braunschweiger's tender care," he replied and walked out of the room.

"Sit down," said Mrs. Braunschweiger. "You know him, do you?"

"I couldn't place him at first." Elissa dropped into the chair. She had sometimes wondered whether Mrs. Braunschweiger kept only one chair in the room to control the number of visitors who came to see her. "Does he come here a lot?"

"He's been coming in here since he was a young man just out of college. Whenever he was in Washington he checked in with me. Of course, he lives here now. He likes to come and find out what's really going on here in town."

Elissa knew that Mrs. Braunschweiger cultivated the image of herself as the confidante of persons in the higher echelons of government and society. She knew that Mrs. Braunschweiger was said to be the repository of many secrets told her by her clients which, if divulged, could compromise many reputations. Perhaps that was true. Certainly there was something in Robert Alden's manner that said that he was thoroughly at home here in Mrs. Braunschweiger's sanctum.

Mrs. Braunschweiger was asking in her deep voice, "Are you interested in him?"

Elissa shrugged. "I don't know much about him. He's a curator at the National Gallery. My friend Clemence works there, so I hear about him."

111

"He has a gift for causin' talk. When I first knew him he was a junior assistant at the Smithsonian Institution. He got into trouble there because he claimed that a piece of sculpture they had on display was a fake. He made everybody mad. But he turned out to be right. He used to come in here wantin' books that would prove what he said. I liked the way he stood up to all those pompous know-it-alls." She paused and looked again at Elissa. Usually her broad, full-cheeked face was impassive, but Elissa had learned to catch the fleeting glimpses of emotion that were sometimes discernible on it. Now she saw that Mrs. Braunschweiger was suspicious of her questions.

Elissa had lit a cigarette and was flicking the ash into an ashtray already brimming with other people's butts. "He's the curator in charge of that painting that's vanished off the wall at the Gallery. You know about that?"

"Yes."

"Did he tell you anything about it? Why he did it?"

Mrs. Braunschweiger's black eyes dwelt on her. "He's not the only person from the National Gallery that comes in here."

"Who else?" Elissa thought of Francis Hearn.

"You're really inquisitive today, ain't you?" But there was an indulgent tone in Mrs. Braunschweiger's voice. "I'll say this for Robert. He has the courage of his convictions. And not only about art."

There was an overtone to her voice that alerted Elissa. Mrs. Braunschweiger, she knew, at one time — probably during the Rosenberg spying trial — had been investigated by the FBI. Mrs. Braunschweiger rarely referred to her own private opinions, but on the other hand she never denied her adherence to the principles set forth by Karl Marx nor her sympathy for Emma Goldman and her views. She had always been a regular subscriber to the Daily Worker, a copy of which lay now on her desk.

Elissa remembered that, when she was first a frequenter of the bookstore and had formed the habit of chatting with its owner — in reality, had for some reason caught Mrs. Braunschweiger's interest and become a favored visitor — she had been fascinated by this aspect of Mrs. Braunschweiger's character. In her own chaotic childhood she had encountered people who claimed radical views and who railed against authority, as represented by the police and the politicians in city government. But Mrs. Braunschweiger was the first person she had met who could validate with intelligence and schooling her own discontents with society as she knew it. Elissa wondered if Mrs. Braunschweiger was actually a member of the Communist Party — which, after all, was legally in existence in the United States, a fact not grasped by many who fulminated against it.

"Do you mean he's a Marxist?"

"That's for him to tell you. He and I do see eye-to-eye about a lot of things."

"He can't be a communist — a member of the Communist Party — because, if he was, he'd never be cleared for his appointment at the Gallery."

Mrs. Braunschweiger looked at her curiously. "Words of wisdom from the informed. He don't talk about that sort of thing any more. Probably thinks it's too dangerous. He's got plenty of enemies who'd like to see him lose his job."

"He must have friends, too. A lot of people in the art establishment, here and abroad, stand up for him. That's chiefly why he can get away with this business about the painting. The Gallery people are afraid to attack him openly."

"That's innerestin'." Mrs. Braunschweiger seemed to appreciate this bit of information. "The trouble is, he's pretty careless about how he treats people and most of them don't take kindly to that sort of thing. Besides, he's not a family man. That's always a handicap when a man's in the public eye."

"What do you mean, Mrs. Braunschweiger?"

Mrs. Braunschweiger's black eyes gazed steadily at her. "Well, Elissa, it was your inquirin' mind that made me notice you at the very beginnin'. You've still got it, haven't you?"

There she goes again, thought Elissa, being evasive. But I think she wants to tell me something.

Mrs. Braunschweiger went on. "Is your friend — what's her name?"

"Clemence."

"Is she interested in him?"

Elissa was silent. Was Clemence interested in Robert? She said she wasn't. But —

Mrs. Braunschweiger was still looking at her. "What's the matter, Elissa? You look upset."

"Oh, no! I just never thought of it."

"You mean she ain't told you. You're pretty close friends, eh? Well, sometimes your close friend doesn't tell you somethin' like this. If you're fond of her, you ought to give her a hint that she's wastin' her time. He's not interested in women. You might save her some grief."

Elissa stared at her. "I've heard rumors."

"You know, Elissa, a good many people know that he is or suspect that he is, but they don't talk about it out loud — because they like him or they've got scruples. He's pretty discreet about it. It's the one thing he is discreet about. I think he pretends to play around with women as a sort of smokescreen."

Elissa thought, is Francis Hearn one of the people who know? She asked aloud, "Do you know Francis Hearn?"

"Never heard of him. Who is he?"

"He is the Director of Purchases for the Gallery. He and Robert hate each other."

"That's innerestin'. You mean this other man is gay, too?"

"Oh, no! But I wonder —" She left her conjecture in the air and Mrs. Braunschweiger dropped the subject.

Elissa did not see Clemence until the following evening. When they were sitting in Clemence's living room with their first drinks of the evening, she tried to weigh the information she wanted to give Clemence, while Clemence talked about Charlie Olsen's infatuation with Kathleen.

"Ah, the knight come to awaken the sleeping princess with a kiss," she said sardonically.

"But, 'Lissa, it would be a disaster if he persuades Kathleen to marry him. He's not using any common sense at all."

"You said that about Regina being in love with Francis Hearn. But Kathleen is not going to marry him unless he converts to Catholicism. Or so I gather from what you say. That's a pretty remote possibility, isn't it?"

"It depends. Charlie always reacts violently when he's thwarted. He tends to lose sight of the consequences when he decides he's going to bull his way through some situation. Opposition makes him more stubborn. He's got to prove he's the winner. He won't stop to think whether it is a good idea or not for him to marry Kathleen. He wants Kathleen and obstacles in the way are just something to be overcome. The struggle becomes an end in itself. He's bound to do something because everybody is against it."

"Hm. What does Regina think about it? Is she one of the obstacles?"

"Regina is preoccupied with her own situation. She tried to get me to tell her mother that I think Francis is a fine man who'll make her a good husband."

"Did you?"

"You know I didn't. I tried to be neutral about him, since I don't like him. The more I see of him the less I like him. This bothers me, because I'm afraid it's just prejudice, that my opinion of him is based on emotion, not reason."

"Are you sure about that? Is it because of Robert?"

"It does seem to me that Francis is calculating. When he wants revenge on somebody, he doesn't come out in the open. He waits for an opportunity so that he can act through somebody else. I know for certain that he is the motivating force behind this attack on Robert. I think the other people involved would be perfectly willing to deal with Robert on a friendly basis. But Francis has created this situation where everybody is hostile."

Clemence went on talking till presently she noticed that Elissa was unusually silent. "What's the matter, 'Lissa? You're not listening to what I'm saying."

Oh, yes, I am, Elissa thought. All I can hear is how you're defending Robert. Does he really mean so much to you? Aloud she said, "Yes, I am listening. You're talking about Francis and Robert and there's something I ought to tell you. Sunday afternoon, while you were visiting Regina's mother, I went down to that old bookstore I've told you about. Mrs. Braunschweiger stays open all the time. Robert was there with her. We talked about him after he left."

Clemence frowned. "Who is this woman?"

"I've told you. She owns that old secondhand bookstore down on the ratty end of F Street. I've known her for years. She's known Robert for years."

"What did she say?"

"Well, she says that a lot of people suspect that

Robert is gay. She says he plays around with women to hide the fact."

Clemence still frowned. "Charlie Olsen said that."

Elissa was astonished. "Charlie Olsen? How would he know?"

"Charlie has a lot of friends in the government. He goes to a lot of cocktail parties. So he hears a lot of gossip."

"This morning I was having coffee break with a fellow who has worked on the Hill for a long time. He remembers when McCarthy accused General Marshall of being either a communist or a fellow traveler. This man said that one of the most serious questions raised about Robert when he was being cleared for his Gallery job was that he is a homosexual. You know, a charge like that is almost certain death to a person's career in government service. Fortunately it didn't stick. Robert had enough powerful friends who denied it."

She looked at Clemence, who sat perfectly still. "Don't be so shocked, Clem. It's a lot more common than you think."

Clemence said bitterly, "This is nothing but nasty gossip!"

Elissa shrugged. "People like to speculate about that sort of thing. It's a change from gossiping about somebody committing adultery with somebody else's wife. But the important thing is — what I've been wondering about — is whether Francis has revived this gossip. Francis strikes me as the sort of man who reacts violently against men like Robert."

Clemence said in a cold voice, "You're assuming that this is true, that Robert is really a homosexual."

"Well, is that something terrible? Do we have to think like the people who excoriate people like us? Don't be hypocritical, Clem."

"People like us?"

"People like you and me."

"That's not the same thing."

"Why isn't it? That's not reasonable, you know. I admit I don't know much about men who prefer their own sex. None of us have to apologize for ourselves, even if we have to hide the fact."

But she saw that Clemence was taking a while to absorb this new challenge.

In fact, Clemence was exploring another facet of what Elissa had just said. She thought of the other women in the office where she worked, suddenly seeing their attitude towards herself in a new light. One or two of them were long-time employees of the Gallery, going back to the first years of its existence. They might well remember gossip that had faded otherwise in the intervening time. Did their speculations about her include this knowledge, this suspicion of Robert's nature? Did they talk about the fact that she was such a child that she did not realize what the real situation was?

"I hate it!" she blurted out.

"What?" Elissa looked at her in surprise. "You hate what?"

"I hate all this petty spying on people, talking behind one's back —"

"Invading your privacy." Elissa nodded. "Of course you do. But I don't know what you're going to do about it."

There was a long silence between them. Then Clemence said, "Father Vincent knows Robert."

"Father Vincent?"

"He's the priest that I met at Regina's yesterday. He brought up the subject of the missing painting. He said that he was upset because the painting had been taken off the wall and that he missed seeing it. I think he may make a point of talking to Robert about it."

"I didn't know that Robert was a Catholic."

"He isn't."

"Are you sure he isn't a lapsed Catholic?"

"No, I'm not. He knows a lot about the subjects of religious paintings. But then Francis does, too. It's part of their training in the background of their work. It's odd to listen to them discussing the settings of the paintings, the saints depicted, the religious symbolism, all in a cool, dispassionate way. Quite different from Father Vincent. He gets very fervid. He talks about the painters' religious faith, religious feeling which to him is more important than their technique."

"But Robert gets wrought up, too, doesn't he, about that sort of thing? You've mentioned how impassioned he can get."

"That's different. That's something personal to him. As it is to me."

III

It was the middle of the afternoon and most of the women in the administrative office had gone down to the snack bar for a coffee break. One or two remained, immersed in work that absorbed them. Clemence, as she did more and more often now, sat on at her desk, unwilling to spend time in aimless talk with people intent on sounding her out about the rumors circulating among the staff. She had a book of art illustrations in front of her, a handsome, ornate volume the publication of which had been paid for by private funds provided by a wealthy

120

art patron. It contained many reproductions, on expensive paper in brilliant color, of paintings in the permanent collections of the Gallery. She had it open at the reproduction of A Flight of Angels, her eye lingering gratefully on this pale image of the original. No matter how effective the photographic technology, how expert the photographer, the developer, the printer, no photograph could capture the entire spirit of the painting, the divine afflatus, as it was called, of the artist who had created it.

She was startled when Francis Hearn spoke at her elbow. "The Bernheim volume of Gallery reproductions," he said, naming the patron who had subsidized the volume. "An extraordinary publication — a tour de force, really. The Bernheims really spared no expense in having it produced."

"Yes," said Clemence, twisting her head around to look up at him.

He looked down directly at the volume lying open on the desk. "I see you are studying our notorious Giardini. What do you think of it?"

"Of the reproduction? I think it is wonderful. But it is a tantalizing shadow of the original."

He paused before he said, "Sometimes a photograph can show us details — minute details — that are not apparent in the painting itself. I don't mean the methods of x-raying canvases and so on, to discover whether the painter has covered up earlier sketches or changes. I mean, sometimes one sees details that are lost in the surface of the painting itself. That is something we learned when we had to identify canvases that had been stolen during the war. Perhaps not when the photograph is reproduced like this. The graphic process may obscure them."

Clemence said nothing. She was surprised by his appearing there at that hour of the day and puzzled by the lecture. Francis was not known for bothering to explain technical details to his subordinates. In fact, she had had very little contact with him for some time now. He had seemed to have systematically chosen one of the other women whenever he needed work done for him — a result, she supposed, of the general belief that she preferred to work for Robert.

Francis said, "Well, in any case, if you are free for a few minutes, would you like to come and join me for the afternoon break?"

Astonished, Clemence said, "Why, yes. Just let me make this safe."

He waited patiently, his hands in his pockets, while she closed the big volume and put it back into the soft cloth sleeve in which it was kept. As they walked out of the door together she was aware that the two women still in the room had stopped their work to look after them.

The snack bar was a small room fitted with soft drink and cigarette machines and a counter behind which a blind person dispensed a few sandwiches and cups of coffee. Francis chose a table in the corner, to which he carried two cups of coffee. He ignored the hubbub of voices and the curious glances. It was not usual for someone of his rank to frequent the snack bar. Clemence wondered what sort of gossip would be generated by his appearance there now.

He began by asking what she heard from her parents. Were they coming home soon? Clemence said no. Their return had been postponed again. They would not be back for Christmas. Did that mean she was unhappy? he asked.

"Well, of course, I'd like to have them back," Clemence answered. "But I am used to their being away a lot."

Francis sipped his coffee. "You've got a lot of friends, I know. They will not let you be lonely."

Mystified, Clemence said, "That's true," wondering at this solemn discussion of a commonplace.

"Does Christmas mean a lot to you — in a religious way, I mean."

Still more mystified, Clemence said, "I think you know that my parents do not give much importance to religious things."

"But you personally?"

"Christmas means something to me. I like the drama of the season, the pageantry, listening to Handel's Messiah, going to midnight mass — all that."

"Just the outward show?"

How persistent he is, she thought. "It would all be hollow if you did not feel something of the meaning of the Christ story."

He seemed satisfied that she was making a distinction between her parents' attitude and her own. He nodded sympathetically. "So perhaps you will not miss them as much. You have your own way of enjoying Christmas."

Clemence glanced at him briefly, anxious to fathom the purpose of his questions. "When I was little my mother always made a lot of Christmas — the pageantry part. I think it was because she remembered her own childhood and how magical it could be for a child. So I will miss having her here. When I was older and came home from school for the holidays she always made a very happy time for me."

"Yes, I remember spending a Christmas holiday with them once, abroad." He was silent for a while, toying with his empty paper cup. After a silence he said, "I miss your father a good deal just now. I had been hoping to hear that you expected your parents home soon. Your father has always understood how I feel about certain things. He was always willing to listen to me and asked the sort of questions that helped me clarify my own mind. Whenever

I've reached a crisis in my life I've been able to go to him for advice and moral support. I was hoping he could help me now."

Good heavens! thought Clemence, he surely isn't telling me that he wants my father's advice about what to do about Robert! She said aloud, "I'm sorry I can't give you a definite date for their return. It doesn't seem now that they'll be back before spring. But sometimes they surprise me and come home without notice."

Francis nodded. "Perhaps by then we'll have this problem in the Gallery cleared up." But he seemed preoccupied, as if this was not the reason he had wanted to talk to her. He added half-absentmindedly, "You know that the next meeting of the arts council is postponed till after the holidays? It was announced this morning."

"Yes," said Clemence. "I heard about it this morning." She waited for what he would say next.

He suddenly asked, "You are very good friends with Regina O'Phelan, aren't you? She mentions you often when I see her."

Clemence suppressed a gasp. He was going to talk about Regina! "I've known her since college. We've renewed our friendship since she has moved back to Washington."

"She is a Washingtonian, isn't she? I believe her family has lived here for some time."

"Yes."

"She finds you very sympathetic. She tells me that she has been having a difficult time fitting in back with her family again after being away for so much of the last few years in a different environment."

Clemence murmured a noncommittal reply.

"I'm speaking specifically about her religious views."

What a strange way to talk about someone's faith, thought Clemence — religious views, as if it was a subject of philosophical debate. But I suppose that is how he sees it. She said aloud, "Regina has always been devout. Her family is very devout. I don't think anything has changed while she has been away."

"You don't think that perhaps she has become more relaxed in the practice of her faith?" Francis leaned back in his chair, a battered thing that creaked under him. "You know, Clemence, we in the art world, to borrow a phrase from the newspaper people, spend a good deal of our time concerned with representations of religious scenes, of the agonies and ecstasies of martyrs and saints. But we see them in non-religious terms — at least, many of us do, though I suppose there are those who see them with the eyes of faith. I often point out to my students — you know I teach seminars on the history of art — that it should be remembered that religious subjects were the only ones that the early painters could earn money by painting when the patrons of art were chiefly churchmen or wealthy men who underwrote the building of churches and religious establishments. In many cases the artists were not particularly religious men themselves. They painted what was acceptable. Take that Giardini — it has no popular name, except perhaps something like " 'Pilgrims visited by the Heavenly Host' —"

Clemence broke in eagerly, "I call it A Flight of Angels."

Francis looked at her in surprise. "Why, that is a very good title for it! So far as we know, none of the pilgrims represent saints or biblical figures. It is the host itself that dominates the scene — the concept of humble, devout pilgrims on the way to a shrine, dazzled by the appearance on the way of a — a flight of angels, as you say — come to protect them from dangers on the road. That is very good, Clemence. Where did you get the idea?"

Clemence said, self-consciously, "From Shakespeare — from *Hamlet*. You know it, of course — Horatio on the death of Hamlet: 'Flights of angels sing thee to thy rest.'"

"I see. That does bear out the idea — heavenly spirits descending to earth to carry upward an earthborn creature. That is the impact of the painting — the burst of glory entering the souls of men."

Clemence gazed at him. He was not looking at her but seemed to be musing over the train of thought she had inspired. "The painting has always meant a great deal to me. I miss it very much — not being able to see it."

She feared for a moment that this spontaneous confession of hers would prompt him to make some complaint about Robert. Instead he said, turning his eyes on her, "I see why Regina finds you such a congenial friend. You understand her feelings about the restrictions her church places on her freedom of action."

"What do you mean?"

"Clemence, I am very much interested in Regina. She is a brilliant girl. I should like to persuade her to marry me. But I'm sure you realize that a divorced man is a persona non grata in her family."

"Well, yes," said Clemence, embarrassed by the earnest simplicity of his manner.

He seemed to be making up his mind to ask her something and she waited.

"Has she mentioned this to you?"

Clemence shook her head. She was annoyed by this attempt, as she saw it, to intrude on the privacy of her friendship with Regina.

"You see, I should like to see more of Regina. I think she responds to me. I think she likes me. But I know that she is inhibited by her family's disapproval."

Remembering Regina's attempt to enlist her help with Mrs. O'Phelan, Clemence said carefully, "Do they disapprove?"

"I don't really know. I have not met her mother. Regina seems reticent about introducing me. I can only suppose that is because she knows that her mother will not approve."

"I think probably she will have to have time to let her family get used to the idea," said Clemence, lamely. "Regina doesn't rush into things without thinking of the consequences."

Francis stopped playing with the paper cup. "I find that one of her attractions. She is a thoughtful person. Yes, you're right. It will take time."

"It sounds Victorian," said Elissa. "Besides, he has a reputation for being devious. I suppose it's his nature. He can't help approaching things obliquely."

"But why should he come and ask me questions? Why should he assume that I'm going to discuss Regina with him?"

"Because he is in love with her, he has a real obstacle in his way, and he doesn't know how else to go about it. I'm amazed, Clem. Do you suppose he was in love with his first wife? He seems so passionless. He must really be carried away by Regina."

"Passionless, perhaps. That's what he seems to be. But he's capable of smoldering. For instance, look how he hates Robert. He probably ended by hating his first wife, when the honeymoon was over. But why ask me? Why get me involved in his personal affairs?"

Elissa grinned at her. "Because you're such a

sympathetic little thing, so ready to rally round anyone who is in trouble, the sort of trouble they can't confide to anybody else."

"Oh, Elissa, be serious!"

"Well, I don't think what I'm saying is frivolous. Of course, I don't know the man — only the gossip I hear about him."

Clemence, sitting on the sofa with her arm stretched along its back, frowned in thought. Elissa, standing, sought a cigarette in the humidor that stood on the table.

When Clemence stayed silent, Elissa said, "Regina really is on the spot, if she is so much in love with him. Except for the religious taboos about being divorced, I should think he would be a pretty acceptable son-in-law."

"Yes, of course. He's a little old for her. He must be at least forty, but Regina would not be happy with a young man who did not have his knowledge and experience. Yes, I think her mother would find him very acceptable — except for that. But I'm thinking about something else. I think they're incompatible, basically, emotionally. She's all fire. He's cold."

"You said just now that he smolders. There must be some fire there somewhere."

"But not the right kind. He's not outgoing. I'm sure it would be a mistake for her to marry him."

"That's because you don't like him."

Clemence did not answer. Elissa waited and then said, "You remember what I told you Mrs. Braunschweiger said about Robert. I've been thinking. Do you suppose that has something to do with Francis hating him?"

"You mean, Francis hates him because he knows he's homosexual?"

"Is he the kind of man who does hate homosexual men — Francis, that is?"

"I don't know. But he is a good hater."

"Some men do detest the idea that some men prefer other men to women."

"That's pretty impersonal, isn't it — like hating somebody because he doesn't agree with your political opinions?"

"There's been plenty of persecution throughout history based on hatred of other people's religious beliefs or cultural inheritance."

"Yes, of course. Well —"

As she fell silent again, Elissa said, teasing, "Aren't you glad we don't have that problem?"

But Clemence looked at her soberly. "We have one just as big, 'Lissa."

Her quiet tone struck a chill through Elissa. She blustered, "Not if we don't let it be an obstacle! It's up to us!"

Clemence answered her glare with a long look. At last she said, "We do have a problem. It's no use pretending it doesn't exist. Neither of us can flout society — just say we can go our own way. You need to have a decent job — something that makes use of your education. I have my parents to think about. I've no idea what I can do there."

Still angry, Elissa declared, "If you love me the way I love you, we can dare anything!"

Clemence shook her head. "Don't be childish." But she did not go on to upbraid Elissa. She realized suddenly that Elissa was using anger to disguise her dismay — and, yes, the fright that had possession of her. She reached up to pull Elissa down beside her and said instead, " 'Lissa, there isn't any need to panic. We'll try to find a way out of this but it won't help to deceive ourselves about what it means for us to love each other as we do."

At first Elissa resisted her, her body rigid with

rejection, but her anger did not last under the touch of Clemence's hands. Clemence put her arms around her and stroked the back of her head. "You're scared, 'Lissa. You always get mad when you're scared. Come on, kiss me."

Elissa surrendered, returning her kiss. She said humbly, "I always get scared when it seems like something awful is going to happen and I can't stop it. Clem, I can't lose you! I can't!" She buried her face in Clemence's neck.

Clemence said into her ear, "Uh huh. You've been conditioned to expect disaster. 'Lissa, there's no use giving way to fright just because we don't see a solution right now."

Elissa's voice was muffled. "The bit about the coward who dies a thousand deaths."

Clemence held her tight. " 'Lissa, you're no coward."

The trouble was, thought Clemence, coming in from the cold street and taking off her coat and hat and hanging them up in the little dark-panelled room provided for the staff, this new knowledge. Yes, this uncomfortable new knowledge which was creating a problem for her in her everyday dealings with the people she worked with. When she had been ignorant of it she had supposed that they had unfounded suspicions of her relationship with Robert and she could dismiss that as ordinary gossip. Now it was obvious that they wondered whether she was pursuing Robert unaware that there was a barrier to any response from him. It was far more difficult now to hide her real feelings, uncertain as she was about them herself.

When she stepped into the big room full of desks and typewriters, she walked quickly to her own, responding with nods to the good mornings tossed at her. She sat down at her desk and drew towards her the big volume of reproductions Francis had found her examining the evening before. If everyone else had suspicions of Robert's private life, Francis must certainly know about that. She still pondered her own reaction to the idea of sexual attraction between men. It seemed somehow to have little connection with the attraction that could so easily exist between women. Yet this was not reasonable and probably was only the result of the hostile stereotypes relentlessly projected by those who had no sympathy for any but conventional sexual morality, reinforced by religious prejudices.

She was startled by someone speaking to her close at hand. It was Flora. She looked up at the tall woman standing beside her. Her gaze focused on the carefully waved grey hair, the skillfully tailored suit, the necklace and bracelets and earrings. Flora was a graduate of one of the New England women's colleges and her manner and her speech proclaimed the fact.

Now Flora was saying, "Clemence, if you're not terribly busy, would you help me sort the Lamberton prints? They are so large that it is hard for one person to handle them. But only if you can spare the time."

Her eyes behind the rimless glasses were fixed on her. Clemence, glad of something on which to focus her scattered attention, said quickly, "Oh, yes," and got up immediately.

She had heard of the Lamberton prints. They were fine photographs in color of a collection of ancient ceramics from South America. At the moment they were stacked on a wide, long table that filled most of the space in the windowless basement room. A wealthy patron had lent them to the Gallery for exhibition and they had now to be sorted and classified. Together she and Flora lifted the big sheets of stiff paper, examined them for injuries and stood together every so often for a few moments to admire the fine images and fidelity of color.

Presently, Flora said, "Perhaps we should take a break. This is exacting work."

They sat down on the long bench of polished mahogany behind which hung a great tapestry darkened by age, depicting the scene of a knight's return from the crusades to his forest-girt castle. For a while conversation was desultory but then Flora, in the midst of a pause, said, "You know, don't you, Clemence, that Robert Alden is in serious trouble. I've been wanting to mention this to you because I believe you have a special interest in him."

Clemence, touched on a tender spot, said quickly, "Yes, I have a special interest in him, but it is not what everybody seems to think it is. I admire him and I'm sorry that he is in such a mess, but —"

As she hesitated, Flora added to her statement, "You haven't a romantic interest in him. It is always difficult to convince people that as a woman your interest in a man is not sentimental. Have you just realized that that is what everyone is saying about you and Robert?"

"Everybody seems to think that I am in Robert's pocket — that he tells me all about what he is doing — that I know ahead of time what they later find out. It makes me a sort of accessory to whatever he does and I don't like that. I thought at first it was because I'm the newest member of the staff and that I am here because my parents used influence. People seem to think that I get special privileges because of them."

Flora smiled at her vehemence. "That sort of thing can be a burden, can't it?" She hesitated before going on. "You don't know much about Robert, do you? At least, what people say about him. You know he has two reputations: one, that he chases women; and two, that he does not like women."

"I've heard something about that."

"The second one is nearer the truth. Those of us who have known him longest have thought that perhaps you weren't aware of his — tastes, and we did not like the idea that you were wasting your time and your sympathy."

Clemence said indignantly, "All this is beside the point. I like Robert. I admire his professional gifts. But I'm not interested in his private life."

Flora observed her indignation. "It hasn't seemed to me that you were the kind of girl who would try to interest a man in yourself."

"Thank you," Clemence snapped, angry.

"Don't let this upset you so much, Clemence. It is something you have to cope with in any group of people like this. Well, I expect we had better get back to the Lamberton prints."

They worked steadily and mostly in silence. When lunchtime came they closed things up and began to leave the room together. Flora stopped and put her hand on Clemence's arm.

"I'm having a group of congenial souls in for drinks at my place this Sunday evening. Would you like to join us?"

Clemence hesitated. Sunday had become the special day for herself and Elissa. Neither one of them willingly allowed other events to interfere. Flora, watching her, said as they began to walk toward the door, "I notice that you have a friend who comes often from the Hill to have lunch with you. Do you think she would like to join us, too?"

Clemence blushed with pleasure. "I'll ask her."

Elissa asked, as they walked along R Street toward Connecticut Avenue, "Why do you suppose she said that to you — that she had noticed me and wondered if I wanted to come along?"

"Just friendliness," said Clemence, but she was not as sure of this as she tried to seem. Nowadays, she thought, so much that hitherto she had taken for granted, had not questioned, seemed to conceal something below the surface. "Why should she have another motive?"

"Doesn't it strike you a little odd that in the first place she notices me when I come to see you, and secondly, that she should sweep me up with you, so to speak, in her very first invitation to you?"

Clemence did not answer. Then Elissa asked, "What kind of parties does she give?"

"I think she has small gatherings of people who are interested in the arts — not just painting — music and books. I know that Robert and Francis have both been to her parties — probably not at the same time, because she is not as foolhardy as I was. She has been at the Gallery a lot longer than I have."

They arrived at a large red brick house with a curved drive in front and a wide passageway back to what had once been a carriage house. Elissa recognized it as a Richardson house — a fortress-like structure with crenelations and turrets in red brick, one of many in Washington that had been designed by Henry Hobson Richardson during the nineteenth century. This one had been transformed from a private dwelling into flats. Flora's name appeared over one of the mailboxes set into the wall of the entryway. Flora's voice said presently through the speaking tube, "Do come up. I'm on the second floor."

The second floor landing was spacious, with a big door that had once opened into a drawing room and a smaller one in the dimness towards the back for the servants. She must have the whole floor, Elissa whispered as the big door opened. Flora stood there smiling at them, the light from the fanlight over the street door glinting up from below onto her glasses. She took their coats from them in the vestibule and held back the heavy curtain for them to enter the big room that was the length of the house on that side. It was a richly furnished room, with overstuffed chairs and deep-piled rugs. It was also empty. They were the first arrivals.

Flora said, following them into the room, "I wanted you to come before anyone else because I'd like to get to know your friend, Clemence. This is —?"

"Elissa Sampson," said Clemence, instinctively placing her hand on Elissa's arm.

Flora's quick eyes caught the gesture and she smiled, glancing from one to the other. "I've seen you often, Elissa, and in fact, we've greeted one another on occasion, haven't we?"

Elissa nodded as they all sat down in a small circle of chairs.

"I believe you are on the staff of a congressional committee. Do you have a great interest in art — in painting?"

"I like to look at paintings." Obviously I must, thought Elissa, if I come to the Gallery almost every day.

"But you really come to see Clemence, don't you?"

Wary, Elissa nodded. "We're college chums. I was very happy to find out that Clemence was in Washington when I came to work here. But how did you know that I work on the Hill?"

Flora's smile broadened. "No, Clemence did not tell me. You don't realize the extreme interest everyone on our staff has in anyone from the Hill. We're very sensitive to the Hill and some emanation, perhaps I might say, warns us when we have a visitor from there."

She's a smart one, thought Elissa.

Clemence interjected, "No, I didn't realize that."

"You haven't been with us long enough," said Flora.

"Our nerves have been sensitized even more now by Robert Alden's doings. Of course, I and one or two others on the staff date back to the time when he first joined us. There was a good deal of controversy about him then. People said, among other things, that he was a communist or a fellow traveler, and other such scandalous accusations. A couple of us were interrogated by the FBI — as if two women like us would have the slightest knowledge of his private life and opinions. I am reminded of all this by current events." Flora broke off to look across the room at a woman who entered from a door at the other end. "Ah, Val. This is Clemence and Elissa. I have told you about them."

Val came across the room towards them. She was a plump, short, grey-haired woman who appeared to be the same age as Flora. She wore a long-sleeved silk dress with elaborate embroidery at the neck and cuffs. She nodded in acknowledgement of Flora's introduction and sat down opposite them.

She said to Clemence, "I have met your father and mother on several occasions. They are extraordinary people."

She was, it turned out, a curator at the Smithsonian Museum of Natural History. Her bright, lively eyes played over Clemence and Elissa, as if she had been told something of interest about them and was curious to compare her own impressions with that hearsay. She questioned them about their ages, their college history, their present jobs. Clemence noticed that she came back again and again to Elissa, as if Clemence she understood at a glance, but Elissa required more study. Elissa seemed to lose her usual stiffness under Val's scrutiny and blossomed into an expansive retrospect of her origins in the Bronx — things, thought Clemence, I haven't known till now. She tried to listen to Flora while watching Elissa's sudden spontaneity with a mixture of surprise and concern. Did Elissa realize, she wondered, how skillfully Val was leading her on to talk about herself with a reckless abandon that Elissa never displayed?

But then Clemence became aware that Flora was talking about A Flight of Angels. She was saying, "You know, Clemence, there is going to be a showdown about that painting when the trustees meet. They are going to have to account for this situation to the congressional committee. The appropriations hearings are coming up soon."

Elissa's ear obviously caught her last statement and she half-turned away from Val, who stopped speaking.

"You mean," Clemence asked, "they are going to force Robert to bring it out of hiding?"

"I should say so. So far he has been able to refuse them, chiefly because they don't want to be seen as harassing him, a man with such a wide reputation as preeminent in his field. But if he is called before a congressional committee he may risk contempt of Congress. I think even Robert would like to avoid that."

"I'm sure he would avoid it!" Clemence exclaimed.

Flora replied, "It is a distinct possibility."

Elissa blurted out, "If he pushed it that far, he'd open up a lot of trouble for himself. He could be questioned about anything, including past scandals."

Flora and Val were both watching her. Val said, "You're referring to the accusations in the past about his personal life. We often wondered how he was able to defeat the FBI inquiry into that. He must have powerful friends — people who are able and willing to defend him."

Flora said, "I believe it is chiefly his reputation in the

art world. The international community of arts people can be powerful. And they admire him in spite of his inclination to go his own way regardless."

Elissa demanded, "Then you think the allegations were true?"

Val glanced briefly at Flora as if for support before replying. "You mean, that he is homosexual. No one who knew Robert at that time had any doubt that he was."

"Well, then, he still is, isn't he?" Elissa said. "It is not something that happens at one time in your life and disappears."

Flora and Val exchanged smiles. Flora said, "Now that is a question I can't answer. I've known a good many men who change their habits of life when they reach their forties. They seem suddenly to decide that they must honor the requirements of their families and marry and produce children."

"But Robert hasn't done that," Elissa protested.

"And doesn't show any sign that he is about to," said Flora, glancing at Clemence.

There was a silence and before anyone spoke again, the buzzer from the street door sounded and Flora went to answer. Presently she returned followed by a couple of women, one of them small and frail who was introduced as the retired president of a women's college. The buzzer sounded frequently after that and the room filled with people, most of them middle-aged or older and most of them women, although several men were sprinkled among them.

Elissa found herself in a corner with a grey-haired man with a youthful face and trim build who eyed her curiously.

"You're on the Hill, I understand," he said.

"Yes."

"Which committee?"

Elissa told him.

"That's the one chaired by one of the New York representatives, isn't it?"

Elissa said yes again.

"I've often wondered what it would be like to have one's finger on the pulse of the nation."

"I wouldn't say it's that," said Elissa. "At least, not as it applies to me."

"What! You mean to say that you're not informed about all these esoteric doings and fateful decisions that affect us common folk in the arts and sciences?"

Playing to his satire, Elissa answered, "No, I'm sorry to say that I'm as much in the dark about the intentions of Congress as you are. Are you all —" she paused to glance round the room "— all of you here, in the arts and sciences?"

"Now, I can't speak for the whole lot. But Flora and Val are partial to the creative types. As a matter of fact, most of us are either now in government jobs or retired from them, jobs that have something to do with the arts and sciences. You —" This time he was the one to pause and glance across the room to where Clemence sat talking to the retired college president "— and your friend are a new departure. In the first place, you're very young —" he paused again to grin at her. "Does this portend something new in Flora's interests? We're not used to seeing such youth and beauty amongst our grey heads."

Disconcerted, Elissa murmured, "I have no idea what you mean."

"Of course not. However, my curiosity is piqued."

Elissa said, "Clemence works in the administrative office at the National Gallery. She and Flora have become friends. I suppose we were invited for that reason."

A slight smile played round the corners of his mouth. "Flora and Val like to entertain and often she does have colleagues and co-workers here. But she does not invite them to such intimate gatherings as this. All of us here

139

have a common bond. I'm sure you understand." He stopped abruptly as Val joined them, a plate of small cakes in her hand.

She said, "I think these are favorites of yours, Steve. Do take one, Elissa."

It was an efficient way of breaking up a tete-a-tete, thought Elissa. Steve proceeded to shepherd her round the room, introducing her to a number of people before he left her. She found herself enjoying the party more than most she had attended in Washington. There seemed to be a congeniality among the guests that first intrigued her and then aroused a new suspicion in her mind.

As they were going home, Elissa said, "Did you figure it out?"

"Figure what out?" Clemence's tone was short, as if she was out of temper.

"Didn't you enjoy it?"

"Yes," Clemence admitted. "They were very interesting people."

"And everybody there was unmarried. Most of them came alone, one by one. And those who came in pairs were of the same sex — women with women, men with men."

"Do you mean —?" Clemence began and stopped. "Elissa, that can't be true! There wouldn't be that many people like that in a small group!"

"Oriented to the same sex as themselves. That's where you're wrong. There are a lot of people like that — beginning with Flora and Val. I found out that they've been living together for thirty years. You've heard about Boston marriages and lifelong companions? Well, you see an example right there. So of course they know all about Robert."

Clemence said stubbornly, " 'Lissa, how can all these people be what you say? They look and act just like everybody else."

"Except that they're better behaved than most. They have to protect their jobs and reputations. In fact, they have to be more like what they're not than most people. One thing I'm wondering about is: what is going to happen if Flora tells all her friends about us? They must all guess, since we were invited to this particular party."

Clemence demanded, "Are you absolutely sure? I mean, are you absolutely sure that all these people are like us, and that Flora invited us because she was certain about us?"

"Yes, I am. Did you see me talking to the man wearing a plaid jacket. Well, he was talking about Flora and Val. He said they're partial to creative people, meaning especially people in the arts. Then he said we — you and I — were something new at Flora's parties, because we're younger than the rest of their friends. I played dumb but he persisted. Flora, he said, doesn't invite the people she works with and other people she knows generally, to this kind of party — intimate gatherings, he called them — and he talked about everybody there having a common bond, which he said I would understand without him explaining. Now, Clem, he couldn't have been plainer if he had come out and said that everybody there was gay."

Clemence pondered what she said for a while. They were sitting in the living room. Finally Clemence said, "But 'Lissa, are we the same as they?"

Elissa looked at her in surprise. "Clem, I can't see a difference. I'm not interested in men. I never have been. You remember when we were at Goucher what a job it was for me to get a date for a dance — you know I hated that sort of thing. I only went to those dances because you told me I had to. I was miserable trying to make conversation with those boys. You've told me I don't know how to act with men — that I go out of my way to antagonize them."

"That's because you're so fervent about what you think is injustice. I've told you that you should be less aggressive. Men don't like women to be aggressive."

"And I say that I don't give a damn, because I don't care what they like. Oh, Clem, we always argue about this! What I mean now is that I know I don't like men."

"You don't always seem to like women, either," said Clemence tartly. Then she was sorry, for she saw the stricken look that came on Elissa's face at her tone of voice. "'Lissa, I'm just anxious that you don't make unnecessary enemies. You're so prone not to pay attention to what somebody else may think or feel, how they'll react to your statements."

"That's not what I'm talking about. I know I'm no good at dealing with people with kid gloves on. You've told me that often enough. I'm talking about you and me. You know I'm not like the other girls you've known. I prefer women and you've certainly given me the right to believe you're the same."

"But I don't like to be put in a category. You and I don't fit into a category. We're simply us."

"Well, we don't fit into any other category, either."

"I'm not sure about myself at all — especially after this evening. Yes, I know how you feel. You've demonstrated it. But I don't see it just the way you do."

Elissa's face reddened. "What you're telling me, then, is that I'm a lesbian — yes, that's the word for it, whether you like it or not — but you're not. Does that mean you're just playing with me — that I don't mean to you what you mean to me — that you're just experimenting?"

"No, I'm not experimenting. If I was doing that, we'd have stopped after the first time we made love. I just don't know what I am and I don't know what I'll want to do in the future. There's no use my saying things that are not true."

142

Elissa had jumped to her feet while Clemence was speaking. She said in a choked voice, "If that's the case, I might as well leave now. I won't burden you with my presence." She started to walk toward the front door. "I'll come back and get my things some other time, when you're not here. And I'll leave the key."

For a moment Clemence sat immobile, still caught in the strange feeling of unreality that had held her since she and Elissa had come away from the party. She was seeing herself from the outside, the Clemence she knew was familiar to the people she worked with. If what Elissa said was true, that image was in imminent danger of being shattered and she had no idea what other image would be put in its place.

But suddenly, as Elissa stormed towards the door, she sprang up and ran after her. It was almost an involuntary motion, since it was purely reactive to the fact that Elissa was about to disappear. She reached Elissa as she opened the door. She laid a firm grip on her arm.

" 'Lissa, 'Lissa, where are you going?"

Elissa tried to wrench away from her. She said through clenched teeth, "I'm getting out of your way."

Clemence clung to her arm. " 'Lissa, come back here. Why do you get so beside yourself? Come back here and sit down."

For a long time they stood striving against each other and then Clemence felt the tension in Elissa's body begin to ebb. After a while Elissa allowed herself to be led back to the sofa.

She sat down with her head in her hands and said nothing. Clemence, sitting sideways to watch her, presently said, " 'Lissa, I can't agree to something I don't understand."

Elissa raised her head and Clemence saw that there were tears in her eyes. "Clem, I love you. I've never loved anybody the way I love you and I never will. Don't you understand that? I've been going along thinking that you knew all about me and how I feel and that you understood what it meant."

Clemence impulsively put her arms around Elissa and pulled her head down to her shoulder. " 'Lissa, I do love you. You're in first place with me and I don't think anybody else could ever be the same to me. Surely you know that."

Elissa protested, raising her head to look at her. "But then why did you say what you did — that this doesn't mean the same thing to you?"

"I didn't say that. You're as important to me as I am to you. But I don't know that I accept the rest of this as if it were inevitable. I don't think that anyone else could ever have induced me to make love with them — any other woman and certainly no man. But that is as far as I can go. I do not see us — you and me — as just another example of a category of women."

Elissa stared at her for a moment and then straightened up. "I don't think it's any use arguing about this. I'm not an advocate for any abstract idea. It is just you and me. Oh, Clem!" Elissa seized hold of her, searching for reassurance in the touch of their bodies.

Later that night, when Elissa slept the sound sleep of emotional exhaustion beside her, Clemence sat up in bed and pondered. She felt peaceful now and fulfilled after their lovemaking. The storm earlier seemed far away, something that had passed into half-forgetfulness. Why, she wondered, did they find themselves, every so often, in this extreme turmoil of spirit, as if there was real conflict between them? Their feeling of unity was usually so deep and untroubled until occasionally shattered by these, to her, sudden, unaccountable flare-ups which Elissa precipitated. Elissa's feelings seemed always so close to the boil. Perhaps she herself was not as free of blame for their few quarrels. Perhaps there was something in her — ambivalence, perhaps? — that drove Elissa every so often into these violent protests. She knew she was given to questioning her own and others' motives, never able to accept at face value what was said and done. But — and pondering now she was astonished by this — one thing she never questioned was her feeling about Elissa. It seemed to be bedrock in her spirit. No one but Elissa could have roused her to this fire of life.

She sank down into the warmth of the bed again and bent over Elissa's sleeping head. She touched her lips lightly to Elissa's forehead, cheek, eyelids. Dear Elissa, so vulnerable always, awake or asleep, to the shocks of existence.

She could not banish a sense of trepidation as she arrived at her desk. The world seemed, over the weekend, to have become an entirely different place. Where before she was oblivious to anything that was not self-evident, now she was wondering about what lay beneath the surface of every remark made to her, every facial expression. Presently she pulled herself up short. This was not sensible. If the people around her had ulterior motives for what they did, hidden meanings in what they said, reserved thoughts that lay behind their attitudes, she should ignore these things and act in her own, uncompromised way, as she always had.

But whenever she persuaded herself that this should be the case, she remembered Flora, Flora's percipience, Flora's calculation in welcoming her into the special group of people with whom she obviously believed that she and Elissa should belong. Then her self-confidence deserted her. She could only reassure herself with the thought that Flora undoubtedly was the soul of discretion in hiding from the world her own private life.

This morning, soon after she reached her desk, there was a summons from Robert's office. She went down the corridor to it nervously, as if everywhere she went now was a journey fraught with the threat of danger. She could not see Robert now with the same straightforward vision as heretofore. Before this she had seen him as a difficult man who both intrigued and annoyed her, whose idiosyncracies she accepted as a facet of his professional brilliance. Now he was something else: a man with not only a complicated past but also a dangerous present.

Robert was obviously out-of-sorts. When she opened the door and stepped into the room, he did not greet her but said petulantly, "I need the acquisition file on the Giardini. Will you get it? I don't think they will make trouble for you."

"They" she interpreted to mean the people in charge of the confidential files of the Gallery. She also supposed that he was sending her rather than go himself because he wanted to avoid some sort of confrontation. She went, and discovered that the file was not available. It had been taken out by the secretary of the arts council. Clemence sought her out. She was a woman Flora's age but without Flora's unobtrusive friendliness. It was, she said, out of the question for the file to be released to Mr. Alden. Yes, of course, Mr. Alden was the curator in charge of the painting. But the council members specifically stated that the file was not to be released to anyone on any grounds.

Clemence, unhappy, started back to Robert's office. She was unhappy that she had not been able to persuade the woman to give her the file, even unofficially for a brief period of time. But she realized she was more unhappy because the woman obviously took a real pleasure in denying her request. Was it only because of a personal dislike of Robert? Or was there also a censorious triumph at being able to thwart a man who usually had his own way — and whose suspected manner of life she condemned?

When she got back to Robert's office he was sitting at his desk writing rapidly on a yellow pad. He paid no attention to her entrance and she finally sat down in a nearby chair and waited. Presently he threw down his pencil and glanced at her.

"Well, where is it?" he demanded.

"Mrs. Blake has it and she says she has been instructed not to release it to anyone."

Robert's face grew fiery red. "The goddamn bitch! Who told her she could sit on it?"

"She says the council members —"

"Have impounded it so that I won't have evidence of some of the things I'm going to accuse them of." He jumped up and strode around the room. He seemed unaware of Clemence except as someone sitting in a chair. Finally he stopped in front of her.

"You know what they want to do, don't you? They want to trip me up by accusing me of lying if I don't quote exactly what I said at the time I was arguing for the purchase of that painting. They know nobody can remember verbatim what he has said or written ten years ago, if he doesn't have the documents." He looked down at her, as if focusing on who she was. "You weren't here, were you?"

"I've only been here since June —"

"Before your time, before your time."

He seemed to calm down as his temper vented. "Well, I'll tell you about it, Clemence. It was 1949. The dust of bombings had hardly settled in Europe. That was when I got my appointment here. I made it a condition of acceptance that I could exercise the privilege of acquiring paintings that I had been able to find in the wreckage of war, provided there wasn't overwhelming evidence that they belonged in some specific collections which were being reconstituted. Nobody claimed the Giardini. Very few people knew where it had been before the war. There were references back to Napoleon, that he had appropriated it during his Austrian campaign. Did you know that Napoleon was a art plunderer, too? But nobody could say where he had got it from or where it had been hidden in the meantime — probably he gave it to someone he owed a favor to, who kept it in a private collection, till it wound up in a dealer's hands. I had a glimpse of it in Italy back in the 'thirties. The acquisition committee were a paling lot, afraid of the congressional committee. I bulled through the purchase."

Listening to him, Clemence marvelled at the way he could be overcome, in the midst of a towering rage, by the history of a painting, by its radiance, by the artist's inspiration. Presently he stopped speaking and she looked up to see that he was standing in one of the big windows, deep in thought. He had forgotten that she was there. But all at once he turned round and asked, "Clemence, has Francis Hearn said anything to you about the Giardini — about me?"

"Nothing in particular —" she began.

Robert gave her a long look and then said, "If he does, will you tell me?"

Her overwhelming feeling was that he should not be asking her to do this. Obviously he depended on her good will towards him. But also it was certain that he did not consider for a moment how this request would affect her. She wanted to say that she could not undertake to do this. But her tongue was reluctant. She felt a fellowship with him that urged her to comply — a feeling she was sure he would never reciprocate.

She looked at him again and saw that his eyes were still fixed on her. She sighed and said yes.

Just before Clemence went to lunch in the cafeteria, Regina appeared at her desk and asked if she could join her. Clemence, thinking of Elissa waiting for her in the corridor, nevertheless realized that she could not say no. She was prepared for the vexed look on Elissa's face and was grateful, when she and Regina appeared in the cafeteria, to her for swallowing her annoyance and making cheerful conversation while they all three sat at lunch.

What Elissa could most readily talk about was the substance of the public debates in the civil rights movement. They had a new girl in her office, she said, a black girl, the first ever hired there. Just before she came to lunch she had found her crying into the files and discovered that the girl had a brother who had been beaten to death in an incident in some southern state. As she was talking Elissa did not notice the horrified expression that appeared on Regina's face and was unprepared when Regina crossed herself and exclaimed, "Sweet Jesus, Keeper of my soul!" Elissa stopped short. She had seen Regina do this before but she was always startled. She had finished her lunch so now she rose and picked up her tray to place it in the rack. She muttered, "I'd better be going now. Glad to see you, Regina," and left them with twenty minutes still to go of Clemence's lunch period.

Regina, who had sat in obvious misery while they ate, managed a smile as Elissa left. Clemence waited.

Regina said, "Oh, Clemence, everything seems to be going wrong for me. The academic council has finally acted on my dissertation. They say they cannot approve the research it is based on. It was Father Vincent who gave me the news. He says it is because some of the more conservative faculty members question the implications that may be drawn from the results. I did not want to tell you while Elissa was here because I know she is not sympathetic to any discussion about religious controversy."

"Does that mean, Regina, that you have to abandon it? Surely not."

"Yes, that is what it means. Oh, Clemence, I am sick at heart. They don't say they are going to cancel the research grant. They just leave it dangling. But they will not authorize funds for my participation in the research, so it amounts to the same thing."

"You haven't any way of appealing?"

"Well, yes, but it would be a long drawn-out business. Research like this has to be carried out consistently. It can't be broken off and then taken up again with any worthwhile results."

"Regina, I'm terribly sorry."

Regina sat biting her lip and flexing her hands. A flick of anger appeared in her eyes. "It also means that I will get no credit for what I have done. Several of the people I have been working with are not Catholics. Some of them are in other universities — it is an inter-university project. This probably will mean that one of the others will take the project over and have the prestige of breaking into this new field. I'll be out of it, of course."

"This is unthinkable, Regina! It was your idea in the first place and you had to persuade the others to join in with you."

Regina nodded, looking down at her hands in misery. Clemence, at a loss for consoling words, waited in silence. Presently Regina looked up at her.

"Clemence, that is only part of it. Francis has been no help."

"Francis?"

"I had to tell Francis what has happened. He saw that I am very unhappy. He is indignant, of course. But he also used this as an opportunity to make me feel how archaic, how senseless — these are his words — the Catholic faith is and how bigoted my family is. He is much more versed than I am in all the arguments against religious belief and how wrong-headed it is to put faith ahead of rational thought. He says it is impossible for a rational person to accept dogma. He says he would never agree to the imposition of any sort of restraint on his own thinking, on the use of his mind. I cannot argue against him, Clemence, because I cannot reach him on this subject. His mind is closed to any objection I might make." Regina stopped and wiped her lips with her crumpled-up paper napkin.

Clemence saw that she was trembling with the effort at self-control and put out her hand to hold hers. "Regina, this is very unfair — and it doesn't show Francis to be kind. Surely he must see that you need his comfort now, not lecturing."

"But you see," said Regina, eagerly, "he feels so strongly about it — I suppose, as strongly as I feel about my faith. He has absolute belief in the rational. He cannot conceive of anyone not acknowledging the truth of what he says. He is not just trying to scold me. He feels he has to rescue me — from myself, I suppose. Yet I cannot abandon my faith. It holds truths that he cannot encompass in his arguments."

"Well, don't you think," said Clemence, slowly, wondering how much she should say on this subject, "that this is a warning to you about your dependence on Francis? I don't think you can change his opinions."

151

"Oh, I wouldn't try to do that! I'm not as —
single-minded as Kathleen." She gave a bitter little laugh.
"Kathleen has a perfectly simple answer to her situation:
just make Charlie a convert. And really she seems to be
on the way to achieve her goal. Charlie is taking
instruction from Father Vincent. Francis is quite a
different kind of man. I wouldn't attempt such a thing. I
can just imagine what he would say if I suggested such a
thing! And I would consider it an impertinence. A change
like that is something one must seek on one's own, from
some inner urging, not through someone else's
exhortation." She stopped again and looked at Clemence.
"You see how far I've come from the requirement that one
should try to bring the heathen into the fold. What I
want is for us — Francis and me — to forbear where
each other's beliefs and opinions are concerned, to respect
our differences and let them resolve themselves through
the action of our — our —"

What she means, thought Clemence, waiting for her to
finish her sentence, is for their love for each other to lead
them to a harmonious relationship. Her love will certainly
lead Regina. But Francis? She said aloud, "That's a tall
order, Regina. Francis would be a much more
extraordinary man than I think he is if he could do that.
He is, you know, very self-centered. Most men are. It
would be better for you if you would just realize how
incompatible you two are. Do think about this, Regina,
before too much damage is done — to you, I mean."

Regina's mouth became set. She said firmly, "That's
not possible. And why should it be? I can't put a distance
between myself and Francis. It would hurt him and
devastate me."

Clemence, aware that her lunch period had run out,
waited for her to say something further. But Regina sat
silent and Clemence thought perhaps she was not going to
say anything further. But then Regina said, in a more

normal tone of voice, "In the meantime I must do something about my situation. I must earn my living. I'll not be able to see you as often, Clemence, as I have. I've accepted a teaching appointment at Rosecroft — the girls' school outside Philadelphia — to fill out the school year for a teacher who has become seriously ill. The nuns there are anxious for me to join their faculty."

"Why, that's fine! Are you going to live there?"

Regina grimaced. "No. I've arranged that I'll stay there through the week and come home for weekends. It's a school for the daughters of very wealthy people and I don't think I could stand spending my weekends chaperoning girls whose parents have sent them there for the nuns to keep them out of trouble."

"Oh, I see. But it is a good fill-in for the moment, isn't it?"

"Well, yes, I suppose so. And of course I can be here for the holidays."

Available to Francis, thought Clemence.

In the evening, when she told Elissa about this conversation, Elissa said, "I wondered what she had on her mind. I saw she wanted to talk to you."

"Yes. She's very unhappy."

"She had better be prepared for a lot of grief. Doesn't she see that?"

"That's the most tragic part about it. I think with her mind she sees that very clearly. But she won't let go of this opportunity to seize life. Francis is the first chance she has had to go beyond the limits of her inherited world. I don't think she realizes that there is more to this situation than simply her infatuation with Francis. Of course she doesn't see it as infatuation. She does love him in a way that blinds her to what may happen."

"But with her religion it's so final — I mean, if she marries him. He does want to marry her, doesn't he? After a while, when she realizes what a mistake it is, she is trapped. She won't accept divorce any more than premarital sex. Unless — come to think of it, Clem, in the eyes of her church she won't be married at all. If he was just not Catholic, they could be married in the sacristy or wherever. But he's a divorced man. And then, in her mother's eyes, she will be living in sin."

"Yes, I suppose that's what it will amount to. I'm sure she hasn't overlooked all that. And if she has, Father Vincent will have pointed it out to her."

After a silence Elissa asked, "What is his position in her family, anyway?"

"Who?" Clemence's thoughts had strayed.

"Father Vincent. He seems to be always underfoot."

"How do you know?"

"I see Charlie every so often. He comes up to the Hill with information from the Archives that he brings to the committee. He's always complaining about Father Vincent. He's taking instruction from him to become a Catholic, I gather. He hasn't told you that?"

"Regina has. I don't see much of Charlie these days. But I'm amazed that Kathleen has got that far with him."

"It's my private opinion that he's having heavy going. His heart's not in it."

"I can't see that it would be. And that's not a good thing, 'Lissa. He's only doing it because of Kathleen."

"I suppose he thinks he'll go through the motions for Kathleen's sake and after they're married he can backslide. But from what he tells me, Father Vincent isn't satisfied with his progress."

"Father Vincent is a very astute man. Charlie would never be able to fool him. Besides, Kathleen won't be satisfied with lip service. She's very rigid."

As usual they were seated on the sofa close together.

Elissa put her arm around Clemence and said, "I never could understand why people put so many obstacles in their own way when it comes to intimate relationships."

Clemence responded to her touch by leaning against her shoulder. "People don't see it that way. They think of it as the hand of fate. They don't see themselves as creating problems. They think they inherit them. In one sense they do. Regina and Kathleen were provided by birth with the Catholic Church. I'm sure Kathleen sees Charlie as a test of her faith and she rather exults in the trouble caused by overcoming his resistance."

"A soul saved from the burning, you mean?"

"Yes."

"But what about Regina?"

"It would be a lot easier for her if she was a bit more like Kathleen. Kathleen doesn't have any doubts. The path for her is straight ahead, well marked. But Regina can't see things so simply. She has to reconcile her faith with her reason and sometimes that's hard to do — no matter how clever Father Vincent is in putting his case."

"There he is again — always in the picture."

"He's very much aware how tempted Regina is to follow her own inclination. He doesn't want to lose such a jewel from the flock."

"I think she should just up and do what she wants."

" 'Lissa, you don't understand about faith, any more than Charlie does. It isn't something that you can take or leave. And Regina would be wrecked if she lost hers."

"I'll have to take your word for that, Clem."

Clemence looked at her soberly. "We're not really in a position to talk about other people and their obstacles. We've got one of our own that's as bad as Regina's, if not worse."

Elissa, suddenly serious, said, "Is it worrying you?"

"Of course. I find myself thinking about it underneath everything else. I think I must be getting neurotic. I find myself wondering if the people who see me on the street can see at a glance that I'm different. I never imagined anything like that before."

"You mean, because of going to Flora's party?"

Clemence hesitated, "Come to think of it, yes."

"It's something that's been there all along."

Clemence gazed at her. "Are you so sure?"

"You think it's just something that's happened to you —"

"Because I met you."

Disconcerted, Elissa looked away from her.

Clemence went on. "The trouble is that our obstacle isn't one we can confess to anyone. Other people may have problems, but they don't have to worry about being thought peculiar. Regina is lovesick for Francis. She has a serious problem, but no one thinks she is abnormal because of it. It's not unnatural for someone to want to marry a foreigner or somebody of a different religion or a different race. It may be unfortunate but it's not unnatural."

"Yes, yes," Elissa interrupted, wanting to stop the flow of Clemence's words. "Let's forget it all for a while."

She took Clemence in her arms. In a few minutes they had truly forgotten everything but each other, the happiness of being together, the touch of each other's hands, each other's lips on skin made moist by pleasure.

It was the end of the business day and Clemence sat alone in the spacious office. Elissa had gone to New York that morning on committee business and the evening stretched ahead of her, empty. So she lingered at her desk, fiddling with small details of work that had no great importance. But what she was doing absorbed her enough that she did not hear Flora come in and approach her.

"You're still here. I wondered who it was when I noticed someone through the door. Are you very busy?"

"Why, hello Flora! No, I'm not. I'm just filling in time."

She wondered whether Flora would ask, "Waiting for someone?" but Flora did not. Instead she sat down at a nearby desk. Even at the end of the day she was band-box fresh, her soft grey hair perfectly coifed. She had on her hat and coat and held her purse in her hand as if she had paused in her way out of the building.

"How are you, Clemence? I haven't seen you for several days. Do Robert's troubles keep your nose to the grindstone?"

"I'm pretty busy but not only for him."

Flora looked at her with a slight lifting of her head, so elegantly poised on her neck. "You get along with him well, don't you?"

Clemence answered warily, "I think so."

"He's an extraordinary man, really. He seems able to survive situations that would be catastrophes for anyone else."

"Has something new happened?"

"New? Well, there has been another meeting of the arts council. You knew that, of course." When Clemence nodded, she continued, "I hope he is aware that the administrative people are about to take a new approach in dealing with him. They know that they must be careful how they deal with him so far as his professional reputation is concerned. He has many friends and supporters in the international art establishment. So now they are going after his Achilles' heel — the weak spot in his armor."

"What is that?"

"His private life. You know, Clemence, that there are many episodes in his past that could be used against him. There is one in particular. You know he was once an assistant curator at the Smithsonian."

"Yes, I've heard that he was."

"When he was a young man, before he had established himself in the art world — some time back in the thirties — his first real professional job was there. In those days the Smithsonian arranged exhibitions of paintings and other art objects — things from some of the miscellany for which it was the custodian. It was really a glorified attic then. The galleries were jammed with all sorts of things of value that could not be properly set out for viewing because of lack of space. These exhibitions were in fact airings of some of the things otherwise lost to view. Of course, Robert was very keen to bring order out of chaos, to identify some of the things hidden in the muddle." Flora paused to glance at Clemence. "Can't you imagine him? Like a child in a shop full of wonderful toys. He got himself put in charge of an exhibit of what he called neglected masterpieces, things he had found in poking around the attic, so to speak, some of them items that were never brought out into the light of day because they were considered unsuitable for public viewing. He mounted the exhibit without anyone objecting until it was too late. Some visitors were scandalized and complained to their congressmen that the show was indecent — too much nudity, suggestive scenes, etc. Probably there were some French Impressionists among the items. No telling what they thought they saw. Anyway, nothing of the sort was current in the part of the country they came from. The trouble was that Robert was pretty far down in the hierarchy and his betters were put out because he had managed to set up the exhibit without calling attention to what he was doing. As he pointed out, they had had every opportunity to stop him before the pictures were on the walls. The way he did it — on purpose, of course — infuriated them even more. It was pretty hard for them to explain away the fact that they hadn't been up to their job of supervising him.

"He lost his job?"

"Forced to resign, is the phrase used. The important thing was that it was then that the rumors began."

"The rumors?"

Flora looked at her. "Clemence, I'm sure you've heard some of the stories about Robert's private life. You know that there are some men who prefer other men to women."

Of course I do, Clemence thought. I met some at your party. In the stillness of the high-ceilinged room their voices were lost beyond a few feet of their seats. Her silence brought a faint smile to Flora's face. "Well, these rumors concerned the fact that Robert was homosexual. There were reasons to believe, so people said, that he had been encouraged in his selection of paintings by friends who were of the same persuasion — men in positions of importance. Robert, as I've said, was young and unimportant at that time, so he became the scapegoat."

"You've known Robert a long time, haven't you?"

"Since that time. I was a young novice at the Smithsonian when he was. Would it surprise you very much if I told you that I had a crush on Robert?"

Clemence stared at her in astonishment. "Why —!"

"Yes, of course it surprises you — for more than one reason, I'm sure. He's the only man who ever aroused romantic feeling in me."

"Did he know it?"

"Oh, yes. He could hardly avoid knowing how I felt about him. I think he was used to women falling in love with him. He was very good-looking — he still is — and he had an off-hand, good-natured way of treating you as if he took your feelings for granted and was kind to you in a noncommittal way. He wasn't like the other men I was used to; in those days I had the usual expectation of meeting an eligible man and marrying him. Robert was never openly arrogant with women. He never has had the slightest interest in women in a romantic or sexual way, but he is ready to accept a woman as his intellectual equal — that is, so far as he is willing to accept anyone as his equal."

Her voice, faint in the big room, ceased. Clemence was too disconcerted to reply. Flora went on talking. "That was why, Clemence, when I began to hear gossip about you and Robert, I wondered whether I should warn you. I wanted to, but I could not think of a way. Do you know, Clemence, that you are quite unapproachable when you do not wish to be approached?"

Clemence listened, uncomfortable. It was another way of saying, she supposed, that her air of innocence became an impenetrable armor. "I'm sorry I gave you that impression."

Flora smiled. "I was worried until I began to notice Elissa. She's an unusual girl, too. Quite a contrast to you. But then they say that opposites attract. And now I want to say what I came to tell you. The holidays are upon us. Val and I always have open house on Christmas Day. We do not have family commitments on that day, so we like to see our friends. We should be delighted if you and Elissa would come."

Clemence smiled in response to her smile. "I'm sure we'll both come. Thank you very much, Flora."

As Flora stood up to go, Clemence gathered her things together and they walked out through the empty corridors to the street.

* * * * *

"Merry Christmas. Have some eggnog," Val urged. She was seated at one end of a large oval table whose dark polished surface reflected the silver punch bowl and many little cups arranged on the big high-sided silver tray.

Elissa took the cup from her. It was four o'clock on Christmas Day and the cheerful warmth of the pleasant interior made up for the damp chill outside the windows. There were several other people in the room, talking in twos and threes. It was like a painting by a nineteenth-century artist, she thought: "Evening in the home of such-and-such a family," displaying tastefully luxurious furnishings and well-dressed people in studiedly correct postures. She was somehow aware that this gathering differed from the evening she and Clemence had spent there before. The idea of anything strange about the assemblage would not cross anybody's mind. In the minds of the people present, Flora and Val were obviously two middle-aged women of similar social and economic background and probably friends for many years, who maintained a joint household for convenience and companionship. There was an air of propriety about the scene that forestalled questions.

Elissa knew that Val was watching her covertly. There was no one near them and at the moment there was no one arriving. Val gestured to a nearby chair and said, "Won't you sit down?"

Elissa sat down. Val said, "I did not have much chance to talk to you when you were here the other evening. You're from New York. I am from Massachusetts."

Elissa nodded.

"And I gather your interests are political, not artistic."

Again Elissa nodded.

"Then it is Clemence who has got you involved in our art intrigues."

"Not involved, really. I'm only a spectator."

"Who sees the best part of the play, I believe. Well, what do you think of the situation at the Gallery?"

Surprised to be asked the question, Elissa protested. "I don't know anything about it."

"But you've heard a good deal, I'm sure. Flora talks about nothing else."

"She knows the people concerned."

"Of course. Apparently, if the truth about the situation leaked to the press there would be a great scandal. Why do you suppose it hasn't?"

"I've no idea."

"It has all the elements that would make for public interest — stolen paintings, forgeries, the misuse of public funds, even scandalous comment about the private life of one of the main characters. You would have thought that before this someone would have confided in a newspaper reporter."

"Perhaps there is nobody who would gain from spreading the story."

"I can scarcely believe that. Someone would surely like to talk just out of the love of mischief, if nothing else."

Elissa, a little uneasy at Val's vigorous assault, glanced at her warily. Was there a motive behind this chat? She did not know Val well enough to judge whether this was her usual way of making conversation with a newcomer. "There's only been a brief mention in the newspapers of the fact that the painting has been removed."

"Of course, to say that it has been removed for reassessment would be likely to start a controversy. Do you know that Robert will be forced to take it out of hiding soon and hand it over to the committee for examination by outside experts?"

"No! Clemence hasn't said anything about that."

"This is Francis Hearn's doing, of course. That's

typical of him — to carry a vendetta to its ultimate, but through the agency of others. You know him, don't you?"

"I've met him once or twice."

"Oh, I know him very well. As a matter of fact, his former wife is my niece, my brother's daughter. If he gets his knife in you, he doesn't take it out. He just twists it."

"You mean, he's getting revenge on Robert. But why?"

Val's glasses glinted as she looked at her. "It's one of those things that are whispered about but not openly stated. It is assumed, not said."

"He doesn't like Robert because Robert is homosexual."

"Yes, that's the basis of his dislike. Francis is fanatical — as he is on other subjects — about deviant men."

"For any particular reason?"

"Well, it is said that one hates what one most deeply fears. Robert makes enemies easily. He rather enjoys doing so. He's never disguised the fact that he is contemptuous of Francis' reputation in professional matters. He thinks that Francis has been successful in his career more because of influence with the right people than any great ability. Francis is very much aware of this. Francis doesn't make enemies, but he doesn't make friends, either. He's very jealous by nature. He was very jealous of his wife — my niece. She led a miserable life with him. He would construct — that's the only way to say it — he would construct circumstantial evidence that she was being unfaithful to him — in the most absurd situations — and then torment her when she tried to defend herself. She's a dear girl but not very clever and finally she had to leave him, to preserve her own sanity. When she did, he was outraged and filed suit for divorce on the grounds of desertion. He'll be free to marry again, I believe, very shortly."

She spoke with vehemence. Francis, thought Elissa,

might not deliberately make enemies, but he had certainly made one here.

They had not noticed that Clemence had come to join them. She said, "Merry Christmas, Val. How are you?"

"Very well, my dear." Val offered her a cup of eggnog. "Merry Christmas. We are settling the affairs of your Gallery. I'm sure you've heard that Robert's painting must be brought out of hiding to have its fate settled soon."

Clemence murmured, "I have heard something." The last time she had seen Robert he had brushed past her in the corridor without a greeting, an angry look on his face. She had known at once that something had happened in the struggle over the painting, something unfavorable to Robert.

Val went on. "I understand that outside experts are to be brought in to reassess the painting. Flora tells me all this. I don't know how she learns of it."

"I haven't any real information," Clemence said. "Do you mean that the authenticity of the painting is to be questioned again?"

"Apparently. It does mean opening up old wounds, doesn't it? That is likely to bring the whole thing out into public debate. Hasn't Robert said something to you about it?"

"No," said Clemence and she was relieved to be spared further catechism by the arrival of another guest.

When they left, Clemence and Elissa walked along the nearly empty street without speaking until Elissa said, "I suppose you know this but it's new to me. Francis' former wife is Val's niece."

"Oh? No, I didn't know. I've never heard anything about his marriage. I'm sure my parents know all the details but they've never said anything to me about it."

"From what she says, Francis is sadistic and insanely jealous. Regina ought to hear Val on the subject."

Clemence said, after a while, "I'm sorry but it

wouldn't do any good to tell her. She would just think he was the victim of people who don't like him."

"You sound pretty unhappy about it."

"Well, I am — because there doesn't seem to be anything I can do about it."

The week after New Year's the Giardini was placed on an easel in a small room reserved for the display of art objects that had to be kept under special guard. Clemence, eager for a glimpse of it after so much time, went to see it at the first moment she was free

At first, when she reached the room, she was thwarted by the crowd standing outside the door. The guard permitted only three or four people to enter at one time; whenever one group came out he admitted another. Most of them were visitors made curious by the notoriety that had erupted when the controversy had at last leaked into the newspapers. In her imagination, during the period when the painting had been hidden from view, it had glowed with a particular brilliance in her mind's eye and on the way down the corridor to see it once again she felt a pang of anxiety, fearful that it would not live up to her memory of it.

But she need not have worried. The moment she stepped into the small room her spirit was captured by the glowing colors, the radiance envisioned and projected by the artist. There the angels were, poised in embodied rapture, aware and yet heedless of the awed humans over whom they hovered. Her eyes sought one angel in particular, the one floating a little apart from the group, looking down her long nose at the pilgrims struggling along the stony path, a gentle, knowing smile on her face, as if she foresaw the outcome of their devotion.

Could it possibly be, she wondered, incredulous, that

this was a fake — the concoction of a modern artist mimicking the fervor of an ancient painter? Or that it was a hodge-podge of brushwork by a chance collection of painters? If it was not by Giardini — whoever he or she might be — then it must be the work of someone unknown altogether, some unknown genius. She noticed a plaque affixed to the bottom of the frame. It was not the one that had been there when the painting had hung in the gallery. That one had stated that this was the work of an artist of the early fifteenth century, who was identified only by his surname Giardini and that it was the only work unquestionably attributed to him. The new plaque read: attributed to Giardini, believed to be a pupil of Girogione, with the appropriate dates.

"That really casts doubt on the whole thing, doesn't it?"

Clemence, startled, turned quickly at the sound of Flora's voice. Flora went on, "It's a marvelous painting, isn't it? And who might Giardini be, that he should have that kind of gift and be known only as someone's pupil or apprentice? Perhaps a woman? Francis must have composed that legend."

Troubled, Clemence murmured, "Could it possibly be the work of some other better-known painter —?"

"Painted on commission for a nobleman or other important personage and then botched up by a journeyman artist to suit another patron, a merchant who had made a fortune and wanted to ape the nobility?" Flora finished for her. "That is the argument that Francis makes. At least, I have seen that argument in the written statement presented to the arts council."

The guard signalled that their time was up and that they should leave the room. But Flora continued as they left, "Furthermore, it is contended that serious changes were made when the painting was repaired after it was found and that Robert conspired with the dealer when this was done."

Angry, Clemence declared, "Robert would not be capable of doing that."

Flora raised her eyebrows. "You mean you don't think Robert capable of double-dealing? I'm afraid I can't agree with you there."

"No. I don't mean that. I mean that Robert would not be capable of conspiring to ruin a fine painting."

"Ah. If that really happened, then the repairer must have been a genius, too. Nothing has been done that diminishes the vision that painting projects."

"Yes," breathed Clemence, thinking of the angels. "You'd have to be made of stone not to be affected by it."

Flora gave a short laugh. "There are some of those, alas, of whom Francis is one."

The Sunday afternoon was sunny and mild for January. There was little traffic on North Capitol Street as it circled around the grounds of the Old Soldier's Home. Several elderly pensioners enjoying the sun on a bench near the high iron fence saw the car coming into sight on the further roadway. They also saw the old pickup truck coming in the opposite direction. The statements they gave later to the police as witnesses of the accident did not agree, except for one detail: they were all surprised to see the two vehicles collide, apparently without any warning. There seemed to be no reason why two vehicles traveling in opposite directions on an otherwise empty street would suddenly crash into one another. A small crowd of people materialized out of the quiet Sunday neighborhood and an ambulance arrived to take the driver of the car to the hospital, bleeding and with broken bones. The driver of the truck walked away.

The accident was not reported in the newspapers. No one had been killed and the injured man was not prominent in public life. It was not until the following Wednesday that Regina called Clemence in the evening and asked if she could come round to her apartment.

When she arrived she seemed taken aback to find Elissa there. "Oh, I didn't know you had anyone here," she apologized. "I just have some news to give you, which you may not have heard."

"It doesn't matter, does it, if Elissa is here?"

"Why, no, not really. I just wanted to tell you that Charlie Olsen is in the hospital. He was in a car accident. You haven't heard? He isn't in any danger, but he has a broken leg and a concussion. I didn't know whether you'd hear about it from anyone else."

"Good grief! No, I haven't heard. How did it happen?"

"He was on the way to our apartment to see Kathleen. He was hit by a truck — not a big one. He doesn't have any family here. Kathleen says his parents live in Milwaukee."

"Kathleen must be very upset."

"Yes, she is, but not so much because of the accident." Regina was gazing at Elissa absentmindedly.

Clemence saw that Regina was vexed and angry. She asked gently, "What is the matter?"

"It's such a senseless situation. Of course Kathleen is sorry that Charlie is hurt. She was ready to do anything he wanted her to. She wasn't prepared for what he did when she went to see him."

Clemence, mystified, asked, "She was able to see him?"

"Yes. He is recovering very quickly. But he will be laid up a while. That annoys him. He is such an active

168

man, very athletic, as you know." Regina's voice was full of irritation.

Elissa, watching them, saw desperation in Clemence's face. Clemence said, "But, Regina, what is the trouble? What has Charlie done that's so upset Kathleen?"

Regina bit her lip in vexation. This time she looked at Elissa for a long moment. Elissa, uncomfortable, got up from her chair, saying, "Clem, why don't I go and get us something to drink? Regina, would you like a drink?"

Regina shook her head. "No, thank you. I won't stay a minute. Elissa, you know Charlie Olsen, don't you? And you've met my sister."

"Yes," said Elissa, poised to walk out of the room. "Regina, if you have something to tell Clemence in private, I don't mind going into the kitchen. I can't hear you from there."

Regina, obviously struggling with conflicting emotions, finally declared, "Oh, why should I mind speaking plainly? It is so ridiculous. It just vexes me that my sister — though Charlie isn't any better."

"But what has happened?" Clemence demanded.

Regina turned her eyes on her. Clemence saw a mixture of mortification, anger — and, yes, contempt — in them. Regina said, "It seems that Charlie has been carrying around with him a leaflet containing suggestions for persons who are interested in taking instruction to become Catholics. It had Father Vincent's name and phone number on it. When the police and the hospital people were trying to identify him — Charlie was unconscious, of course, when he arrived at the hospital — they found this and called Father Vincent. Charlie's wallet was missing — it was found later under the seat of the car — and he did not have any other identification on him. Father Vincent was able to give them his name and address but nothing more. He called and told Kathleen. She was already upset because she had been waiting for

Charlie to come to our apartment as he usually does on Sunday afternoon and there was no sign of him. Kathleen wanted to go to the hospital right away but they told her he would not be able to see anyone for a day or so. This morning I went with her — she called me at Rosecroft and I canceled class periods for the day — to the hospital. Charlie is in a private room. Kathleen had told them who his parents are and how to reach them and they said they wanted him in a private room. Fortunately."

Regina said the last word angrily. She stopped and put her handkerchief to her lips. Clemence and Elissa waited. Then Regina said, "I wanted to wait in the corridor but Kathleen pulled me into the room. Charlie was sitting up. His leg is in a cast, of course, and he had a bandage around his head. When he saw Kathleen he said, 'Don't come near me! You and your damned saint have caused me enough grief. Let me alone. Get out of here!' "

Regina's eyes flashed and her voice rose as she repeated Charlie's words.

Clemence exclaimed, "What on earth was the matter with him?"

Regina went on as if she had not spoken. "You can imagine how shocked we were. At first Kathleen was indignant and then she thought it might be something to do with his concussion. She pleaded with him but he was downright nasty. He was babbling some nonsense about 'that damned idol sitting on his dashboard' and that this was the last he wanted to know about all that superstition. When Kathleen began to cry, I took her out of the room. After a while, when we got home, she was able to explain to me. Charlie seemed to be getting along so well with Father Vincent's tutoring that when he told her he was getting a new car, she said she would give him a present for it. She meant a statuette of St. Christopher." Regina glanced at Elissa. "St. Christopher is the patron saint of travelers. It is a very usual thing to have one which has been blessed, of course, in your car. Charlie had picked up his new car on Saturday and he was coming on Sunday to take Kathleen for a ride in it. He put the little statue on his dashboard, as she had suggested. The car is a total wreck now. Charlie thinks it caused his accident."

Elissa thought, who's superstitious now?

Clemence said, seeking to soothe, "I think Kathleen ought to give Charlie a little while to get over this. He's probably suffering from nerves."

Regina fired up. "You wouldn't say that if you'd been there to hear him! No woman should forgive a man for saying the things he said! And I don't think that Kathleen will. After the first shock she was pretty angry. Father Vincent talks about forgiveness, but for once I don't think that Kathleen is very receptive."

Elissa thought, a woman spurned —

Clemence said, "Regina, listen to me. Kathleen is going to be sorry after she gets over being angry, isn't she, sorry that she hasn't been more forbearing with Charlie? I thought he meant a good deal to her."

Regina sat silent for a while, looking down at the floor. Clemence, watching her, thought: what a lovely woman. How different from her sister. The image of Kathleen came into her mind — the blind-eyed goddess of antiquity — Hera-Juno. Yes, Kathleen could be ruthless.

Presently Regina said, "Nothing means as much to Kathleen as her beliefs. I don't mean her faith. I mean her own, personal beliefs — which are, I suppose, what she has fashioned out of what her faith teaches her. If Charlie — if any man — cannot accept these, she will feel she is well rid of him. That is how she feels now.

Oh, Clemence, I know that sounds like a terrible indictment of her but that is not what I intend. She has a strength I do not."

Clemence, the image of Kathleen still before her, said nothing. Kathleen's mind was closed to all doubts. But Regina — she looked back at her. Regina, the vulnerable, the sympathetic — would not have the armor that saved Kathleen.

Elissa also was silent, and Clemence glanced at her, apprehensive. Elissa sat still in the big armchair a little way from them, obviously watchful but giving no sign that she reacted to what was being said.

Finally Clemence said, "Regina, it's too bad for things to end this way between Kathleen and Charlie, but they've never been a very good match. After a while, when they've got over being upset, they'll probably realize that. I think that Charlie has been building up a lot of resentment over Kathleen's pressure and that resentment has come out like this. And I'm sure Kathleen has deceived herself about him, imagining that he is much more willing to accept what she requires of him than was true."

"Father Vincent agrees with you. Yes, you're right. It just seems so cold-blooded — so cold-blooded for Charlie to be so quick to push Kathleen out of his life — and —" Regina hesitated — "Yes, cold-blooded for Kathleen to cut him off, as if they had not spent the last months —"

"Vowed to deathless love," Clemence finished for her. "Well, so much the better. Their attraction for each other obviously couldn't stand any real strain. I don't think they would have been very happy people in future years."

If Charlie didn't walk out, thought Elissa.

Regina seemed to be slowly relaxing under the influence of Clemence's calm. She rubbed her forehead and sat back in her chair. After a moment she made a move to get up, as if feeling she should leave. Clemence stopped her.

"You don't really want to go home just now, do you?"

Regina gave her a rueful look. "It is not very pleasant at home right now. Kathleen is very bitter and she won't stop talking. I am exhausted trying to comfort her. She won't be comforted. She seems to batten on this situation, getting strength from going over and over Charlie's behavior and her own indignation. My mother says just let her talk. But I can't close my ears."

"How does your mother take it?"

"I really think she is relieved. She doesn't dislike Charlie, but she has not felt that he belonged with us. She seems quite calm about it all."

"Well, then, she doesn't need you back there. Why don't you go out to supper with Elissa and me? We can talk about something else."

Clemence glanced across at Elissa as she said this, wondering how Elissa would take it. Elissa responded with a shrug. "You can call your mother and tell her where you are."

"Thank you, Clemence." Regina obediently got up and went to the telephone on the other side of the room.

Clemence said to Elissa, "You don't really mind, do you? She needs a breather."

"Just as you say," Elissa responded, trying not to show her dissatisfaction.

IV

There was a bustle in the Gallery's administrative offices, caused by the arrival of various art dealers and art historians who had been invited to come and make fresh appraisals of the Giardini painting. Among those who specialized in the evaluation of ancient paintings the Giardini had become a cause célèbre. Clemence, watching the new arrivals, decided that though some had come because they were intrigued by the questions raised in the controversy, there were others who were drawn chiefly by the notoriety. The room where the painting was displayed had been closed to the general public. The corridor outside

174

it was filled with a chattering throng. Clemence joined it, curious to see what would happen when the Gallery officers arrived to open the door. Looking around for familiar faces she saw only several employees like herself, no doubt brought there by the same curiosity. Then she spotted Francis. He looked in her direction but gave no sign that he saw her. Probably he was only surveying the crowd in general.

Presently the Director of the Gallery arrived with a retinue and the crowd parted to let him pass. At his order the guard unlocked the door and the people jockeyed for position to pass through it. Clemence, unaggressive, followed with those at the end of the crowd. Since the room was not large, it was difficult, at first, to get near the painting on its tripod. After the first jostling, people formed into small groups commenting and arguing. One group whom Clemence took to be dealers were especially interested in the details of the painting. From time to time one or another of them would return to the painting, elbowing his way through the throng in front of it and examining the canvas sometimes with a magnifying glass. The guard standing nearby motioned people away when they got too close.

"It's like a holy relic, isn't it, with the devout seeking a sanctification through touch." Flora had found her way through the crowd to where Clemence stood. "Or through breathing the same air. It's getting pretty close in here, isn't it? I had to use my pass to get in. Did you? Oh, I see." She had glanced down and saw the sheaf of papers in Clemence's hand. "Did Robert tell you to come here?"

Clemence nodded. "I'd have come anyway. But he hates to carry anything anywhere. So he told me to bring these and have them ready for him when he arrives."

"Then he's on his way. I see that Francis is already here. Or was. Has he left?" Flora looked round the room.

"I think he has. He probably just came to have a

175

look, to see who was present. He wouldn't want to confront Robert."

"No, I'm sure of that. And I'd better be getting back, too."

Flora left and Clemence sought a corner from which she could watch what was happening and not be jostled. She was especially interested in several men whom she recognized as well-known art historians. Unlike the dealers, they stood close to the painting for long periods of time, silently scrutinizing it. She supposed that they had already seen the x-ray photographs of the canvas, the infra-red photographs and had heard the opinions of their colleagues, and had read not only the contemporarily published articles but also those that had been placed in the file years before when Robert had fought to a successful conclusion the battle to have the Gallery acquire the painting. Some of these men were older than Robert. They were probably well-acquainted with his career, with the accusations and counter-accusations that had surrounded his reputation for years. She wondered how many of them were still his friends, tolerant of his acerbic tongue, and how many he had made into implacable enemies.

It was sometime later, when some of the people had left the room that, as the door stood open while those departing stood talking as they left, she heard Robert's voice. His was a penetrating voice that carried well beyond his immediate surroundings. It was a voice whose tone seemed to challenge the attention of anyone within its reach. She had often observed its effect. Some people were instantly intrigued by it, while some seemed irritated, ready to object to anything he might say. It was the challenge that did that, she thought. She believed that Robert himself was aware of how his voice affected his hearers and deliberately honed the edge of flippancy it frequently held.

He came into a room that was suddenly quiet. All those still there had instantly recognized him and were eager to see what he would do. He acted as if he was unaware that there was anyone present except himself and his companions. He walked to the painting and stood for a moment silently contemplating it.

Clemence looked at his companions. They were a white-haired couple dressed in expensive clothes. The man was taller than Robert and massive, as if in his prime he had been either an athlete or someone who earned his living at work that required unusual strength and endurance. The woman was almost as tall as her husband, a big woman obviously used to dominating any group in which she found herself. She looked round the room, while her husband followed Robert and stood beside him, examininig the painting. Neither of them spoke.

The quiet in the room seemed unnatural, as if the scene itself were a painting. But Robert turned away to face the woman and said, "What do you think?"

She said, "If I had not seen it before, I'd be overwhelmed. It is flawless." Her voice was not loud but it reached everyone. Her husband continued to look at the painting, finally shaking his head as if unable to find words to express what he felt.

Clemence saw Robert grin, something she had learned he never did unless he was under considerable stress. He suddenly looked round the room and she realized that he was searching for her. She stepped over to him and handed him the papers she had been holding. He snatched them from her without a word and turned to say to his companions, "If you will come with me to my office, I can show you the material that will establish the provenance of the painting and a resume of the controversies that have surrounded it."

She knew what the papers were: Robert's own account, in the minutest detail, of where he said the painting had been first noticed, in an Italian parish church during the nineteenth century, its fate during the Second World War, and his own recognition of it among the treasures discovered by the Allied armies at the war's end. She knew that almost every detail had been disputed by Robert's rivals. She wondered what he had said to the couple accompanying him. She knew the account he had prepared intimately, since she had typed these papers in several drafts from Robert's handwritten yellow sheets; he hated to dictate to a stenographer.

But she could not guess the identity of the couple he had brought to view the painting. She watched the three of them leave the room. As she walked toward the door she glanced once more over her shoulder, catching a last glimpse of her special angel, whose graceful outstretched arm and hand seemed to point the way for the pilgrims below.

"They are Mr. and Mrs. Stulman, from Texas," said Flora.

Clemence wondered, as she had before this, how Flora learned these details. It must be that she gleaned them from the gossip that circulated at her parties. Flora's father had been a senator from a western state and her grandfather a state governor and a member of a presidential cabinet. Her circle of acquaintance among government people must be vast.

Flora went on. "And why are they so interested in the Giardini? Ah, I wonder. So do a lot of other people. He is very wealthy. Oil, among other things. Once upon a time he was a roustabout in the oil fields. She is the one who has decided that they should be patrons of the arts. But I do them an injustice by seeming to look down on them. After all, who were the great patrons of the arts in the

Renaissance and before? The bankers, the merchants, the ship chandlers."

"But why is Robert so anxious to show them the painting? It is as if —"

"He wants them to buy it."

Although Flora was only putting in words the thought that lay in the back of her own mind, Clemence was shocked. "The Gallery would not sell it."

Flora smiled. "If it is not authentic, why not?"

"But in that case the Stulmans would not buy it."

"It depends on who thinks it is inauthentic."

"But Robert thinks it is authentic. How can anybody dispute him?"

"The members of the board of trustees. Of course, it is true that the trustees, exalted personages though they may be, are quite incompetent to give an opinion on the authenticity of a painting by a fourteenth century artist. For instance, no matter how astute they may be in their own spheres, I think you will agree that the Secretaries of State and the Treasury and the Chief Justices of the Supreme Court are not what one would consider well-versed in the technical qualities of the Italian Old Masters. The Secretary of the Smithsonian Institution might come closer, though I believe he is more at home in the sciences."

Clemence, aware that Flora's satirical tone disguised a deeper intent, merely murmured, "Well, there are others."

"But few of them are able to detect art fraud. So they depend on experts. And who is better prepared and respected in that field than our own Francis Hearn?"

"I see. You think that Francis has persuaded the board of trustees that the painting is not authentic."

"Perhaps not as definitely as that. Probably he has persuaded them that, though it may be what it seems, it has been so damaged and tampered with that it cannot be accepted really as the canvas that Giardini painted. Of

179

course, the implication is that Robert knows all about this and has foisted this imperfection onto the Gallery's collection, no doubt in league with an unscrupulous dealer."

Horrified, Clemence said, "Do you really think that Francis would accuse Robert of doing that? He would have to prove it."

"Francis would not accuse him directly. That is not his way. He has insinuated into the minds of the people responsible for the Gallery and its collections, that there is a serious doubt about the painting. Francis understands that people who are in positions of public trust are sensitive, very sensitive to the winds of public blame, even if it is unreasonable. Francis has raised the fear in the minds of several that they have spent a large sum of public money on a fraud, and they would be inclined to dispose of a valuable painting rather than be thought to be housing something of dubious value."

"But Robert couldn't possibly be found guilty of such a deception. I know he is certain that the painting is genuine. He must be right."

"Most people who are knowledgeable would be certain of that. If Robert says it is the Giardini, it is the Giardini. He has an uncanny sense for such things. And he would not lie about it. Robert may not think anything else in the world worth fighting about, but he certainly believes it is a terrible sin to betray an artist's work. But I am afraid Francis has won in this case."

Clemence said in despair. "Then you think it will be sold?"

"It will be, if Robert sees that that is the only way out for him." Flora paused a moment and then added, "And it would be his revenge, wouldn't it? To deprive the Gallery of a jewel it was too unenlightened to keep."

* * * * *

Elissa followed Clemence into the apartment. She had been aware, ever since they met at the bus stop, that Clemence was profoundly upset, presumably about something that had taken place during the day. As they stood together in the living room, still wearing their hats and coats, and kissed, she knew that Clemence's preoccupation did not dissipate even under the influence of their desire for the touch of each other's lips and hands.

Elissa waited until they had settled down on the sofa before she said, "What's the matter, Clem?"

Clemence's gaze was still abstracted. "Nothing. I can't take in what it all means."

"What all what means?"

"I couldn't have lunch with you today because of what was happening at the Gallery. I called you and left a message. Did you get it?"

"Oh, yes. I figured there was something going on."

"They had a showing of the painting. I told you that they've had it locked up for several days, not allowing anybody to see it. This showing was for the people they've invited to give an opinion on the questions that have been raised — whether or not it is really the Giardini."

"So?"

"Robert told me to be there and wait for him. The last few days he's had me typing up a sort of handbook on the painting. I don't know what else to call it. He gives an account of when he thinks it was painted, who he thinks Giardini was, who he thinks Giardini's patron was. Then he gives his explanation of the changes that seemed to have been made in it, back in those days and during the war years and after. He goes on to tell about recognizing the painting when he saw it among the treasures stolen by the Nazis. He says he kept track of it up to the time when it was shipped with all the others to

181

France for restoration. When he saw it again it was in the hands of a dealer who claimed he had bought it from a farmer who got it from somebody who used it to pay for a pound of butter. You see, there is plenty of room for doubt in this story. It was the dealer who had had it repaired. Robert says he spotted the repairs right away, that they were badly done, and he made the dealer hire a good artist, somebody Robert knew, to re-do them so as to restore as much of Giardini's brushwork as possible."

Elissa objected, "But if it's been mended and re-mended and mended again —? Isn't it by now fatally flawed?"

"No. Robert has a marvelous gift for the integrity of a painting. It probably looks more like what Giardini painted than it has at any time since."

"You were saying that Robert told you to be in the display room with these papers."

"Yes. But when he arrived, he wasn't alone. He had a couple with him, wealthy people he was showing the painting to. He acted exactly as if he was trying to sell it to them. He didn't say anything to me, just took the papers and went off with these people. 'Lissa, he really is trying to sell the painting!"

Surprised at her agitation, Elissa said matter-of-factly, "Well, obviously he can't sell it. It isn't his, though I must admit he has been acting as if it was."

"No, no! I mean he must have decided that the trustees want to dispose of it and he is trying to get these people to buy it."

"Doesn't that look as if he's admitting that there is something wrong about it?"

"No. You don't understand. It is Francis Hearn who has persuaded the trustees that they should sell the painting, even if it is not established that it is inauthentic. Robert knows it is the Giardini and for that reason he wants these people to buy it. Oh, 'Lissa, if it is sold, it will be lost to me forever!"

"Now calm down, Clem. If these people buy it, I should think they would display it somewhere. Or do they intend to hide it away in their own collection, wherever that is."

"I don't know anything about them. It's Flora who told me who they are. She says their name is Stulman."

"The Stulmans!" Elissa exclaimed.

Clemence looked at her in surprise. "You know them?"

"I know who they are. God, Clem! Robert really has pulled this off! Stulman is one of the wealthiest men in the oil industry. His influence in Congress is enormous. He has a reputation of being pretty rapacious, but now he wants to rehabilitate his name. He gives a lot of money to charity. His wife has persuaded him to use some of it to bring culture to the masses in the part of the country they live in by founding a museum and filling it with art treasures. Robert knows how to protect himself, doesn't he? He obviously learned that Stulman was going to be in Washington to talk to the Government about oil leases. He probably met him at a cocktail party."

"Have you heard anything about Robert when people were talking about Stulman?"

"No. That's why I'm so flabbergasted. I haven't heard anything connecting Robert and the Stulmans and the Gallery." Elissa paused thoughtfully. "Do you know that Francis visits the Hill almost every day? He's always having lunch with somebody in the Congressional dining room. Or I see him walking down a corridor talking to a congressman. Everybody on our committee knows him by sight."

"What do you think he's doing?"

"If my guess is right, something that is really very clever. He is acquiring a reputation among political people as a valuable man to consult on matters of interest to those who appropriate money for the Government's artistic institutions. It's a funny thing but a recognizable human weakness. If you don't know anything about a subject, you need to depend on somebody who does. If you know that somebody personally, you're inclined to exaggerate his importance. So Francis is busy making himself visible to people who count, so that they'll come to believe that he is the fount of all knowledge in artistic matters."

"But Francis really is an expert in the arts."

"Oh, I'm not saying that Francis isn't the real thing. But being something and being known to be that something are two different things. Francis is making sure he will be known. Robert doesn't bother with that sort of publicity, does he?"

"Robert knows how to persuade people who show any appreciation for the arts. But he doesn't care about anybody who doesn't. He has a way of saying: 'Follow me and learn the true marvels of a painter's vision.' But otherwise he doesn't care. He wouldn't stoop to do what Francis does."

Elissa contemplated her for a moment. Resentment was rising in her. She knew she should hold her tongue but did not succeed in doing so. "He certainly has you in his thrall. It's always Robert you try to protect."

Clemence, drawn away abruptly from her own preoccupations, exclaimed impatiently and without forethought, " 'Lissa, why do you always have to be so touchy when I say anything about Robert?"

"Because he's so important to you. You think about him all the time. Everything he does — everything he says — you talk about him constantly." Hearing the jealousy in her own voice, still Elissa could not stop herself from venting it.

Clemence, her patience exhausted, exclaimed, "What difference does it make? I've got to deal with him every day. He depends on me because there isn't anybody else he trusts —"

"So he makes you feel you're very important to him and you know very well that he forgets you the moment you've provided him with what he wants. Why do you have to be so goddamned eager to be his little helper? It makes me sick to see him use you —"

"Please stop talking such nonsense." Clemence was pale with anger. "Why do we have to quarrel like this, just because somebody needs my help? What does it have to do with us?"

Elissa, suddenly frightened, stammered, "I'm sorry, Clem. It's just that there are so many people who are important to you that I get lost in the crowd."

Clemence made a disgusted sound. " 'Lissa, I'm tired of your always telling me that I don't pay enough attention to you. All right, have it your way. I don't. If that's —"

Fury took possession of Elissa. "Well, then, I'll leave. I won't stay around to bother you." And not giving Clemence a chance to protest she snatched up her hat and coat and flung out of the door.

Clemence did not try to follow her. She felt sore from the emotional upheavals that she seemed constantly involved in. It seemed to her that she had borne the brunt, in the last few days, of other people's distresses, had been caught up in currents of hatred and intrigue that swirled around her. Elissa gave her no support. Perhaps it was just as well if Elissa experienced a few hours of anguish. Underneath all this she felt the pain of real loss: A Flight of Angels seemed lost to her. That was the crowning touch to the accumulation of discords.

For a while these feelings kept her from regretting Elissa's sudden departure, from fully realizing that Elissa was not there, Elissa had not come back. But where was she? Where had she gone? For a moment she felt helpless, thwarted. But then she remembered what she had learned in the months of their intimacy: it was impossible for Elissa to make the first overture for a reconciliation after they quarrelled. There was a stiffness in Elissa, an inability to express contrition, that had been bred in her by the circumstances of her life. Elissa could be abjectly contrite once Clemence made the first gesture but otherwise she would dwell in outer misery. She must seek Elissa and open the door for her. They could not remain for a moment longer in this state of alienation. But how? Elissa lived in a boardinghouse and had no private phone. The only way to reach her was to call the house phone. If Elissa was not there, she would have to leave a message with whomever answered and hope that it would be delivered. She did this and then sat waiting.

Midnight came and she gave up hope of hearing from Elissa. Should she call again and risk waking somebody up? Finally, in desperation, she did so. The phone rang and rang in the hall of the boardinghouse. She had visited Elissa there and could envision the scene. She was about to hang up, anxious not to hear a blast of angry words from some irate person awakened by the telephone, when she heard the sound of the receiver being lifted from the hook. Elissa's voice, hoarse and angry, said, "Hello."

"Where have you been, 'Lissa? I called hours ago. Didn't you get my message?"

"No. I've just come in. Everybody is in bed."

"But where have you been?"

"Working."

"You mean you have been in your office?"

"Yes. I had work to catch up with." She knew that Clemence did not believe this. In fact she had sat at her desk, facing a future so bleak without the presence of Clemence in it that she could scarcely bring herself to imagine it. These passages through the anguish of loss were familiar to her. Something in her nature which she could not exorcise led her through these purgatories — yes, that's the word Regina would use — that were chiefly of her own contriving. She had to have Clemence. Life was not supportable without Clemence. It would have no meaning. It could not be endured. So, then, why did she let her tongue betray her in this way, reproaching Clemence for something that was as natural as breathing to Clemence — the bringing of comfort to others in distress?

Clemence's voice over the phone broke in on her brooding. " 'Lissa, please, talk to me. Why do you do this? Do you really want to hurt me?"

"No."

"Well, then, why don't you say that you love me, that you're coming back here."

There was a long silence. Clemence said anxiously, " 'Lissa?"

Elissa gave a long sigh. Her voice thick with the misery of the last few hours, she said, "I can't stand it, Clem. I know I shouldn't provoke you. But — but —"

Clemence's voice said decisively, "Well, come on back here and talk about it."

Half an hour later Elissa rang the nightbell at Clemence's apartment house. When she reached the apartment, Clemence stood in the doorway. They stood just inside, gripped in each other's arms.

A Flight of Angels was once more under lock and key in the display room, with a guard at the door. Several days passed without any announcement concerning its fate. Robert did not appear in his office at the Gallery. When Clemence mentioned this to Elissa, Elissa said that he was probably preoccupied with the Stulmans, who were

187

still in Washington. They were present at a White House reception. She had seen Stulman himself in a group of men present as spectators at a committee hearing, not concerned with art but oil drilling rights. Francis, she said, was as much in evidence as ever on the Hill.

One afternoon Francis himself came into the administrative office. This in itself was an unusual event. When Francis wanted something from someone in the administrative office he sent for them to come to his. Now he nodded briskly to Clemence but walked past her to Flora, who stood beside the desk of the supervisor.

"Miss Kelso," he said, "can you give me any information about Mr. Alden's whereabouts? I understand that he has not been in the Gallery for several days."

Flora's face registered polite surprise. "Why, I haven't the slightest idea where Mr. Alden is. Perhaps Miss Barrett," — she looked down at the woman seated at the desk — "or someone else here —" She did not finish her sentence but looked around the room, in the end bringing her eyes to bear on Clemence.

Francis turned his head to follow her gaze. "Oh, yes, Clemence." He walked across to Clemence's desk and stood looking down at her. "Can you tell me where Robert is?"

Clemence shook her head. "I haven't seen him."

"I'm told he has not been in the Gallery since Tuesday. Did he say anything to you about a possible absence?"

"No. I have no idea why he hasn't been in. He said nothing to me."

Francis frowned at her. She realized that it was not a frown intended for her but simply a symptom of the anger he was carefully supressing. "You don't see him at other times, outside of office hours, elsewhere?"

Annoyed, Clemence said stiffly, "I haven't seen him anywhere since Tuesday." She supposed that in his present state of mind he would not notice that she did not like his questioning. She thought spitefully that she might suggest that he call the Stulman's hotel, knowing that Francis valued any connection with the wealthy and powerful, a connection Robert had apparently achieved.

Francis stood silent for a moment. "It is very important that he should be informed that there is a special meeting of the board of trustees set for Monday. It is at short notice, of course. I've been to great pains to arrange this. It is a difficult thing to bring so many high officials together without a reasonable warning. Robert must be present. The purpose of the meeting will fail if he is not."

Without saying anything further he walked out of the room. As soon as he was gone Flora beckoned to Clemence and she got up and followed her out into the corridor.

Flora demanded, "What did he say to you?"

To Clemence it seemed that Francis had spoken loudly enough to be addressing the whole room. But now she realized that he had spoken in a low, tensely controlled voice that had not carried beyond the two of them. "He wants to know where Robert is. He seems to think I know everything Robert does, that it's my business to keep track of him."

Flora, intent on her own suspicions, ignored the tone of grievance in Clemence's voice. "Why is he so anxious?"

"He says that there is a special meeting of the trustees set for Monday and Robert must be present. He made a point of the fact that it is hard to get so many important people together at such short notice."

"Of course he can't get all the trustees together at

long or short notice. They'll send their deputies. I wonder what this means. I suppose he tried to get Robert where he lives and didn't succeed."

"Yes, but he seems to expect me to get a message to him."

"I'm afraid I can't help you, my dear," said Flora, ending their conversation.

In the evening she told Elissa about it. "The point is," she said to Elissa, as they sat down to a meal in the apartment kitchen, "Robert really should be notified. It probably is very important for him — at least as important as it is for Francis."

"I would guess so, if Francis is so eager to find him."

"Where do you suppose Robert is?"

Elissa thought while they went on eating. Presently she said, "There's only one way I could probably find out. Mrs. Braunschweiger is bound to know."

Clemence looked up from her plate in surprise. Elissa reminded her. "You remember, the woman who owns the bookstore."

Clemence's face brightened. "I wish you would go and see her. It would be wonderful if she knows where he is."

Elissa looked at her glumly. "It seems to me that Robert ought to be more alert — more on the ball. He might know that Francis would be up to something and that he should keep an eye on him. But maybe he thinks he has everything arranged the way he wants it and doesn't care."

"Well, I guess that this meeting is crucial for a decision about the painting. Robert must be warned."

"All right, I'll go and see Mrs. Braunschweiger, tomorrow when I get off work. I'll come and tell you what she says right away."

She was only half an hour late leaving her office the

next day and since the evening was mild, she decided to walk to the bookstore rather than wait for a crowded streetcar. She could make better time, she thought.

There were several customers in the bookstore, standing in the narrow aisles between the high bookshelves or waiting at the counter that filled the one corner of the front window. The hunchback was busy taking money and wrapping books, but he waved cheerfully at her when she made a gesture toward the back and began to find her way there, edging by a couple of men immersed in books they had reached down from the shelves. When she got to the room in the rear she put her head around the doorjamb, hopeful that Mrs. Braunschweiger was alone.

The room was empty. The upper floors of the house were used as a sort of warehouse for overflow stock but presumably Mrs. Braunschweiger had some sort of living quarters there also. Elissa stood in front of one of the bookcases that lined the walls, reading titles. The books back here, she knew, were the more valuable stock, which Mrs. Braunschweiger kept under her own eye. Before she could become engrossed, Mrs. Braunschweiger's gruff voice said close to her shoulder, "What brings you here at this hour? Your friend's not home?"

Now how, Elissa marvelled, has she figured out that I don't come here in the evenings the way I used to? Obviously she has picked up a lot of chance remarks I've made about Clemence and put them all together. Elissa had heard that Mrs. Braunschweiger had a reputation as a clairvoyant. In Washington even the rumor that someone had such a gift was enough to endow that person with a certain fearful respect, complete with a pocketful of anecdotes.

Mrs. Braunschweiger stared into her eyes and Elissa

tried not to flinch. "As a matter of fact," she said, "my friend wanted me to come here this evening to ask you for some information."

"What kind of information?" Mrs. Braunschweiger turned her large bulk and moved behind her desk to sit down.

Elissa sat down in the visitor's chair. "It's about Robert Alden. Nobody seems to know where he is."

"I presume that means he don't want them to know."

"Yes. But there is something about to happen that he should be told about."

"Be more specific." It was obvious that Mrs. Braunschweiger was not discounting the importance of what Elissa said.

"Has Robert told you that the Gallery is going to sell that painting?"

Mrs. Braunschweiger was evasive. "I know more or less what's goin' on."

"There's going to be a trustees' meeting on Monday. He ought to be there."

Mrs. Braunschweiger did not respond for a long moment. Then she said, "Sometimes he won't do somethin' just because he don't want to."

"But could you let him know about the meeting?"

Reluctantly Mrs. Braunschweiger said, "I'll see what I can do. You understand, I don't know where he is every minute of every day. It depends on whether he comes in here to see me."

Elissa nodded. "We just want to make the effort, so that something won't happen without his being warned."

Mrs. Braunschweiger raised her eyebrows just a shade and then nodded her head.

Coming into the apartment half an hour later, Elissa said, "I've seen her. I told her what was going on."

Clemence, in the midst of getting a meal, demanded, "Does she know where he is? Can she reach him?"

"She said she'd try. She doesn't see him unless he stops in to visit her. Or so she says."

"That's not very hopeful, then."

"I'm sure she knows all about his private life. When he disappears for a few days or weeks — I gather from something she said that he's apt to do that — she probably knows who he's likely to be with and where. Right now I'd guess he is likely to be on a binge — fired up by his success with the Stulmans."

Clemence murmured, "That's all the more reason why he ought to be at the meeting on Monday. If there is some sort of decision to be made, it could affect his deal with the Stulmans."

"We'll have to rely on Mrs. Braunschweiger."

On Monday Clemence saw nothing of Robert. Occasionally she glanced around the room, wondering if the tension she felt was also felt generally. But there was no evidence of this, though she knew that all the women were aware that a special trustees' meeting was being held and this in itself was cause for rumor and speculation. The hours passed and still, by the end of the day, neither Robert nor Francis had been seen. The trustees met in a remote room that had its own elevator and entry.

That evening Elissa was held overtime in her office and Clemence did not expect to see her. She wondered idly about Charlie Olsen. He was out of the hospital. She called his apartment and asked him if he would like her to visit. He said yes, enthusiastically. When she got there and rang the doorbell he called out to her to come on in, the door was not locked.

He sat in a chair with his leg in a cast propped on another. A pair of crutches was leaned against it within his reach. In spite of his injuries he looked healthy and cheerful — the reason being, no doubt, his habit of vigorous outdoor exercise which provided him with a reserve for just such emergencies.

"Hi, Clem. Join the party. This is Janis and that's Ted." He pointed to the girl who sat in the armchair opposite him and the young man by the sideboard pouring a drink. "What'll you have? The usual? Scotch with some water, Ted."

The girl, a pretty brunette, nodded to her. Clemence sat down in the nearest chair. "You look as if you're doing all right, Charlie."

"Oh, outside of this" — he rapped on the cast — "I'm OK. Sometimes I get a little woozy. The doctor says that's normal after a concussion. Sometimes this thing" — again he rapped on the cast — "makes me feel as if I had a ball and chain on." He laughed. "As a mater of fact I'm not as woozy as I've been for the last three months and didn't know it. Take my advice: don't fall for girls who want to convert you to something."

Clemence glanced briefly at Janis and saw that she herself was under discreet scrutiny. Ted thrust a glass of scotch under her nose. She had a vague recollection of having seen him before. He grinned at her and said, jerking his thumb at Charlie, "I'd say he's had a narrow escape, wouldn't you?"

Clemence, discomforted, did not answer. Janis said in her pleasant contralto voice, "You're a friend of Kathleen's, aren't you? Is she pretty upset about Charlie?"

Clemence, recognizing her effort to remind Charlie that he should be less aggressive in his remarks, said, "I haven't seen her since Charlie had his accident. But I'm sure she is."

"She sent him a card — didn't she, Charlie?"

The spreader of oil on troubled waters, thought Clemence. But Charlie said, "Yes, she did. I was afraid to let it into my room at the hospital. No telling what might come with it."

Clemence could not refrain from exclaiming, "Charlie! You know she meant well."

"Oh, sure, sure. As a matter of fact, she sent Father Vincent to see me — no, I don't think she did. He came on his own. I admit I didn't welcome him. But he said I'd get over how I felt and that the Church would always be ready to receive me. Meaning: accept your punishment here to cut down on your stay in Purgatory, you know. I don't buy that." He was aware that Clemence did not like the heavy humor he was attempting but there was a stubborn look on his face, as if he was daring her to voice her objections. When she said nothing, he went on, "Anyway, I told him not to expect me back for any more instruction. Well, let's talk about something else. I'm going back to work next week. The sooner the better. I don't take to this sedentary stuff."

Other people arrived, strangers to Clemence, and Charlie seemed to make a point of joking about the dangers of having a religious symbol anywhere around. The Devil, he said, must be laughing up his sleeve. Clemence, unhappy at his determined pursuit of the subject and his remarks about Kathleen, said she would be going. Charlie objected. "You haven't finished your drink. What do you want to leave for?" He stared at her belligerently.

But she set down her glass firmly and got up and left. Ted went down the stairs with her. Charlie, he assured her earnestly, was doing just fine. He liked having a lot of people around. His friends took good care of him, bringing him food from the nearby Chinese restaurant and taking him to the doctor. His parents hadn't come East when it seemed that he wasn't dangerously injured. Janis was always available when he wanted somebody to talk to.

Clemence, saying goodnight, thought this was typical of Charlie. He had never had trouble attracting girls. Janis' discreet scrutiny had been self-explanatory. She was eager to learn what she could about the woman Charlie had been so seriously pursuing. It would not be surprising if it was Janis who would eventually nail down Charlie.

Ted was standing at her elbow. "Would you like me to take you home?" he asked. "My car is parked across the street."

"Oh, no!" Clemence realized that in her dismay she had spoken too sharply. "That's nice of you, but I'd rather walk."

"How far away do you live? I'd like to walk you there. I can come back for my car."

He stood poised, looking at her hopefully. "Well —" Clemence began. "Well, all right."

They began walking down the street. "Don't be too hard on old Charlie," said Ted. "I think he's really upset about Kathleen."

Clemence said coolly, "That's a funny way to show it."

"Tell you the truth, he's not used to all this talk about saints and supernatural forces. Charlie hasn't been around religious people much — at least, not Catholics and people who take the idea of evil influences seriously."

"Then he must be more superstitious than I thought he was."

Ted, realizing that his apologies for Charlie were not being well received, changed the subject. Thereafter he talked mostly about himself and what he was doing until they reached Clemence's apartment house. There she firmly said good night.

The morning after the trustees' meeting Clemence entered the office to be at once aware of a sense of

196

excitement under the calm surface. She supposed it must be caused by news of the outcome of the meeting; there was as yet no official announcement. She passed Flora as she came in, but Flora merely waved and walked on by.

She had not been seated at her desk for more than ten minutes when the little buzz of the signal from Robert's office sounded. So he was in the Gallery. She surmised that he must have arrived very early, before the usual working hours.

She speculated apprehensively as she walked down the corridor and warily opened the door of his office. There was no one in the outer room and no sound of voices, so he must be alone.

He responded to the door opening as if he had been waiting. "Clemence," he said, "I want you to help me clear out my desk and files. We'll begin here."

He pulled out a drawer in the cabinet in the corner of the room, a wide piece of furniture with many shallow drawers for the storage of large reproductions of paintings. He went on with his instructions. "I want you to help me identify anything that belongs to the Gallery. When I leave here I don't want any accusations about stolen property." His tone was defiantly jovial.

Clemence exclaimed, shocked, "But, Robert, you're not leaving the Gallery!"

He looked directly at her, noting the dismayed surprise on her face, and smiled. "You might have guessed, Clemence. I'm sure this place has been a hornet's nest of gossip and rumor. The question is, am I leaving or have I been fired?" When she did not respond, he looked at her. "It was you, wasn't it, who sent that message to me about the trustees' special meeting? I almost didn't heed the warning. I'm glad I did. I got my two licks in before they could fire me. I didn't let them have that satisfaction. I told them I was going because I have a better opportunity, where I will get greater appreciation for my knowledge and judgment of Italian art. So I will. If they don't have me, they have second-best. I told them I just hadn't decided to make the move — until that meeting. That threw them. They're such a bunch of old women."

"But, Robert, you are really going?"

"Yes. I'm going. I suppose you can guess where. The Stulmans have a museum with an art gallery, out in the midst of a desert, I'm told — a beautiful, empty museum with a beautiful empty new art gallery. It will be mine to fill with all the art I deem suitable. To begin with, the Giardini — your Flight of Angels, hovering over the awe-stricken multitude of sinners below, grovelling before the rapture, the glory they can feel but not understand. Don't you think that will be a fitting introduction to the marvels that are to come?"

He paused long enough to turn away and bend over the cabinet. Pulling out one of the drawers he said over his shoulder, "Come and tell me when I'm appropriating something I shouldn't. Mind you, I may accept your decision and leave something behind and I may decide that it has a higher destiny with me."

Clemence, mute, listened intently to his words and also the tone of his voice. There was in them a tautness, a strung-up quality that projected the tension in his body. Robert's self-contradictions battled in him. She knew he was triumphant, suspicious, wary, overweaningly self-conscious, all at the same time. She went over to help him take the big sheets of photographs from the drawer. For a while their attention was concentrated on what they were doing. Clemence was struck by the efficiency with which Robert made selections, without comment except about the nature, date, origin or source of the material. In spite of his threat to appropriate what he wanted, regardless of its ownership, he seemed to be scrupulous in setting aside only those things that were clearly his.

When they had gone through the cabinet, he straightened up and walked away from the piles on the floor. He obviously did not intend to go through the chore of replacing the sheets that were to remain. Instead he said, pointing to the smaller pile, "You'll have that lot packed up for me. I mean now, today. I don't propose to linger around here. I'll give you an address to send them to."

His attention seemed to have shifted completely to other things. He walked back to his desk and sat down, opening the drawers on one side and reaching out whatever was in there and placing it on top of the desk. "I don't think any of this stuff is any use to me." He was, Clemence supposed, searching through to see if, in his usual carelessness, he had dropped personal items in amongst the clutter. Clemence lingered, though she supposed her usefulness was finished. She felt a number of emotions competing within her; irritation with Robert's callousness threatened to drive out the rest. But that irritation was underlaid by a real sense of distress. Robert's presence in the Gallery, the volatile quality of his behavior, had colored much of her attachment to her work in the Gallery. Without him there she realized that her job would become for her what theirs were for most of her co-workers: a nine-to-five occupation for the sake of a wage.

Her rumination was interrupted by Robert's voice. "Of course, if you find anything of mine that I've left behind by accident, I'm sure you'll keep it for me. Sometime or other I'll be in touch with you, let you know where to reach me."

"But, Robert," she protested. "I'm terribly upset that you're leaving the Gallery this way! It's so —"

He looked at her in genuine surprise. "Why, this is the best way to leave anywhere — at the drop of a hat, without a lot of procrastination."

"But I wish things were different. I don't like the idea — things are left dangling this way — that you're —"

She was floundering and he spoke with sardonic clarity. "That I'm leaving under a cloud, shall we say. But who made the cloud? Let me tell you, Clemence, you should never let anyone try to put you in the wrong, in any situation. The cloud stays there, over the board of trustees — and Francis Hearn. He has talked them into getting rid of me — me, the preeminent art expert of this age in this country — and of a painting that is worth two or three of any they are keeping on their walls. Time will tell, Clemence, time will tell. So you need not be upset." He paused and looked at her with sudden kindness. "Though it's certainly nice of you to feel that way."

He got up and came over to her and put his arm around her shoulders. "You're a good sort, Clemence. I appreciate what you've done for me since you came here." He was not much taller than she and his fair-grey head was just a little above hers. He leaned over and kissed her on the lips. Why, she thought in surprise, his lips are as soft as a woman's. Then he squeezed her shoulder and moved away.

Clemence, stunned, stood for a moment immobile. But this time Robert had really dismissed her and she walked out of his office.

She reached the nearest gallery just as Francis entered it with a group of people. His keen eyes lit on her instantly and then glanced behind her, as if he guessed at once where she had been. He nodded briefly and walked on with his companions.

* * * * *

It was half-past eleven at night when the phone rang. Clemence, in bed alone, roused from the beginning of sleep and opened her eyes in the half-darkness of the room. A street lamp outside gave a faint radiance on the ceiling. She had grown so used to Elissa's presence beside her in bed that she felt at once vulnerable and unprotected. Elissa, she remembered, was in New York with her congressman. The phone rang several more times. Feeling cowardly, she let it go on ringing, hopeful that whoever it was would tire and hang up. But then she thought, perhaps it is Elissa.

She got up hurriedly and went to it, hoping now that it would not cease before she could get to it. In answer to her hello she heard Regina's voice, full of sobs.

"Oh, Clemence! I thought you were not home! I must come and talk to you."

"Where are you?" Clemence asked, foggily.

"I'm at Union Station. I've just got here from Philadelphia. I couldn't call you earlier. There was no opportunity. Oh, Clemence —" Her voice broke again into half-suppressed sobs.

Clemence came wide awake. "Can you get a cab and come here? Or do you want me to meet you there?"

"Oh, no! I want to come to you. My mother doesn't know I've come to Washington. If you had not been home, I don't know what I would have done." There was an hysterical note in her voice.

"Well, get a cab. I'll be waiting for you downstairs."

Clemence put down the receiver and stood thinking for a few minutes. The distress in Regina's voice had brought her fully awake. Whatever was the matter, it was obvious that Regina was desperate. Clemence went back into the bedroom and put on her street clothes. Downstairs, in the lobby of the apartment house she waited anxiously. Regina, she knew, was not used to acting alone in an emergency. She hoped the cab driver who picked her up was the staid sort who would be sympathetic to a young woman in obvious distress.

With a sigh of relief she saw the cab arrive in front of the apartment house sooner than she expected. Regina got out and fumbled frantically with the clasp of her handbag. Clemence opened the door and went to her. "What's the fare?" she demanded of the driver and, taking the handbag from Regina, she found the required cash.

She put her arm through Regina's and walked her up the steps and into the apartment house. She could feel her body trembling against her own. As soon as they were in the apartment she led her to a chair and pushed her gently into its overstuffed comfort.

"I'll get us something to drink. Do you want tea?" She remembered that Regina did not really like whiskey.

Regina, mute with unhappiness, nodded.

"Then I'll put the kettle on. I'll only be a minute."

When she came back from the kitchen she saw that Regina had not moved but sat sunk in the chair with her head thrown back and her eyes closed. Clemence sat down at the end of the sofa and waited. The stillness in the room had a portentous quality, as if the very furnishings were part of a tableau. It was several minutes before Regina stirred.

She brought her head down and looked at Clemence. Hers is the very face of tragedy, thought Clemence, unnerved. But she said nothing, waiting for Regina to speak first.

Presently Regina gazed about as if searching for something. "Where is my handbag?" she asked, at last.

Clemence looked about the room and saw it on a small three-legged table by the door where she had automatically deposited it when they came in. She got up and fetched it, holding it out to Regina, who took it eagerly and began to search in its depths. She drew out an envelope and held it out to Clemence.

Clemence took it reluctantly, with a mixture of dread and embarrassment at the idea of entering in on someone else's privacy. But Regina, half weeping, urged her, "Read it."

Clemence unfolded the sheet of heavy quality writing paper embossed at the top with Francis Hearn's name and a string of letters which she recognized as the initials of several organizations of which he was a member. The letter began: "My dear Regina, I find it very difficult to write this. However, I cannot shirk doing something necessary because it is distasteful. Several times lately, when we've been together, I have tried to tell you that I don't think we should go on seeing one another. I blame myself for allowing our relationship to reach this stage of intimacy. I should have realized earlier that to you it would have a deeper meaning, that I cannot reciprocate your devotion with the ardor you have a right to expect. I know now that our natures are too different. I cannot love you as you believe you love me. I do not think I can give any woman that depth of devotion. Forgive me, if you can. I shall always treasure the moments we had together. They will live in my memory as something unique, marvelous, unduplicatable. But they must remain that — a dear memory of the past. I think in the future you will realize that I am being a truer friend to you than if I did not call a halt to my courtship of you."

Clemence, her indignation making it impossible for her to read further, dropped the sheet of paper on the table where the lamp stood. A wave of immense anger enveloped her, anger greater than any she had ever felt before, so great that it burned in her like fire. For several moments she could not speak. Regina sat with her handkerchief pressed against her eyes.

Finally, Clemence got up and going over to her said, trying hard to control her own feelings, "When did you get this?"

"This morning. The mail is delivered at the school about nine o'clock, just before my first class. I always pick mine up as soon as it comes. But of course I could not read it till after the class period."

Clemence, through the cloud of indignation that gripped her, recognized the meaning of what she was saying: Regina had waited, with quickening heart, every morning for some message from Francis. He must have been in the habit of writing to her frequently and she did not want the other people at the school to recognize and speculate about his letters. Clemence glanced down again at the sheet of paper lying in the lamplight. There was something practiced about Francis' way of expressing himself. Calling up his image, she thought, perhaps it was not as calculated as it sounded. Perhaps this was really the essential Francis — always coolly in control of emotions that threatened to overwhelm him and which he feared.

Clemence's voice was crisp. "Dear, this is dreadful. I am very sorry. But you know, he is right in one thing: it is fortunate for you that you should learn about how he feels now, not later, when you would be made even more unhappy."

Regina looked up at her. Even now, with tear-swollen eyes and tragic lines in her face, thought Clemence, she's the most beautiful woman I've ever seen. Regina put out her hand to take hold of Clemence's arm. She tried to speak but instead gave a small cry and buried her face in Clemence's breast. Clemence put her arms around her and held her close. Presently, in an effort to return things to normal, she said, "He says he has tried several times to tell you that he wanted to break off with you. Is that so?"

Regina moved her head. "I had no idea what he meant."

"But you realize it now?"

204

Regina did not answer for a while. Then she said, piteously, "Clemence, how can he say this? I thought he felt as I did. You remember the party you gave last year? It was the first time I met him. I thought he was a very attractive man, but I did not think any more about him. It was he who followed up on that introduction. He called me up and asked me to go out with him. I was so surprised. I did and after that he called me frequently and we went out together often. He was always very careful how he acted. He realized that I wouldn't accept any sort of equivocal invitation. He never suggested that we go to his apartment. He seemed to understand that I would not do that. I invited him to come to our apartment and meet my mother. But he refused. That meant that we could only spend the evenings in restaurants or other public places or sometimes just sitting in his car in some quiet spot. He never made any sort of pass. I knew — I know — that there in the beginning he really did love me, Clemence. I was so happy, underneath all the problems. I've talked to you about them — my faith, how my family would feel about him as a divorced man. He has always said a lot of things derogatory of the Catholic Church — or any sort of faith. He said it is all illusion, any belief in an eternal soul, a hereafter — an illusion that has been used by self-seeking people to control others foolish enough to believe. In the beginning I discounted all this, because I was very much in love with him. But I couldn't help but notice that as time went on he seemed to grow more and more critical. For instance, when I went to confession on Saturday, he would stand just inside the church by the holy water basin and when I came out he would say sarcastic things, hurtful things. Sometimes, when I protested, he would claim that it was his duty really to try to open my eyes to the mistake I was making in not leaving behind all I had been taught. He has made me very unhappy on more than one occasion. I suppose I should have been warned by this, but I was not. I thought he did this becuase he was unhappy about our situation, that it was his way of showing his unhappiness because there was a barrier between us. In between whiles he was so consoling, so loving —"

She seemed overcome by her own words, and standing up, clasped Clemence fiercely in her arms. "I cannot believe he could mean what he says in that letter! I love him! I love him! He must love me!"

Clemence, trying not to flinch in her ardent grip, said hastily, "Dear, you mustn't try to make him into something he isn't. Yes, I know. I think Francis did fall in love with you. I can believe that he pursued you after he met you at my place. I think he was carried away as he has never been carried away by anyone or anything before. But, Regina, listen to me. You must listen to me. It did not last with him. He isn't a man who can let his heart govern him when obstacles arise. The more he realized that you would not change, that he had to accommodate to your feelings about your faith, the more he realized that he had made a mistake. He couldn't change his own nature. He wouldn't want to. He is himself and what you were doing was confronting him with a demand that he should modify his ideas. He had been taken by surprise, that first time he met you. You were a sudden vision that swept him away from his mooring. But it could not last with him, unless he could make that vision over into something of his own. It didn't occur to him that if he tried that he would destroy what had attracted him. He could not allow you — or anyone — to make him come to terms with some concept that was not his own. Don't you see, dear, that he could never accommodate to the idea that you would have thoughts and feelings beyond what he allowed you?"

Regina did not answer her but was still, her head on

Clemence's shoulder. Clemence, anxious to convince her that she should welcome her escape from future misery, nevertheless dreaded to defeat her own efforts by provoking a stubborn reaction in Regina. She sat down on the sofa and drew her down beside her. Regina was no longer weeping. She seemed exhausted and Clemence sat quiet, afraid to disturb this first sign of returning calm.

At last Regina lifted her head. "I know you believe what you've been saying to me, Clemence. To you — to anyone looking on from outside — what you're saying is reasonable. But, Clemence, I cannot believe that he does not want me the way I want him — that he does not feel about me as I feel about him. There must be some dreadful compulsion that has made him write this letter."

Clemence sighed. "Regina, are you going to try to get in touch with him? You should not, for your own sake. You must not demean yourself like that!" In her indignation Clemence sat up straight, dislodging Regina's weight from her shoulder.

Regina gave her a wan smile. "I don't think personal pride should stand in the way, if I can do something to change his attitude. If we were face to face, if we can talk face to face — he must realize that he has deceived himself — how unhappy he will be — as unhappy as I am now."

Clemence took a deep breath. "Regina, you have admitted that lately he hasn't been acting the way he did at first — that you realize now that he had tried to waken you to the fact that he has changed his mind about your relationship with him. Don't you see that if you try to confront him, he will be forced into saying things more brutal than those he has said in the letter? He has tried to avoid that by writing to you. You will embarrass him and make him feel that he isn't behaving well — which he knows anyway — and you will make him feel small and he'll take revenge for that. Believe me,

Regina, Francis will never let anyone humiliate him with impunity."

"But I'm not going to humiliate him! That's the last thing I'd want to do. I'm just going to tell him that I don't believe he really feels the way he says he does in the letter."

Clemence turned to face her, gripping her shoulders. "Regina, listen to me. In the first place he won't see you, unless you take him by surprise somewhere. He'll make it impossible for you to see him — at least, not without a scene of some sort. Secondly, if you should succeed in seeing him, he will be as cruel as he can be. Don't you understand that he wants to get out of any further involvement with you? He feels guilty as it is and he wants to put as much time and space between you as he can, so that he can forget it all. If you pursue him, he will be only more determined to drive you away."

At first, seeing Regina bridle at her words, Clemence thought she had failed, that nothing she could say would penetrate Regina's self-delusion. But suddenly Regina collapsed once more on her shoulder and began to sob, rending sobs that shook her body. She knows I'm right, thought Clemence, striving to soothe her with gentle pats and murmurs. After a while the hysterical sobbing died away and for a long time they once more sat perfectly quiet.

Then Regina stirred and raised her head as if she was trying to regain some composure. She was passive while Clemence wiped the tears from her face. She said, "I don't know what to do, Clemence. I can't go home tonight."

"You'll stay right here. What you need is a rest. In the morning we can decide what you should do. Tomorrow — I mean today — it's way past midnight — is Saturday. You usually spend the weekend with your mother, don't you? So the people at the school won't be surprised if they don't see you around."

Regina made no response. Clemence stood up and reached down to bring her to her feet. "Come on. I think you're better off in bed." Regina allowed herself to be drawn up but she put her arms around Clemence, clinging to her with a desperate strength. Eventually Clemence was able to lead her to her own bedroom. The other beds in the apartment had been stripped and left open till she was sure of her parents' return. If she could get Regina into bed, she herself could find somewhere else to sleep.

When they reached the bedroom, Regina docilely visited the bathroom, taking with her a pair of Clemence's pajamas. When she came back to the bed and Clemence was helping her into it, she suddenly seized hold of Clemence.

"Clemence, Clemence, please, please don't leave me alone! I need you near me. I'm afraid of something — there seems to be a shadow over everything —"

"Afraid of what, dear?" Clemence asked reasonably.

"I don't know. Oh, Clemence, stay with me! I've never felt like this before."

Clemence looked down at her and saw a profound terror in her eyes. She could feel the hysterical trembling in her body. She said, "All right. Lie down and I'll get ready for bed."

When she came back into the room, Regina was sitting up, anxiously waiting for her. She got into bed beside her and was immediately seized in Regina's arms. They lay down, Regina burying her face in Clemence's neck. Clemence lay still, not drawing away from her, uncertain what she should do. Obviously Regina did not want fondling, except as a reassurance of her sympathy. Regina had reached out to her with a tremendous demand for comfort, desperately clinging to her as if she was drowning in a sea of her own fear. She would be lost without me, thought Clemence.

After a few minutes Regina's grip loosened. Clemence, raising herself on her elbow, saw that she had fallen asleep, overcome by the emotional exhaustion of the despair that had overtaken her. With a sigh of relief Clemence put out the light and nestled down beside her to seek sleep herself.

But before she could sleep she found herself trying to understand Regina's feelings. Ever since she had first met Regina at Goucher she had been aware that, under the intellectual brilliance that dazzled many people there was a fire that burned in her, a fire that was the very essence of an extraordinarily sensitive and creative person. It was that fire, Clemence realized, that, in her opinion, had been threatened by Regina's infatuation with Francis. There was no possibility that a man like Francis could ever comprehend or accept that element of vital force in a woman, much less his wife. He would have killed it. And Regina would have contributed to her own destruction, unwilling to deny him what he demanded and tied to him by a religious code that forbade the severing of the bond between them. Could Regina ever be convinced that this cruel rejection was in fact her own salvation? Listening to Regina's deep breathing she sincerely hoped so.

She heard the faint tinging of the old clock on the mantel in the living room striking three o'clock as she drifted into sleep.

It was late the next morning when she came awake. For the first second or so, feeling the warmth of Regina's body close to her, she thought Elissa was in bed with her and reached out a hand. But instantly the sense of the emotional upheaval of the night before came back to her. Carefully she got out of bed, anxious not to arouse Regina. She put on her dressing gown and went into the kitchen to make coffee. She had seen Regina drink coffee, so she supposed this would be appreciated. She had left another robe on the chair by Regina's side of the bed.

She made the coffee and drank a cup, standing by the kitchen table, wondering whether by the clear light of day the events of the night before would seem less stark, less crushing. But she found that the cheerful daylight did little to dissipate the anger and pity that filled her. How could she tell someone like Regina that she must look on the bright side, cast off the months of ecstatic joy that had filled her relationship with Francis as if it had never happened, chalk it all up to the need to learn what the reality of the situation was? This was the brightly rational way to advise someone else to overcome grief. But could grief be banished in that way?

She sat musing, long after her cup of coffee had been drunk, unaware of the passage of time. She was startled when a sound called her attention to Regina standing in the doorway. She looked lost in Clemence's pajamas and dressing gown; she was a little shorter than Clemence but a good deal thinner — thinner, thought Clemence, than I remember her to have been. Obviously the last few months had taken a toll. Regina, she guessed, was the sort who might forget eating in the pursuit of something far more valuable. And she had not noticed the gradual change. After all, it was Elissa who had filled her own thoughts.

Regina pushed her dark hair away from her face, which was pale and pinched. Her eyes were heavy-lidded as if still not completely free from sleep.

Clemence said, "I've made some coffee. Would you like some?"

Regina said timidly, "Tea, perhaps?" She came across the kitchen and sat down in the other chair at the kitchen table.

Clemence poured the boiling water into the teapot and

brought it to the table. "I'll toast some muffins," she said, fetching the butter from the refrigerator. Regina was silent while she prepared the breakfast. Sitting down again Clemence waited uneasily for her to speak, uncertain how much of the night before's conversation Regina wanted to revive.

After she had drunk the tea Regina said, "I'm very grateful to you, Clemence, for having me here. I know I couldn't have been very coherent last night. You must have known I was beside myself. You are always so patient with me."

The humility in her voice made Clemence writhe inwardly in embarrassment and her indignation rose again to the surface. "I'm very glad you came here to me, Regina. You were much safer here than you would have been anywhere else. I just wish —" she broke off, afraid of reviving more than she intended of the night's distress by venting her own emotions.

"You're always kind, Clemence. I did not think of going to anyone else. I could not have explained to my mother. You've always understood my inner conflicts." She paused and for a while was so abstracted that Clemence thought she had forgotten what she had said. But then she added, "Is it because you have conflicts of your own, Clemence? I have never considered that possibility before. Which shows you how selfish one can be when one is wrapped up in one's own distress."

"You mean, do I have conflicts and therefore that's why I have a fellow-feeling? Well, perhaps there is something in that. I suppose everyone has some inner conflict that is not brought out in the open."

"I remember that you told me once that you do not have the same outlook as your parents when it comes to religious belief. They do not understand what you feel. They are agnostics, aren't they?"

Clemence nodded. "They don't understand my need for

212

a spiritual interpretation of life beyond scientific speculation. But there is no real conflict. They are always sympathetic to me."

"Always?" Regina's question seemed half-preoccupied and Clemence realized that, though she had been listening politely to what she said, Regina was still sunk in her own misery. When Clemence fell silent, Regina said, "I must gather myself together. The day is half gone already, isn't it? I don't know whether to go to my mother's apartment or return to Rosecroft. I can call her from there and explain that I decided not to come home this weekend. I shall have to pretend that I had something to do that would keep me busy through the weekend. But I'm afraid that if I go back to Rosecroft today the people there will wonder about that." She seemed to notice an expression of concern on Clemence's face, because she hurried on with a quirk at the corner of her mouth. "I've learned to be less than candid about what I am doing from day to day. It was never necessary before I met Francis. Very often, in order to spend some time with him, I've had to lie." Suddenly smiling mischievously, she declared, "Lying is a sin, Clemence. You know that. It is the Devil who leads you into practicing deception. Would you say that Francis bears some of the responsibility for leading me into sin? He'd certainly scorn the idea. My sins are my own, he'd say. But then he denies the existence of sin."

Clemence stared at her in perplexity. Up to this moment she had assumed that, Regina being Regina, her relationship with Francis had been chaste. Now she wondered, alerted by Regina's words. "Regina, have you gone to bed with Francis?"

Regina's head jerked up in indignant surprise. "Oh, no!" Then a scornful expression came into her face. "Thank God, no! I don't have that memory to humiliate me. Of course, there were moments when I was nearly

213

swept along with what he wanted. But I always made it plain to him that I was not going to bed with him unless we were married. I thought you would certainly know that."

"Well, in fact, that is what I supposed. But you were talking about sin."

Regina cut in, "Which to most people means sexual transgression." Her tone was sharp.

"Yes. It occurred to me that, if you had, that might have been an added reason why he cooled off. He had had what he wanted."

"He had not. But," Regina hesitated for a moment, gazing into space. "You never did like Francis, did you, Clemence?"

"No. I have never really liked him."

"I should have been warned by your attitude." Regina's tone was dry.

"Oh, no! One can never — one should never — be governed by someone else's feeling in that way. But don't get bitter, Regina." Clemence spoke anxiously. "Betrayal of one's inmost feelings is always a blow. But don't let this lead to bitterness. It won't be good for you."

Regina shrugged, as if shaking off Clemence's caution. After a long silence she suddenly asked, "Where is Elissa? I've been so lost in my own despair that I haven't even noticed that she is not here. Isn't she usually here with you? I always think of the two of you as a couple."

Clemence's immediate reaction was shock. It had not occurred to her that Regina would so easily have penetrated the façade of her relationship with Elissa. "Why," she began lamely, wondering what to say.

But Regina interrupted. "I know that Elissa means a great deal to you, Clemence. And I think you mean even more to her than you do to me. And that is a very great deal. Don't be upset, Clemence. I only wish that there was a solution to my situation as simple and right as your own."

Clemence answered slowly. "It is not as simple as you think, Regina. Yes, Elissa means everything to me. It has taken me some time to realize that. But what are we — she and I — to do now? What am I to say to my parents? In fact, there is nothing I can say."

"But you have told me that they are always sympathetic to you."

Clemence looked at her hard, trying to see whether there was a less than kind meaning in her words — the reflection of her own bitter grief. But Regina returned her gaze frankly. Clemence said, "I assure you that this is one thing I do not think I can discuss with them. You've said that you have learned to be devious because of your need to be with Francis. That is what I must learn now with my parents. I've already begun to disguise from the people I work with, the people I see every day, what Elissa is to me and I to her. It has been happening without my realizing it."

Regina looked at her sadly. "Clemence, you at least have Elissa's love to make it valid."

For a while they sat silently together, drinking another cup of tea, till presently Regina seemed to rouse herself and said, "Thank you, Clemence, for looking after me. But now I must make some plans."

"What do you think you'll do? Go to your mother's?"

"No. I don't think my nerves would stand that."

Clemence, remembering her visit to Mrs. O'Phelan's Sunday at home, silently agreed. "Then what are you going to do? You can stay here. Elissa comes back this evening, by the seven o'clock train from New York."

"Then I shall take the seven o'clock train to

Philadelphia. I shall go back to Rosecroft. I must fill out
the school year. By then, perhaps, I shall see the way
clear ahead of me."

Elissa, sitting in the club car, felt the train begin to
move slowly and smoothly out of the Baltimore station.
She was probably the only one to notice, she thought,
because the people around her were talking and laughing,
excited by the end of the trip back from a hectic week in
New York. Most of them were fellow members of the staff
of the congressional committee to which she was attached.

She sat in an armchair at one end of the car,
surrounded by people but not really a part of any of the
several small groups. Her fellow workers bored her
outside of the office. She had never learned to adapt to
their way of socializing so as to feel comfortable with
them. She knew she was considered to be a loner,
somebody whose loyalty to a shared political and social
outlook could not be questioned but who did not seem to
fit into any group, who never sought a close relationship
or responded to friendly overtures.

It was a fact that she never wanted a close
relationship with anyone — only Clemence. Besides, if she
spent time cultivating other friendships, she would
jeopardize the time she could spend with Clemence.
Sometimes somebody said something to her about her
aloofness, about the fact that she did not spend more
time with her fellow workers. Who was the friend that so
absorbed her attention? The questions obviously arose
from suspicions that she had a private life she kept
hidden. She gave elusive answers and was aware that the
evasiveness was recognized and speculated about. She
thought it was possible — and she hoped this was the
case — that she was suspected of having an affair,

probably with a married man, and possibly with someone whose reputation might be at stake. She remembered Flora and Val. At their age people had ceased to speculate, if they ever had. But with herself and Clemence —

But right now it was Clemence she was worried about. Try as she might, she did not seem to bring Clemence face to face with the problem that loomed ever closer — the problem of what they would do when Clemence's parents returned to the apartment. Clemence's father and mother were well-known people with an active social life and it stood to reason that when they returned, Clemence would revert to being the child expected to conform to their routine. Clemence never answered the questions she asked about this. She simply shook her head and said they would have to wait and see.

Every evening, while she was in New York, she had tried to call Clemence as soon as she could return to the refuge of her hotel room. The second evening Clemence had reported that she had received a letter from her mother. Her parents were coming home, her mother said. They were coming by ship, for two reasons: one being that her mother did not like to fly, especially on long trips like these across the Atlantic; and two, which was more compelling, they were returning with a party of other scientists, all of whom had elected sea travel as being a relaxing and refreshing way to recover from the long months of intensive work.

That meant, said Clemence, that it would be another two weeks at least before they arrived in Washington. Well, what about it, then? Elissa had demanded. What are you going to do? Do? said Clemence, why, I'm not going to do anything.

Elissa had been so busy going over and over again this conversation and its implications that she had not noticed that the forty minutes from Baltimore to

Washington had almost vanished. It was the club car waiter, coming to collect her glass and gather up her ashtray who alerted her to the fact the train was already gliding into the railroad yards of Union Station and that they would be alighting within minutes. She glanced out of the window and saw that they were running rapidly alongside the platform shelters. She hurriedly picked up her belongings and made for the exit, finding herself immediately caught up in the throng of people eager to get out and find their way home. Finally she reached the steps and jumped down to the platform, looking wildly down its length to find Clemence. Usually Clemence, when she came to meet her, stood halfway along the platform, ready to catch a glimpse of her in either direction. But there was no Clemence in sight and she began to walk quickly towards the gates. It was only when the crowd thinned that she spotted Clemence standing just within the nearest gate. But there was someone with her. Elissa's heart bounded, as it always did when she glimpsed Clemence after a separation, but then her joy was checked. Who was with her? It was a moment or two before she recognized, with a mixture of surprise and relief, that it was Regina.

"Clem!" she exclaimed, eager to kiss her but held back by Regina's presence.

"'Lissa!" Clemence stepped boldly forward and kissed her, ignoring her reluctance. "Regina is catching the train back to Philadelphia, so she came along with me."

"Hi, Regina," said Elissa, aware that Regina was smiling at her in amusement.

"Hello, Elissa," said Regina. "Did you have a successful week? Did you settle the affairs of the nation?"

"Oh, yes. But I'm glad it's over."

They heard the trainman's whistle and his voice calling out, "Baltimore, Philadelphia, Wilmington, New York. All aboard!"

218

Clemence said, "That's your train, Regina. Write to me. See you soon." And she leaned forward to receive Regina's kiss and kiss her back.

"Oh, I shall!" Regina promised. "Thanks so much. Goodbye, Elissa." She raised her hand in a gesture and turned away to walk rapidly to the next platform to join the stream of passengers hurrying towards the train that stood there.

Clemence and Elissa walked in silence across the concourse of the station to the cab rank and waited. In the cab they spoke very little, both of them inhibited by the presence of the cabdriver. Only when they were inside the front door of the apartment and Elissa had dropped her suitcase, did they hold each other in a long embrace.

Then, from sheer nervousness, Elissa began to talk rapidly and in detail about her days in New York. She talked about what she had done, about the maneuvers the group had engaged in, the political developments that the trip had brought about. Clemence listened patiently, aware that Elissa's job, her future in Washington, were bound up in the political life of the man she worked for.

Presently Elissa slowed down and in a break in her account Clemence asked, "Are you hungry?"

Elissa shook her head. "I had something to eat in the club car. They were all doing a lot of drinking, complaining about leaving little old New York to come back to dull, slow old Washington. They'll all be hung over in the morning."

She sat down in one of the big armchairs. She yawned. "I'm short of sleep. I could never get more than five minutes to call you. We were working at all hours."

Clemence put a drink down beside her. "Well, we can celebrate all day tomorrow. It's Sunday." She sat down at the end of the sofa. "I've got a lot to tell you. You didn't have time to listen to me on the phone."

Elissa, alerted by the calm but meaningful tone in her

voice, looked at her. The events of the last few days vanished into the air as she concentrated on Clemence. This was a different world, a personal world, their world. "Why was Regina going back to Rosecroft tonight? Doesn't she usually spend the whole weekend with her mother?"

"She wasn't at her mother's this time. She spent the night here, with me."

Elissa sat perfectly still, caught up suddenly in a violent conflict of emotions. Her immediate response would once have been to speak out her jealousy, her anger. But she knew now that whatever Clemence did there was an underlying reason that was not subject to indignant outbursts of temper. She managed to say quietly, "Why?"

Clemence glanced at her, having anticipated an angry outcry. " 'Lissa, you've got to understand what has happened to her. She was beside herself when she came here Friday night. She had had a letter from Francis. Of all the lowdown, stinking cowards —"

The fury in her voice and the words she used astonished Elissa. "Whoa, Clem! What's up? What's this about?"

"He wrote her this letter, saying he had to break off with her because he was not in love with her any more, and therefore, the affair — would you call it an affair? — she never went to bed with him — is over."

Elissa stared at her for a long moment. "Do you mean to say he just said that to her in so many words?"

Clemence, sitting back, said quickly, "Even that would have been better than what he did."

"Better! Good God! How could anything be worse?"

Clemence hesitated, trying to control her own anger. "I told you he wrote her a letter, addressed to the school. Evidently he tried to tell her, when they've met lately, that he wanted to break off with her. But Regina did not understand. How could she? She has been so infatuated with him that nothing short of a flat statement would have made an impression on her. He didn't have the courage to do that. So he wrote the letter. Can you imagine the kind of letter Francis would write? You'd think he was writing to a retarded child."

"You saw the letter? How did you find this out, Clem?"

"Last night — Friday — she called me around midnight. She was crying and hysterical. She was at Union Station. She had missed the seven o'clock train and you know there isn't another for several hours. She was coming to see me. When she got here she was half out of her mind. She had received the letter in the morning mail, just before a class period. She had no time to open it till the noon break. Apparently she had been getting letters from Francis. She had noticed that they were not coming as often and that made her especially anxious to read this one. You can imagine how she felt when she did."

"I haven't seen the letter, but I'll take your word for it." Elissa's manner was stiff.

She was not looking at Clemence as Clemence studied her face in silence. Finally Clemence said, " 'Lissa, don't act this way. Regina did not invent this situation in order to come and spend the night with me. She was really distraught. I'm the only friend she has who can sympathize with her. Can you imagine her going home to her mother in that state of mind — or sticking it out at the school under the eyes of all the women who had been watching her?"

Elissa sat with her head down on her joined hands, silent. Clemence got up and went to fetch whiskey and ice. Before she had finished, Elissa followed her into the kitchen.

"I'm sorry, Clem," she said humbly. "I didn't really think that about Regina. I think she has had rotten luck, having Francis as the first person to arouse her. Damn

221

religion, anyway. She should have waked up years ago to how she's been victimized by it. She's been trying to be dutiful and keep her mind under wraps. And her body, too. She hasn't any protection against this sort of thing."

Clemence looked up from what she was doing. She said ironically, "You sound as if you'd had quite a bit of experience in that line."

Elissa, stung, answered, "You know that's not so! But I've seen this sort of thing happen."

Clemence relented. "Yes, of course, 'Lissa. I don't think anybody else would have put up with you." As she spoke, Clemence put her arms around Elissa's neck. "I'm so glad nobody has tried."

Elissa kissed her fiercely. "At least we don't have to fight off the religious fanatics."

"It's not as simple as you think, 'Lissa. Somebody is not a fanatic because she believes in something. Look at me. In Regina's case, it is more than just walking away from something you've been taught. But I'm so glad she came here to me. She spent the rest of the night with me, frightened to death of her own emotional collapse. Once she got to sleep she didn't wake till close to noon."

"She slept with you?"

"She slept in my bed, yes, like a child."

Elissa took the tray from her silently and they went back into the living room. Elissa asked, "What is she going to do now?"

"What she has been doing all along — teaching at Rosecroft. She knows she has to give herself time to get over this. Don't you realize, 'Lissa, what a terrible year this has been for her? First the disappointment over her dissertation and the suspension of the research she was doing for it. And now this. I have told her she must keep in touch with me. I'm uneasy about the long-term effect of all this. I don't want her to become bitter."

222

"Women have got over being jilted before this. I think Regina is too intelligent to let it get her down."

Annoyed by her cool tone, Clemence asked, "What would you feel if I wrote you a letter like that and told you that now my parents are coming home, it isn't convenient for you to be around any longer?"

Elissa's face flamed. "Clem! You couldn't do that!"

"No, of course I couldn't. Because I really love you, 'Lissa."

"But it's not the same thing!"

"Why isn't it? It is to Regina. I'm afraid she'll never really get over Francis — what she thought he was, how much she thought he loved her. Something like that keeps coming back to you. If someone you trust with all your heart destroys that trust, it takes you a long time before you can learn to trust someone else. I think you know that, don't you?"

Elissa's eye fell under her gaze. That was like Clem, to put her finger on the sore spot. "I never found anybody before who wanted to love me."

"But you thought you had and then found out they didn't want you. Oh, 'Lissa, you've never told me anything about all that but I've surmised it."

Elissa had poured their drinks and they sipped in silence for a while. Then Elissa said, in a tentative voice, "Clem, don't get mad at me, but it is true that Regina loves you."

"Yes, I'm sure she does, as I love her. But she doesn't love me the way you do. And I don't want from her what I want from you." Clemence got up from her chair and went to pull Elissa out of hers and draw her over to the sofa where they could sit close together. "I can't be happy that Regina has lost Francis, because she loved him so deeply — perhaps she still does, underneath her anger. But it is true that she has had a lucky escape. He'd never be able to give her the unreserved loving that would overcome the obstacles in the way of marriage for them. He'd never sacrifice anything and the only thing Regina could do would be to give way to him in everything, submerge herself completely. She's too valuable for that — any woman is too valuable for that with any man."

"Did you point all that out to her?"

"I tried to tell her that she'd come to realize that Francis was right. It was a mistake, their attraction for each other. But she was so devastated that she did not seem to be able to take it in. When I got her to bed she fell asleep immediately. When I got up in the morning and went into the kitchen to make coffee, I was pretty discouraged. She had talked about going to see him and to talk to him face to face, convince him that he's got it all wrong."

"Oh, no! She'd be an awful fool to do that!"

"Well, I told her so, but she didn't seem to see it. But when she woke up and came into the kitchen she was the old Regina — no, that's not quite so. I'm afraid she'll never be the old Regina. She's had too big a shock. But she was in charge of herself."

"Innocence lost," Elissa murmured.

"What did you say? Yes, I suppose that's it."

"You say she's gone back to her job?"

"Yes, she's gone back to Rosecroft, to finish out the school year. She's a very responsible person. I expect it will take her a while to sort things out in her own mind." Clemence stopped and gazed at Elissa for a while. Then she said, " 'Lissa, she envies us — you and me."

"You mean she knows about us?"

"She has all along. Not only that, 'Lissa, she is very sympathetic towards us."

"I never gave her credit — well, no, I didn't really think about it. I just assumed that, because of her religion, she wouldn't countenance our relationship. But now that you tell me I see that's shortsighted. Regina would look beyond that, wouldn't she? Especially —"

"Especially since you think she would want me," Clemence finished for her, mischievously. "No, you're right. There's nothing narrow-minded about Regina." She looked at Elissa and raised her glass. "Come on. To an absent friend."

Surprised, Elissa was a little slow but imitated her. "Yes. To an absent friend."

They were both silent for a while, preoccupied by their own thoughts. Then Clemence said, "There has been a lot more going on while you've been gone. I told you about Robert, how he just packed up his things and left, without a word to anybody but me."

"I suppose that's one way of thumbing your nose at people."

"But I don't think he did it for that reason. He just doesn't care what people think. He's contemptuous of most people, I suppose."

"I wouldn't worry about him. He seems to have done pretty well for himself."

Clemence's yes was so brief and preoccupied that Elissa looked at her attentively. She asked, cautiously, "But you aren't happy about him. What is it, Clem?"

"The angels."

Elissa looked blank and then exclaimed. "The painting! It does mean a lot to you, doesn't it, Clem?"

"Yes. I doubt if I'll ever see it again — unless it comes on tour in an exhibition. I hope that will be the case. I think Robert would want to do that, to prove he's right." She paused and then added, wistfully, as if she had conjured the painting up before her mind's eye, "It gives you such a wonderful feeling — that heavenly host that seems to hold such a wonderful promise."

"Well, you and Regina — you both believe in something."

"You know what faith is, don't you? 'The substance of things hoped for, the evidence of things not seen.' That's what the angels mean."

Elissa did not answer. She did not feel on sure ground here. But after all Clemence would not be Clemence without this touch of otherworldliness. It was a funny thing — to reach for something you did not really visualize. But Robert, of all people, shared this feeling with Clem, about the power of things unseen — or seen only through the eyes of master painters. Sometimes, briefly, she wished that this other dimension was in her own life.

While she was musing, Clemence went to turn on the radio to the good music station. The stately, sonorous strains of Monteverdi's music came over the air. More of the same, thought Elissa, listening to the grave and somber arias, plumbing the depths of feeling. It was time to say something to Clem about themselves. When Clemence came back she said soberly, "Clem, there's something else we have to talk about — something closer to home."

Clemence turned to face her. "My mother's letter." She sat down and gazed into space. "We have a couple of weeks to decide things. I know. You've been worrying ever since I told you they're coming home."

Feeling desperate, Elissa declared, "It's vital, Clem. We've got to have some sort of plan."

Clemence contemplated her silently. Presently she said, "We can't make plans until we know what is to happen."

"Well, what is to happen? Are you going to tell your mother about me — about us?"

"She already knows about you. I've talked about you in my letters to her. She knows about you just as she knows about Regina and Charlie Olsen and Robert and Francis and Flora — who they are and what they do. I reminded her that you and Regina were at Goucher with me in my senior year. I've said you sometimes sleep over here with me in the apartment when it gets too late for you to go home safely. She approves of the idea that I have a close friend like that."

Elissa did not answer. A feeling made up half of rebellion and half a sense of helplessness welled in her. The fatefulness that had dogged her all her life as far back as she could remember, back to the days of her first encounters with the world — in the foster homes in which she was placed as an infant, in elementary school, in the often squalid tenements she inhabited with the people in charge of her — suddenly grew strong again. For the last few months, in Clemence's quieting company, the old dread of disaster lurking just around the corner seemed to have died down, so completely that she had never even noted its absence. Now, with the uncertainty posed by Clemence's statement, it came flooding back.

Clemence was waiting for her to speak. Elissa said, "Could I see her letter?"

"Of course." Clemence got up and went to the desk in the corner of the room and brought the letter back. She held it out to Elissa. "Read it."

Elissa took it from her and read: "We are definitely coming home to Washington by the middle of the month. The last maddening details in the project have been cleared up, finally. I will resist any further delays, no matter by whom suggested, including your father. I am so anxious to learn how you have managed while we have been gone. Letters are no substitute for personal chats. When we left you had just received your appointment at the Gallery. It certainly was not my intention to be away for so long. Your father has dismissed any anxiety I have voiced, saying that of course you would do well under any circumstances. You're a sensible girl and have always had to do many things for yourself when we have been gone. We have both been most entertained by your letters, telling us about all the extraordinary things going on in the Gallery. We have heard gossip here in London about the to-do over the Giardini painting. It is recognized here as one of the special treasures rescued at the end of the war. We remember Francis Hearn well, of course. He has always been a disciple of your father's. I believe I've met Robert Alden at some official gathering. I've certainly heard about him. His latest escapade, concerning the painting, has reverberated here in circles where such things are of interest. It is surprising how many people in the art world here remember him from the period just after the war. He has his partisans — people who believe him to be unusually gifted as an art expert and who think he therefore is justified in some of the things he does in spite of their somewhat shady character. And there are those who like to gossip and tend to heighten the more scandalous aspects. But I'll not take up any more time with that now, since we'll be together so soon and can discuss it all at length."

Elissa looked up from the letter. "Does your mother know about Robert's reputation for being gay?"

"I would guess that she does. She meets all kinds of people and she hears all kinds of gossip, as you can tell from her letter."

"But she doesn't say anything about it here."

"No, she wouldn't."

"Why not?"

"Well, because she doesn't discuss that sort of thing with me."

"So how are you going to talk to her about us?"

"I don't suppose I am."

"What do you mean?" Elissa's alarm grew greater. "Do you mean you're just going to walk away from me — as if I didn't exist?"

Clemence started to be flippant but grew serious when she met Elissa's burning eyes. " 'Lissa, don't be so silly. No, of course I'm not going to pretend you're — you're just a casual friend. She knows already that you're close to me. I know you think I've been shutting my eyes to what will happen when my parents are back here. But I have been thinking about it. But whatever I do, I have to do it in a way that they'll understand. I've come to the conclusion that there is one thing I must do to begin with."

Elissa's alarm, which had brought her to the point of shaking, subsided a little. This was Clem, who never did anything without due consideration. She wanted to jump up, seize her in her arms, kiss her all over, vent some of the pent-up desire within herself. But it was a desire that was only partly a physical need. She wanted Clem as she had always wanted her, all of Clem, in a way that she could not articulate even to herself. Clemence was the world, the sun and the moon and the stars, the horizon. Without Clem —

Clemence was saying, "You know, 'Lissa, my mother is a very reasonable woman. She will always listen if you have something serious to say to her, even if she doesn't agree with it. I've been taught all my life by both my parents to be tolerant — tolerant of other people's opinions and actions, at least until you understand them.

But when you act you must act in good faith. I've always tried to act in good faith, because then they will be tolerant of what I want to do."

She stopped and sat in thought for several minutes. Elissa, suspended in air, waited.

Clemence said, "When my mother gets home, I think she will think it is perfectly natural that I shall want my own place. I'm sure she won't believe that I should remain a child forever. I'm over twenty-one. I have my own income, which I earn at a responsible job. While they've been gone, I've made my own friends. Of course they'll be sad about it. They're used to having me around. You know, when I was growing up I thought I must have been an accident — my parents were so much older than most of my friends' parents. A child wasn't very convenient for my mother. But when I told her this she said no. She had decided she wanted a child, a daughter, in fact, and so I'm here."

Elissa burst out, "She's lucky she didn't get twin boys."

Clemence's smile was sly. "Lucky for her or for you?"

After a moment's blankness Elissa laughed nervously. "Clem!" She caught Clemence in her arms. "Me, of course! So that's what you are going to do — move out?"

Clemence answered her embrace. "It's a perfectly natural thing for me to do. Flora says there is a one-bedroom apartment becoming available in her building. Somebody is retiring and leaving Washington. That will be just right for us. And, you know, my mother will much prefer me to have somebody living with me than my being alone."

"Really, Clem? This isn't just wishful thinking?"

Clemence looked into her anxious eyes. "No, it isn't wishful thinking. I don't know how much my mother will guess. And if she guesses, I don't know whether she will want to face the fact. Perhaps in time she will figure out what our real situation is. Perhaps she will accept it and perhaps — well, there isn't any point to looking too far ahead. We'll just have to go along our own way and see."

In bed that night Elissa reached over to turn off the radio as the voice sang, "The object of my affection can change my complexion from white to rosy-red —" Clemence giggled as Elissa's hands moved over her body. How safe, how comforting, how thrilling it was to feel Elissa, warm, eager, pressing her naked body against her own. They were one.

After a while, as she sank into sleep, a vision came before Clemence's eyes of the Giardini, floating in its sea of radiance, and she murmured, "I wonder where they are now."

Elissa asked drowsily, "Who?"

"The angels."

"Oh."

A few of the publications of
THE NAIAD PRESS, INC.
P.O. Box 10543 • Tallahassee, Florida 32302
Phone (904) 539-5965
Mail orders welcome. Please include 15% postage.

A FLIGHT OF ANGELS by Sarah Aldridge. 240 pp. Romance set at the
National Gallery of Art   ISBN 1-56280-001-9 $9.95

HOUSTON TOWN by Deborah Powell. 208 pp. A Hollis Carpenter mystery.
Second in a series.   ISBN 1-56280-006-X   8.95

KISS AND TELL by Robbi Sommers. 192 pp. Scorching stories by
the author of *Pleasures*.   ISBN 1-56280-005-1   8.95

STILL WATERS by Pat Welch. 208 pp. Second in the Helen
Black mystery series.   ISBN 0-941483-97-5   8.95

MURDER IS GERMANE by Karen Saum. 224 pp. The 2nd
Brigid Donovan mystery.   ISBN 0-941483-98-3   8.95

TO LOVE AGAIN by Evelyn Kennedy. 208 pp. Wildly
romantic love story.   ISBN 0-941483-85-1   9.95

IN THE GAME by Nikki Baker. 192 pp. A Virginia Kelly
mystery. First in a series.   ISBN 01-56280-004-3   8.95

AVALON by Mary Jane Jones. 256 pp. A Lesbian Arthurian
romance.   ISBN 0-941483-96-7   9.95

STRANDED by Camarin Grae. 320 pp. Entertaining, riveting
adventure.   ISBN 0-941483-99-1   9.95

THE DAUGHTERS OF ARTEMIS by Lauren Wright Douglas.
240 pp. Third Caitlin Reece mystery.   ISBN 0-941483-95-9   8.95

CLEARWATER by Catherine Ennis. 176 pp. Romantic secrets
of a small Louisiana town.   ISBN 0-941483-65-7   8.95

THE HALLELUJAH MURDERS by Dorothy Tell. 176 pp.
Second Poppy Dillworth mystery.   ISBN 0-941483-88-6   8.95

ZETA BASE by Judith Alguire. 208 pp. Lesbian triangle
on a future Earth.   ISBN 0-941483-94-0   9.95

SECOND CHANCE by Jackie Calhoun. 256 pp. Contemporary
Lesbian lives and loves.   ISBN 0-941483-93-2   9.95

MURDER BY TRADITION by Katherine V. Forrest. 288 pp.
A Kate Delafield Mystery. 4th in a series.   ISBN 0-941483-89-4   18.95

BENEDICTION by Diane Salvatore. 272 pp. Striking,
contemporary romantic novel.   ISBN 0-941483-90-8   9.95

CALLING RAIN by Karen Marie Christa Minns. 240 pp.
Spellbinding, erotic love story   ISBN 0-941483-87-8   9.95

BLACK IRIS by Jeane Harris. 192 pp. Caroline's hidden past . . .
ISBN 0-941483-68-1 8.95

TOUCHWOOD by Karin Kallmaker. 240 pp. Loving, May/
December romance. ISBN 0-941483-76-2 8.95

BAYOU CITY SECRETS by Deborah Powell. 224 pp. A Hollis
Carpenter mystery. First in a series. ISBN 0-941483-91-6 8.95

COP OUT by Claire McNab. 208 pp. 4th Det. Insp. Carol Ashton
mystery. ISBN 0-941483-84-3 8.95

LODESTAR by Phyllis Horn. 224 pp. Romantic, fast-moving
adventure. ISBN 0-941483-83-5 8.95

THE BEVERLY MALIBU by Katherine V. Forrest. 288 pp. A
Kate Delafield Mystery. 3rd in a series. (HC) ISBN 0-941483-47-9 16.95
                                    Paperback ISBN 0-941483-48-7 9.95

THAT OLD STUDEBAKER by Lee Lynch. 272 pp. Andy's affair
with Regina and her attachment to her beloved car.
ISBN 0-941483-82-7 9.95

PASSION'S LEGACY by Lori Paige. 224 pp. Sarah is swept into
the arms of Augusta Pym in this delightful historical romance.
ISBN 0-941483-81-9 8.95

THE PROVIDENCE FILE by Amanda Kyle Williams. 256 pp.
Second espionage thriller featuring lesbian agent Madison McGuire
ISBN 0-941483-92-4 8.95

I LEFT MY HEART by Jaye Maiman. 320 pp. A Robin Miller
Mystery. First in a series. ISBN 0-941483-72-X 9.95

THE PRICE OF SALT by Patricia Highsmith (writing as Claire
Morgan). 288 pp. Classic lesbian novel, first issued in 1952 . . .
acknowledged by its author under her own, very famous, name.
ISBN 1-56280-003-5 8.95

SIDE BY SIDE by Isabel Miller. 256 pp. From beloved author of
Patience and Sarah. ISBN 0-941483-77-0 8.95

SOUTHBOUND by Sheila Ortiz Taylor. 240 pp. Hilarious sequel
to *Faultline.* ISBN 0-941483-78-9 8.95

STAYING POWER: LONG TERM LESBIAN COUPLES
by Susan E. Johnson. 352 pp. Joys of coupledom.
ISBN 0-941-483-75-4 12.95

SLICK by Camarin Grae. 304 pp. Exotic, erotic adventure.
ISBN 0-941483-74-6 9.95

NINTH LIFE by Lauren Wright Douglas. 256 pp. A Caitlin
Reece mystery. 2nd in a series. ISBN 0-941483-50-9 8.95

PLAYERS by Robbi Sommers. 192 pp. Sizzling, erotic novel.
ISBN 0-941483-73-8 8.95

MURDER AT RED ROOK RANCH by Dorothy Tell. 224 pp.
First Poppy Dillworth adventure. ISBN 0-941483-80-0 8.95